STOP AT NOTHING

KATE SERINE

sourcebooks
casablanca

Published by Sourcebooks Casablanca, an imprint of Sourcebooks, Inc.
P.O. Box 4410, Naperville, Illinois 60567-4410
(630) 961-3900
Fax: (630) 961-2168
www.sourcebooks.com

Printed and bound in Canada.
MBP 10 9 8 7 6 5 4 3 2 1

For Z.L.S....
my very own happily ever after

Chapter 1

WELL, SON OF A BITCH.

The little bastard had decided to run. Didn't that just fucking figure? It was at least ninety degrees, and the air was so thick Kyle might as well have been trying to inhale the gumbo that the citizens of New Orleans found so enticing. And now that freaky little shit Harlan Rhodes was sprinting down Decatur Street wearing nothing but a Speedo, tube socks, and glittery gold sneakers.

No one even raised an eyebrow—except for a random tourist or two who hadn't quite figured out that natives of the Big Easy were rarely surprised by anything.

"Dawson!"

Kyle groaned inwardly when his partner, Dave Peterman, called out to him. He could already hear the ass-chewing he was going to get later for pissing on protocol. But screw it—Kyle wasn't letting Rhodes give him the slip. No way in hell. He'd been working this case almost since he'd arrived in New Orleans a year ago and finally had the key witness needed to put an end to one of the biggest human-trafficking operations in the country. Peterman was just going to have to get his ass moving.

Rhodes suddenly darted into the street, sprinting toward Jackson Square, causing cars to come to a screeching halt. Kyle raced after him, ignoring the cacophony of blaring horns and shouted obscenities.

Sweat soaked through his shirt. His suit jacket and tie began to feel like a wet straitjacket, restricting his movement. But the adrenaline pumping through his veins pushed him forward.

For all his wiriness, Rhodes was struggling just as much as Kyle in the heavy air, his strides beginning to slow even as he vaulted over a couple picnicking in the grass. The muscles in Kyle's legs were on fire and his breath sawed in and out, but he surged forward in a burst of speed.

When he was within a few feet of Rhodes, Kyle lunged, tackling the other man. They crashed to the pavement, sliding along the concrete path and nearly taking down a bride and groom making their vows before a preacher dressed in a Colonel Sanders-like white suit, string tie, and goatee. Ignoring the couple's startled cries, Kyle wrapped his arm around Rhodes's neck, putting him in a headlock and rolling until the man was on his stomach. Kyle scrambled to his knees and twisted Rhodes's arm behind him. The man bucked, trying to throw him off, forcing Kyle to press his knee into Rhodes's back to keep him down.

"Now," Kyle panted, having to yell as the brass band on the other side of the fence struck up their first tune of the afternoon, "I think you had a few things you wanted to tell me, Harlan…"

"Suck my dick!" Rhodes spat. "I ain't tellin' you shit, Dawson!"

Kyle shrugged, slapping handcuffs on Rhodes and dragging him to his feet. "That's what you think, asshole."

———

Kyle popped a handful of peanut M&M's into his mouth just as Peterman stormed out of the assistant director's office and halted abruptly to give Kyle a shitty look. So, pretty much business as usual.

He'd been catching hell from the moment he set foot in the New Orleans office. The other agents treated him like a piece of shit that'd been dumped on their lawn. Whatever. He didn't give a rat's ass what anyone else thought of him personally. He wasn't there to make friends; he was there to do his job. If they felt threatened by that, then screw them.

So instead of kissing their asses to ingratiate himself into their good-ol'-boys' club or slinking off into a corner to lick his wounds, Kyle had fallen back on the arrogance and insolence that had served him so well before. He'd figured out a long time ago how to get under people's skin and turn their own attitudes around on them, thanks in no small part to the decades-long pissing match he had going on with his father.

"You guys have a nice chat?" he taunted Peterman. "Or were you just dropping by to polish Skinner's knob before demanding a new partner?"

"Fuck off, Dawson," Peterman sneered. "I gotta get home to my kid. I don't have time for your shit."

Kyle leaned back on the hand-carved wooden bench that sat in the hallway outside his boss's office, regarding what he figured was now his *former* partner, and feigned a concerned frown. "How *will* I go on? First Hughes and now you? I'm heartbroken, Peterman."

Peterman's already florid face turned an alarming shade of purple. When he opened his mouth to respond to Kyle's sarcasm, Kyle held up his hand. "No, no.

Please don't give me the 'It's not you, it's me' speech. Let me spare you the effort. You're right, Peterman—it *is* you. I accept that. And I forgive you."

"Forgive—?" The vein in Peterman's forehead began to pulse. "You're an arrogant prick, you know that?"

"Dawson!"

Kyle hopped to his feet. "Sorry, gotta run. Boss wants to see me." He shivered with mock excitement. "Can't wait to see what he has to say. Our private chats are always so scintillating."

Peterman snorted derisively then stormed away, shaking his head and mumbling something under his breath.

Ignoring the way his gut clenched in apprehension, Kyle cleared his throat and plastered on his most carefree grin before swaggering into his boss's office. "You know, I don't think Peterman knows what *scintillating* means," he said, jabbing a thumb over his shoulder.

Assistant Director Skinner eyed Kyle with his bland, dispassionate gaze and asked on a sigh, "Beg pardon?"

"Scintillating," Kyle explained. "That's how I described our private chats. But it was totally lost on Peterman. Really, sir, I just can't stay partners with someone who has such a limited vocabulary."

"Well, good thing you won't have to," Skinner replied.

Kyle's brows shot up. "Really?" he said, dropping into the chair across from Skinner's desk. "Sweet! So, who's up next? *Please* tell me my new partner's a hot redhead named Scully."

Skinner blinked.

Kyle gaped at him. "Seriously? You're an assistant director at the FBI who's named Skinner, and you've *never* seen an episode of *The X-Files*? Not *ever*?"

"No, Dawson," Skinner retorted, leaning back in his chair and folding his hands over his stomach. "I'm happy to say I learned how to be an agent from shutting my piehole and listening to the more seasoned agents who knew what the hell they were doing, instead of acting like a self-important, smart-ass prick."

"I thought I was an *arrogant* prick," Kyle corrected. "You and Peterman really need to coordinate your insults better. It's confusing."

Skinner's eyes flashed. "Arrogant, self-important— take your pick. You've been here less than a year, Dawson, and you've already pissed away two partners. No one wants to work with you because you're reckless and dangerous and have no respect for authority or for the badge you carry."

"That's not true," Kyle shot back, his indignation genuine. "I have a *great* deal of respect for the badge."

The muscle in Skinner's jaw twitched, but he maintained his composure. "I knew you'd be trouble the minute you walked in the door."

Kyle's internal shit-storm alarm started blaring loud and clear, so he took his cockiness down a notch, ready to play nice. "Sir—"

"Oh, I've heard all about your family, Dawson," Skinner interrupted before Kyle could make good on his shift in attitude. "What'd you think? You could come down here, do whatever the hell you wanted just because your granddaddy's got his name in the history books?"

When Kyle merely clenched his jaw, Skinner continued. "Heard all about your daddy too. About his renegade methods of dispensing justice, how he runs his county and expects all you boys to follow in his footsteps. Except you didn't, did you? Well, let me tell you something, son. If you need to work out your daddy issues, you can head on back up north."

Kyle's spine stiffened, but he managed to maintain his blank expression in spite of the mention of his father, torn between defending his father's unorthodox but extremely effective ways of fighting the crime that trickled into their county from Detroit and Chicago, and distancing himself from the infamous Mac Dawson as he'd been trying to do his entire life.

"I don't have any contact with my father," he replied, his words as stiff as his posture. "Not anymore."

Eh—what could he say? Old habits die hard.

"Well," Skinner said, cracking a smile that seemed rather menacing. "Guess that's about to change."

Kyle's blood went cold. "What?"

Now Skinner's smile was positively smug. "You're being transferred."

Kyle's stomach sank. "Sir," he said, ditching the devil-may-care act entirely, "if this is about Harlan Rhodes and what happened in Jackson Square today, I had to do what was necessary to bring him in. Peterman and I have never seen eye-to-eye on how to deal with this case, but soon we'll have what we need to—"

"It's not about Rhodes," Skinner interrupted, "even though I've got that little asshole spewing excessive-force allegations against you to anyone and everyone who'll listen. I've already had two phone calls about it—one from that weasely little bastard who calls himself a lawyer. You're damned lucky Rhodes is spilling his guts, or you'd be even farther up shit creek than you already are."

Kyle shook his head. "Then what gives? I'm one of the best agents you have." When Skinner grunted, Kyle added, "Tell me I'm lying."

"You don't get it, do you?" Skinner said, leaning forward to rest his elbows on his desk and clasp his hands together. "Dawson, you could be the greatest agent of all time, but we have a little thing we like to call the Law around here. And I expect my agents to abide by it."

"Sir—"

Skinner narrowed his eyes. "You waltz in here with your cocky attitude and your blatant disregard for the rules and regulations, and you think you should get a pat on the back for it? Well, that dog might hunt with some folks, son, but not with me. I've been working on eighty-sixing your ass since you walked into my building. I'm just disappointed it took me this long to kick you to the curb."

Kyle's temples began to throb as it hit him that Skinner had been planning this since he'd waltzed— yeah, he'd waltzed, no question—into the New Orleans office. He'd been cocky, complacent, smug.

And he'd seriously fucked up by not playing nice in the sandbox with the rest of the kids.

He'd been shitting on authority for so long just to spite his father that he hadn't considered what it might eventually cost him when he'd decided to walk away from his job as a deputy in Fairfield County and flip the proverbial bird to his father by joining the FBI.

Oh, sure—he'd won *that* battle, showing his dad that the guilt trips and harsh code of honor that had governed their family for generations couldn't sway him. But his heart had been the ultimate casualty. Because in finally breaking away from the Old Man's will, he'd also left *her* behind. Abby Morrow. The woman who'd captured his heart like no one else ever had—and then shattered it into a million jagged pieces. Even thinking of her now made his chest tight with heartache and regret.

He gave himself a quick shake, pushing away the image of Abby's sensual smile, bright cornflower-blue eyes, and flawless fair skin and forcing his attention back to the news that he was being reassigned. He cleared his throat. "Where're you sending me?"

Skinner's lips twitched. "Well, since the apple doesn't seem to fall far from the tree, it seems only fitting that you go fill a spot in one of our northern Indiana resident agencies."

Kyle suppressed a resigned, bitter laugh. The irony of being forced back home when he'd worked so hard to break away was not lost on him. But it was too late to confess that his attitude and brash behavior were all an act, that upholding the law was in his blood—no matter how much he wanted to deny it—and that getting scum off the streets was not just his job, but his calling. Any protestations of the sort would just look like he was a whiny bitch trying to save his own ass.

So, instead, he donned his most unconcerned demeanor and flashed what he imagined was an infuriatingly undaunted grin. "So when do I leave?"

Chapter 2

Three weeks later...

ABBY MORROW FROWNED AT THE DATA DISPLAYED ON her monitor. It didn't make any sense. But she'd pulled the files four times and received the same results each time. There was no way she'd made a mistake.

She'd never been so sorry to be right in all her life.

Damn it.

She ran her hands through her already disheveled blond hair, then dropped her face into her hands with a groan, not wanting to believe what she was seeing. But as much as she hated to admit it, facts didn't lie. That was the beauty of being a digital forensics investigator and the primary reason she'd chosen the specialty.

Other facets of law enforcement could be murky and not as clear-cut. How many times were convictions based on mostly circumstantial evidence? Even the science of law enforcement had a certain margin of error. But when it came to digital evidence, the information was either there or it wasn't. She let the detectives draw their own conclusions from whatever facts she uncovered.

In this case, those facts were most definitely staring her right in the face. The texts, the photos, and the call logs that the individuals had tried so desperately to hide were right there on her screen.

Her stomach churned with the implications.

Just how in the hell had she managed to get sucked into this mess?

Oh, that's *right*... She'd asked to take on this particular freelance job. No, no. Not asked. *Begged* was far more accurate. She'd bugged the hell out of Sheriff Dawson, assuring him that taking on a paying client in a private investigation wouldn't interfere with her duties for the Sheriff's Department in any way, until he'd finally relented and had given his okay for her to take on the very lucrative opportunity.

There was nothing Abby loved more than a challenge, and this job definitely fit that description. She'd jumped at the chance, eager to take on something more than the standard cell-phone data pull or hard-drive extract.

Great call there, Abby. Sheer brilliance.

Of course, she never could've guessed what she'd find. That had been a total—and devastating—surprise.

She glanced at the clock in the lower right corner of her screen and cursed under her breath. She'd have to sort everything out later when she had time to mull it over. Right now, she had to get her butt moving or she'd be late picking up her nephew, Tyler. And that was the last thing the boy needed right now.

She quickly saved the reports to her encrypted flash drive, then grabbed a couple of Tums from the top desk drawer while her laptop powered down. She'd pull the data one last time later, just to make absolutely *certain* she hadn't missed anything before she turned in her final report to her client.

If she turned in her report to her client.

She considered denying the findings, claiming she couldn't hack the technology, which certainly could happen if a device was too new. She shook her head and pressed her lips together in a frustrated line. She had fought seriously freaking hard to establish her reputation in the male-dominated field. Her client was the sort of man who had the power to ensure her career came to a grinding halt. Under any other circumstances, she would've just turned over the data to him and let those involved worry about what happened next. And yet…

Damn and double damn.

She shoved the flash drive into the pocket of her capris and grabbed her cell phone from her desk. She impulsively dialed a number on her way to the front door, desperately in need of a second opinion. But she came to an abrupt halt, her thumb hovering over the Call button, and stared at the phone number on the screen. Her heart skipped a beat and her breath hitched in her lungs when she realized who she'd been about to contact.

Since the day she'd met Kyle Dawson at the police academy, he'd been her best friend, her confidant, her go-to guy when she had a case she couldn't quite figure out and needed a fresh set of eyes.

But he was the last person she should be calling right now. Or ever, for that matter. She'd made damned sure to burn that bridge, hadn't she?

Of course, that hadn't stopped her from thinking about him every single freaking day in the three years since she'd broken things off, missing the warmth of his arms around her even after all this time. How many times had she almost dialed his number, wishing she could confide in him, laugh with him, make love with him as she had countless times that summer before he'd left for Quantico?

She shoved her phone into her purse sitting on the credenza next to the front door. No, there'd be no running to Kyle for advice. She already knew what she had to do.

Walk away.

Which meant passing up the crap-load of money her client was offering, money that would've paid for the treatment center where her mother was in rehab. Again.

But for the sake of everyone involved, Abby needed to turn the case over to the feds, let them pursue the leads she'd uncovered, and let the chips fall where they may—which was going to be way closer to home than she'd ever dreamed. And once again, she was going to be left to pick up the pieces.

Typical. So freaking typical.

Abby dropped into the driver's seat behind the wheel of her ten-year-old Camry, shoulders sagging. If things could go more to shit, she wasn't quite sure how. And to add insult to injury, she was once again going to have to break the news to her nephew that his parents were letting him down. Although, she had to admit, considering her sister and brother-in-law's track record, she hadn't been entirely surprised when her sister had called her a few days ago from Chicago to let Abby know she'd decided to stop off on her way home from France to see an old friend.

Yeah right.

Abby knew all about Emma's "old friend." A playboy billionaire, he was one of the most sought-after *married* men in the United States and had a penchant for bedding other men's wives while leaving his own to deal with the fallout in the press. He was also chairman of the board for one of her brother-in-law's international security firms.

She shook her head in exasperation. Her sister's affair with the man was certainly no secret to the social elite of the Midwest. But the wealthy had a way of turning a blind eye to the tawdry goings-on within their circle—until that information could benefit them in some way. That was a truth their mother had learned the hard way. Abby could only protect her sister from scandal for so long. And that time was rapidly running out…

———

"You're a prick."

Kyle grinned in spite of himself, glad to hear his brother's voice on the other end of the line. "Yeah, I've been hearing that a lot lately. But usually there's a colorful adjective in front of it—arrogant, self-important. Get with it, bro."

His brother Joe wasn't amused. "Imagine my surprise when a buddy of mine over at the South Bend FBI office asked me how I liked having my kid brother back home. I didn't know what the hell he was talking about and sounded like a major jackass when he told me you'd been transferred and were now assigned to one of their resident offices up this way. What the fuck, Kyle? You can't pick up the goddamn phone to let us know?"

Kyle set down the last box of his stuff on the office floor and straightened on a sigh. "I'm sorry, Joey. I wasn't ready for Dad's shit. I just got in yesterday and wanted to get settled before I had him bustin' my balls about screwing up again."

"What happened?" Joe asked. "I thought you liked New Orleans."

Kyle sat down on the corner of the desk and stared

out the office window that had an oh-so-scenic view of the dumpsters. Nothing like being the FNG—the fucking new guy—all over again. "Yeah, well, turns out I wasn't such a good fit."

"One too many *X-Files* jokes to Skinner?" Joe chuckled.

Kyle ran his hand through his thick black hair, wishing it were that simple. "Something like that."

"You can tell me about it over dinner tonight," Joe informed him. "I'll throw some steaks on the grill."

Kyle's mouth began to water at the thought of a home-cooked meal. After so many years as a confirmed bachelor, he rarely bothered much with cooking. Pizza and Chinese takeout were easier and didn't make it so blatantly obvious that he was eating alone. "Sounds good. But you'd better run that by Sadie."

"Already did," Joe said. "She said to getchya ass over here by seven."

Kyle couldn't suppress his grin. It was good to see his big brother happy again. Joe had had one hell of a time of it when he'd returned home from his last tour in Afghanistan. The physical scars he'd suffered were bad enough, but the emotional ones… Well, thank God for Sadie Keaton and her love. They'd nearly lost Joe in more ways than one, but thanks to Sadie, his brother was happier than Kyle had ever seen him. As far as Kyle was concerned, if that woman asked him to walk through fire, he'd slap on some sunscreen and get to steppin'.

"You're one lucky bastard," Kyle told his brother. "You know that, right? Sadie grows up next door to the four of us Dawson boys, and *you're* the one she falls for? How the hell did *that* happen?"

Joe chuckled. "I guess she came to her senses after one date with you."

Kyle grunted, remembering well that night back in college even all these years later. He'd never stood a snowball's chance. After just a few minutes into the date, it'd become painfully obvious that the girl next door would never be his, that there was only one Dawson brother for her. And that brother had been on his first deployment to Afghanistan.

"Yeah, well, all she did was go on about you the whole time," he admitted. "It's about damned time you two finally figured out you were in love with each other. I was getting sick of Sadie calling me all the time to talk about your sorry ass."

"You can kiss this 'sorry' ass," Joe shot back. "You only *wish* you could be the fine specimen of manhood I am."

Kyle's smile grew. The only thing he didn't regret about being reassigned was that he was now within a two-hour drive of the brother he'd worshipped while growing up and had missed like hell since leaving home. "Dream on, loser. I'll see you tonight."

"Hey, Kyle."

"Yeah, man?"

"It's good to have you home."

Kyle disconnected the call and stared at his phone for a moment. His brother's happiness brought a dull ache to the center of his chest, and Kyle wondered for the millionth time what his life would've been like if things had gone differently that summer three years ago. If Abby had just asked him to stay.

The memories he'd managed to keep barricaded in

the back of his mind most days came flooding back to
him as if his mental dam had finally crumbled under
the stress of keeping them in check. He'd worked with
Abby at the Sheriff's Department for a couple of years,
had flirted mercilessly with her in spite of his strict
"don't shit where you eat" rule about dating. But when
he announced that he was leaving for Quantico, everything had changed.

It'd all started that day at the lake when his friends
had thrown him a party on the beach to celebrate. Even
now, he could see Abby coming out of the water in that
pale blue bikini that showed off her long, tan legs, pert
breasts, and smokin' hot figure. He'd seen the look in
her eyes as she caught his lustful gaze and knew it was
on. And when she'd seized the beer bottle in his hand
and taken a drink before handing it back with a wink,
he'd been glad to have a towel wrapped around his waist
to hide the effect she had on him.

It'd been sheer torture the rest of the day until he could
get her alone. Finally, as the party was winding down,
they'd gone out for a boat ride together at sunset and had
ended up anchored in a secluded cove, screwing their
brains out. He was grateful for the sport yacht's T-tops
that at least partially shielded them from view—in the
captain's chair, Abby's long legs straddling him as she
rode him; Abby on her knees on the speedboat's bench,
bent over the stern as he clutched her hips, drilling her
from behind; or down on the floor of the boat on the
cushions as he thrust again and again, watching in fascination as rapture played over her beautiful face.

When they were too exhausted to go at it again, they
settled for huddling together under beach towels, kissing

and making out, stroking one another into smaller, mewling releases most of the night. He hadn't been able to get enough of her. His hands and lips constantly sought her out, craving the feel of her velvety soft skin. And her hands had been just as eager to explore his body, bringing him more pleasure than he'd ever imagined possible.

The entire summer had been that way. The sexual tension that had always simmered between them erupted with such explosiveness that they'd been swept away. But it was more than just sex. She'd brought a light into his life that had been sorely lacking, a love that had filled him with the kind of happiness that he hadn't believed existed. And it'd come to an abrupt end the night before he had to leave when he'd told her he loved her and that he wanted to spend the rest of his life with her.

How many times had he wanted to call her over the years, just to see how she was doing? Find out how she was? Try to figure out if she missed him even half as much as he missed her? It's not like he couldn't have found out how things were going for her. He worked for the FBI, for chrissake. Or, hell, Abby was Sadie's best friend. He could've just asked about Abby during one of Sadie's many calls to talk about how much she missed Joe. But he never had, too afraid of the answer he'd get. And Sadie hadn't volunteered any information.

His thumb smoothed over the screen of his phone as his frown deepened, wondering what Abby would say about him being back in town. Did she already know? Had Sadie told her?

He should at least call her, offer to take her out for drinks, catch up. But, shit. Did she have a boyfriend? Or worse—was she *married*? The thought that she might be happy with someone else—someone worthy of her love—gave him peace and made him want to hurl at the same time.

Fuck it.

He had to hear her voice. He had to know. It was hard enough to avoid thinking about her when he was hundreds of miles away and busy building a career, but now that he was back home, she was all he could think about. If he was ever going to move on, he had to get this over with.

Kyle went to his contacts before he lost his nerve and paged through until he found Abby's number. His blood was pounding so loudly in his ears that he almost couldn't hear the phone ringing.

———

Abby had only been on the road to her nephew's school for a matter of moments when her phone rang, startling her from her thoughts. Worried it might be Tyler trying to reach her, she fished the phone out of her purse and glanced down at the display.

Her stomach sank when she saw the number, even though she'd known this call would be coming. She heaved a sigh, silently berating herself for how her voice shook when she answered, "Abby Morrow."

"Good day, Deputy Morrow," came the smooth voice on the other end of the line. "I believe you were to have some information for me today."

She'd already talked to her client's personal assistant in an effort to explain she needed just a few more days, at which time Abby had been assured she would have to answer for her "lack of cooperation." She only hoped her client was more understanding than his harpy assistant had been.

Abby cleared her throat. "As I explained to your assistant, I've pulled the data you requested, Mr. Hamilton, but I'd like to have a little more time to run the reports again to determine—"

"That won't be necessary," he interrupted. "You've already had ample time to go through the technology I provided, Deputy Morrow. And I have every confidence in your abilities. After all, my connections assure me you are quite talented."

"Well, thank you, sir," she demurred, ignoring the beep in her ear that indicated another call was coming in, "but—"

"I have a great interest in learning what you've discovered," Hamilton told her, cutting her off in that particular manner unique to men not used to being denied. "It would be unfortunate if you were unable to satisfy the terms of our contract."

"Mr. Hamilton," Abby began, struggling to keep her tone even and calm, "I just need a little more time. A day or two at most. Regrettably, the data is a little more complicated than I'd anticipated."

There was a heavy pause before Hamilton finally said, "That is regrettable, indeed."

The phone beeped in Abby's ear, signaling the end of the call as she rolled to a stop at a traffic light. She shuddered, her skin prickling.

What had Hamilton meant? Was his parting remark permission to take a couple more days or a thinly veiled threat? And there was something in the way he'd said *regrettable* that had the little spot at the small of her back tingling, sending little tendrils of dread slithering up her spine. She shrugged a couple of times and rolled her head, trying to push the feeling away, but it persisted.

Abby closed her eyes for a moment and took a deep breath, letting it out slowly. She wouldn't give in to the paranoia. *Couldn't*. It had taken her two years to stop constantly looking over her shoulder after her father's murder. And she'd promised herself back then that she'd never devolve into the fearful, timid little mouse she'd been as a teenager. She'd seen what that kind of paranoia could do to a person, had witnessed her mother's never-ending series of breakdowns far too intimately.

That was the primary reason she'd gone into law enforcement—to feel empowered, to make a difference and do her damnedest to ensure that what had happened to her family didn't happen to anyone else's. It was a pipe dream, sure, but she had to do *something* or else the bad guys won.

A horn suddenly blared, jolting Abby from her stupor. Realizing the light had changed, she shook her head, then waved a hand in apology to the driver behind her before moving on. She was still rattled, her mind racing, when she pulled up in front of Tyler's school a few minutes later.

The boy stood at the edge of the sidewalk, away from the other groups of chatting, laughing children milling around nearby as they waited for their rides home. Smaller than most children his age, Tyler seemed even younger than he was. His heavy backpack was slung over one shoulder, his hands deep in his pockets. His shaggy blond hair fell across his forehead, hiding his eyes.

As always, Abby's heart broke a little at seeing how dejected her nephew was, how lost and alone he seemed. One of the wealthiest boys in the Midwest should have lots of friends, should be involved in sports, music lessons, academic teams...

But not Tyler.

He was painfully shy and had difficulty making friends with the other kids. Even though the other students in the exclusive prep school were certainly well-off, Tyler didn't want to call attention to himself, didn't want anyone to know that his father probably made more in one month than their parents made in an entire year. And that was saying something. He even refused to allow his father's "personal security specialist" to pick him up from school, instead preferring Abby in her aging sedan, which could use some work after the most recent spring hailstorm.

"Hey, monkey," Abby called through the open window. "Ready?"

Tyler gave her an exasperated look, his eyes wide with embarrassment at the nickname. But after a quick glance around, he hopped into the backseat. "I told you not to call me that," he mumbled. "I'm *ten*, Aunt Abby."

Grinning, Abby cast a glance over her shoulder. "Sorry, kiddo. Habit. I keep forgetting you're growing up."

His mouth hitched up in a hint of a smile, his expression hopeful. "Well, since you admit I'm growing up, will you let me play *Disaster Zone 4* tonight?"

Abby laughed. "Fat chance, pal. Your mom would lose her mind if she found out I'd let you play that video game."

Tyler shook his head, his mood going dark again.

"No she wouldn't. All she cares about is her stupid spa. She could've stayed *here* and gone to a spa."

Yep, Abby should have a hazmat suit hanging in her closet, considering all the messes she'd been cleaning up.

"Well, your mom will be home tonight," Abby reminded him, leaving out the part about her having been only a couple of hours away in Chicago for the last week. "Why don't you talk to her about it? Tell her how you feel?"

Tyler grunted. "Won't do any good."

"Your mom loves you," Abby assured him, the words sounding hollow even to her ears. She glanced in the rearview mirror in time to catch the skeptical look Tyler sent her way, which pretty much confirmed he had his doubts.

"Yeah right," he murmured, turning his wide blue gaze to the window, the conversation over.

Abby sighed, wishing she could offer more encouragement. But apparently her sister, Emma, had learned her parenting skills from their own socialite mother. To both of them, children were merely trophies to be polished and put on display when company came to call.

"Have you heard from my dad?" Tyler asked.

Abby squirmed a little in her seat. She hadn't heard from Curtis Maxwell directly since he'd left for a spur-of-the-moment business trip, leaving Tyler in her care. She knew he wasn't where he'd claimed he was going, but she wasn't about to out him to the boy. She'd let the bastard do that himself after she told him what she'd found and turned the info over to the feds.

"No," she told Tyler. "I haven't heard from him. But he's traveling today, and it's a long flight from Bogotá, Ty. I'm sure he'd call you if he could."

He caught her eye in the mirror, giving her a wry look. "He has a phone in the jet, Aunt Abby. It's not like he *can't* call. He just cares more about his business than he does about me."

"Well, he said he'd be home tonight, right?" Abby reminded him, forcing excitement into her voice. "He probably just figures he'll talk to you when he gets in." When her words didn't lift Tyler's spirits—probably because she was a lousy actress and couldn't lie worth a damn—she tried a different tack. "Okay, I tell you what. Since it's a Friday night, I'll let you stay up until your parents get home."

Tyler's eyes lit up at the idea, which only served to break Abby's heart all over again. No matter how her nephew pouted or pretended he didn't care about his parents' continued disinterest, the boy desperately longed for their attention and affection.

She forced a smile that was at odds with the furious words she was going to have for her sister and brother-in-law when she saw them again. "Sound like a plan?"

Tyler's smile grew. "Sounds like a plan."

Chapter 3

KYLE HAD CALLED HER.

Abby sat on the deck overlooking the private lake on her sister's property, listening to the water gently lap against the boats moored at the dock. She stared at his phone number, her heart pounding as her stomach performed an acrobatic act that would've put Cirque du Soleil to shame.

She'd been so rattled by the call from Hamilton that she hadn't even bothered checking to see whose call she'd missed until now. And there his name was, like it was the most normal thing in the world for him to have called out of the blue after three years.

At the sight of his name her stomach had dropped at warp speed, bringing a flush of heat to her skin. Which pissed her off. She wasn't some silly little schoolgirl with a crush. She was a grown woman, for crying out loud!

So why was calling him back so freaking *hard*? After three years, she should be able to handle talking to Kyle Dawson. What had happened between them was amazing, incredible. But it was over. Had been over for some time now.

And now, suddenly, he'd called *her*. If she'd been a person who believed in fate, she would've considered it a sign that the universe was trying to tell her something. Even so, she couldn't overlook the fact that the cosmos seemed to be giving her a giant smack upside the head.

She knew Kyle wasn't married, didn't even have a serious girlfriend. Working with his three older brothers at the Sheriff's Department made it impossible *not* to hear the latest Dawson family gossip. So what was the harm in an old friend calling another old friend to say hi? Right? Just a friend. It'd be fine. She could be aloof, indifferent. No problem. No problem whatsoever.

She blew out a harsh breath, then before she could talk herself out of it yet again, she pressed the screen over his number. But just as the line connected, a text message notification popped onto the screen, disconnecting the call.

With a groan at her thwarted attempt at forced nonchalance, Abby glanced at the message, expecting to see yet another message from her sister, another excuse for her late arrival. But it was from a blocked number. Frowning, she opened the message.

Enjoying your wine?

Attached to the message was a picture of her as she sat now on the deck in an Adirondack chair, a glass of Chardonnay in hand.

Her head snapped up, and she scanned the surrounding woods, searching the heavy shadows cast by trees in the twilight.

The sound of another text message coming in drew her attention back to her phone.

How's Tyler?

Abby launched to her feet, her wineglass falling to the deck and shattering as her blood turned to ice in her veins. "Tyler!" she shouted, searching for the boy at the edge of the lake where he'd been skipping stones. Her heart began to thunder in her chest when she didn't see him standing where he'd been just seconds before. "Tyler, answer me!"

—◆◆◆—

A contented smile curled Kyle's lips as he watched Sadie stroll toward his brother and hand him a beer.

Joe's eyes sparked with desire as he slipped his arm around Sadie's waist and pulled her close for a lingering kiss.

The look that passed between Joe and Sadie when the kiss ended was one of such profound love that Kyle couldn't *help* smiling as he looked on, even as he felt that familiar ache of loneliness. "Hey, you two, get a room!" he called out through forced laughter that sounded authentic thanks to loads of practice over the years. Deflect with humor and sarcasm. That was his standard operating procedure whenever things got a little uncomfortable—or straight-up painful. "I didn't drive all this way just to watch you make out all night."

Joe chuckled and released the woman he loved before closing the lid to the grill and returning to the patio table.

The fact that Joe winced a little as he took a seat, his bum leg apparently still giving him trouble, didn't escape Kyle's notice. Joe had been working out, toning up and working his ass off to get back in shape after an IED in Kandahar landed him in a hospital bed for weeks and rehab for months longer, but he still had a way to go.

Kyle tipped his beer bottle slightly toward Joe's leg. "How's that doing?"

Joe shrugged. "You know. About as good as can be expected. Doesn't hold me back where it counts." He sent a playful wink Sadie's way, bringing a slight flush to her cheeks.

"God, you two are incorrigible," Kyle said, shaking his head.

"I gotta say, this is a sorry excuse for a party."

Kyle's head snapped around at the sound of the quiet drawl behind him. He launched to his feet with a laugh when he saw his brother Tom sauntering toward them, as tall and trim as the last time Kyle had seen him. Of the four brothers, Tom and Kyle shared the most similarities—from their black hair to their angular features. But their personalities couldn't have been more different. And with more than six years between him and Tom, he'd never been particularly close to his eldest brother. But, damn, it was good to see him.

Tom's leisurely, long-legged gait and easy smile were a welcome sight that unexpectedly made Kyle's throat go tight. Or maybe the emotion choking Kyle had something to do with the sorrow he saw etched in Tom's features. It'd been a few years now since Tom's wife, Carly, had been killed in the line of duty as a DEA agent during a drug bust gone wrong, but it was plain to see that her loss still weighed on Tom.

"Yeah, well," Kyle said with a jerk of his chin, "we were holding off on the fun until after you leave. Didn't think you could take it at your advanced age."

Tom's quiet chuckle rumbled in his chest, his clear blue eyes—their mother's eyes—sparkling with humor as he extending his hand to Kyle. "Advanced age, my ass," he said with a grin as Kyle accepted his handshake. Then, to Kyle's surprise, Tom pulled him in for a hug before playfully shoving him away and ruffling his hair. "What the hell did you get yourself into this time, you little shit?"

Kyle groaned. "Oh man. I'll fill you in later. I just want to devour these steaks Joe's got going and get totally shit-faced." He craned around Tom, glancing toward the front of the house where he could see Tom's squad car was parked. "You coming from work?"

Tom gave him a curt nod. "Got called to an investigation as I was leaving the house. Gang hit over in Nelliston. Wanted to stop by and check it out."

"Shit, really?" Kyle said, genuinely surprised. Gang violence? In Fairfield County? *Damn...* Had he been gone *that* long? "Is it really getting that bad over there?"

"The county's changed a lot just in the few years you've been away," Joe chimed in. "The gangs from up in Chicago and Detroit are coming down here where they're a little more off grid, especially in cities like Nelliston and Hollisburg. Then you have Dawsonville and North Fallon where all the McMansions are sprouting up. The people who live there still have a small-town mentality and think crime isn't going to come to their doorstep."

Tom grunted. "Yeah, just ask 'em. They'll tell you that kind of thing only happens over in Gary or down in Indy. And yet when someone walks in their unlocked garage door and cleans 'em out, they want to bitch about not having enough patrols in their neighborhoods."

"And don't get me started on the meth houses," Joe went on. "Cooperstown has turned into a total shit-hole."

"Seriously?" Kyle shook his head. "That's gotta have the Old Man out for blood."

"Well, crap," Sadie interjected on a sigh. "Speaking of being out for blood, Kyle—Gabe's here."

Kyle turned to see his brother Gabe charging toward him, that powerfully square jaw of his clenched tight with rage. He heaved a sigh of his own.

Well, shit. This oughta be fun...

"I'm right here, Aunt Abby."

Abby spun around to see her nephew standing at the top of the deck steps. Relief washed over her at the sight of him and she rushed forward, sweeping him into a hug that made him squirm to get out of her hold.

"Abby, I can't breathe!" he protested.

She eased up just enough to shuffle him toward the house, shielding him with her body while she glanced around them, keeping an eye on her surroundings.

"What's the matter?" Tyler asked. "What's going on? Why do you look so scared?"

Abby quickly ushered him into the house, ignoring his questions. She'd just slammed and locked the French doors when another notification pinged. Abby dropped the venetian blinds into place to hide their movements from view before checking the message.

Hide-and-seek, Abby? Very well. One... two...three...

Abby's eyes went wide. "Shit."

"Abby? What's going on?" Tyler demanded again, his voice shaking.

Whoever it was knew her name. Knew Tyler's. And was coming for them.

But why?

Was it Hamilton, pissed about her not handing over the data? *Damn it!* She'd have to figure that out later. Right now, her priority was keeping Tyler safe.

"C'mon," she said, grabbing Tyler's hand and pulling him after her as she raced toward the door to the garage where her car was parked. "We need to leave. Right now."

"What?" Tyler demanded, digging in his heels. "We can't go—my mom and dad will be home soon."

Abby took hold of his upper arms. "Honey, I need you to trust me."

Tyler's suddenly calm blue gaze met hers, and she saw understanding there that was beyond his years. "We should go to the safe room," he told her. "Dad told me to go there if I was ever in danger."

Of course! Abby had completely forgotten about the little room of concrete and steel hidden behind the bookshelves in the mansion's massive library. The fact that Curtis had ever feared his family might be in danger to the extent that they'd have to take refuge in a panic room made Abby want to strangle the bastard. She gave a curt nod. "Go. I'll be down after I set the alarm system."

Tyler spun on his heel and bolted down the hall. Abby sprinted toward the panel that hung on the kitchen wall. Immediately, she pushed the panic button that was supposed to alert the guard at the gates to any trouble, but he didn't pick up. Goose bumps raced up her arms.

Damn it.

She'd have to call for help the old-fashioned way.

"This is Deputy Abby Morrow," she said in a rush to the 911 dispatcher as she punched in the code to arm the system, but before she could enter the final number, the power to the entire house went dead, that sensation at the small of her back so strong her knees nearly buckled. She swallowed hard, her gaze darting around the room as she said softly, "I need to report an intruder."

The backup system should've come up right away, allowing her to still arm the security system. But the keypad failed to respond. She rattled off her sister's address to the dispatcher as she tried the code again. Whoever had taken out the electricity had taken out the security system as well. As she glanced around the kitchen in the growing darkness, she made a not-so-sizable leap of logic and added in a whisper as she glanced around in growing darkness, "The intruder is likely armed."

"We'll send a unit right away, Deputy Morrow," the dispatcher assured her. "Please stay on—"

Abby disconnected, hating to be rude but needing to reach her sister before she walked right into whatever crap was about to hit the proverbial fan. She rushed from the kitchen to the hall where her nephew had gone just a moment before, bringing up her call list as she hurried toward the library and hitting her sister's number.

"Pick up, pick up, pick up," she muttered when the phone rang once, twice. Suddenly, the high-pitched notes of a cell phone's ringtone brought Abby up short.

The hairs on the back of her neck stood on end when she realized the ringing was coming from one of the other rooms along the hall—a room that she had to pass in order to get to the library and the safe room where she hoped Tyler was already hidden. With fingers that trembled, she hung up. The ringing cut off abruptly, confirming her fears.

Oh God.

She swallowed hard, wishing like hell that the overnight bag containing her service weapon wasn't in the guest room upstairs. Her phone pinged with another text message, startling her so badly that the device fell from her hand, falling with a dull thud on the carpeted floor. She cursed under her breath, then dropped into a squat to retrieve the phone—keeping her eyes trained on the hallway ahead of her—and popped back up, her pulse pounding in her ears.

Steeling herself, she glanced down at the text. Her hand flew to her mouth to stifle a sob when she saw the picture on her screen. It was her sister, Emma, bound and gagged, her eyes wide with terror. Her hair was a tangled, ratty mess, blood darkening her silky tresses from a gash at her hairline.

Abby's head snapped up on a gasp. She felt the presence in the hallway a split second before she saw the hulking figure emerge from the room to her right. She pivoted and bolted in the opposite direction, but the intruder was surprisingly quick for his size. Before she could go more than a few feet, he grabbed her shirt, clotheslining her as he yanked her backward.

Abby stumbled, ass-planting so hard it knocked the air from her lungs. But she recovered quickly, scrambling to get to her feet. She didn't get far. The guy was on her in an instant, grabbing a handful of her hair and shoving her against the wall.

She instinctively squirmed and flailed, fighting to get free of his hold until the pressure of a gun in her ribs made her go instantly still.

"Where's the data?" the man demanded, his tone even, unperturbed, almost conversational. He was a pro, no doubt about it.

She realized then that by some miracle she still held her phone. She covertly moved her thumb, tapping her phone screen where she knew the back arrow had to be, trying to mentally tally the number of times it would take to get to the call list. She tapped one last time, hoping that whoever answered would tell the car en route to hurry the hell up.

"Gabe," Kyle greeted his brother with a grin, spreading his arms wide. "You came all this way to welcome me home. I'm touched!"

"You're gonna be touched all right," Gabe growled, his broad shoulders hunching over as his hands balled up at his sides. God, the older Gabe got, the more he could've been their father's clone. The same powerful build, same golden-blond hair kept high-and-tight, same piercing gaze, same scowl whenever he looked at Kyle.

Tom smoothly stepped in front of Gabe, placing a restraining hand on his chest and bringing him to an abrupt halt. "Back off."

Gabe knocked his hand away, making to go around him, but Tom grabbed his arm. "I said, back off, *Deputy*," Tom ordered, his tone leaving no room for argument and making it very clear that he was pulling rank—not just as the eldest brother but as executive deputy and Gabe's boss. "If you have something to say to Kyle, you can do it from right here."

Gabe sent such a menacing look Kyle's way that it brought Joe to his feet and to his younger brother's side.

"Good to see you again, Gabe," Kyle said, keeping his voice as sincere as he possibly could, all things considered. It honestly *was* good to see his brother again— even if the last time they'd seen each other they'd had a knockdown drag-out that had started with Gabe calling Kyle a traitor to the family for turning his back on all of them and ended with Kyle breaking Gabe's movie-star-perfect nose. A vast improvement, in his opinion. Now, if he could just do something about that arrogant dimple in Gabe's chin… The damned thing had always made Kyle want to nail his brother with a well-placed uppercut.

"You might be able to convince Tom and Joe to just forget what happened," Gabe spat, absently moving his hand to his left hip and turning down the radio that crackled loudly with an exchange between dispatch and another deputy, "but I can't forget what you did to Dad."

Kyle laughed in a harsh burst before he could check it. "What *I* did to Dad? Are you kidding me?"

Joe grabbed Kyle's arm and walked him back a few steps, putting more distance between him and Gabe. "Come on, man," Joe urged softly. "Let it go."

"Like hell I'm gonna let it go." Kyle sent an indignant look Gabe's way. "Jesus, Gabe, you're so far up Dad's ass, do you even know whose shit you're wiping every morning?"

Gabe surged forward, spoiling for a fight, forcing Tom to physically restrain him.

But Kyle wasn't about to back down. He strode forward to meet Gabe, trying to shake off Joe's restraining hand. "Let him go, Tom," he said. "I'll clean his clock. Again."

"Knock. It. Off."

Sadie's voice immediately cut through to both brothers, bringing them to heel in an instant. When Kyle turned his gaze toward her, he almost grinned at the woman who'd been like a kid sister to the Dawsons for as long as he could remember. Her expression was chastising, and with her arms folded across her chest and one hip jutting out at a defiant angle, she was damned adorable. He could only imagine what all those horny high school boys thought of their English teacher when she put the smackdown on them with that look. And he'd never envied Joe so much in his life.

"This is *my* house," she reminded them. "If you boys want to fight, you can take it somewhere else. But you're not stupid kids anymore. You're grown men, for crying out loud. You both need to get over yourselves and stop all this nonsense!"

Joe pegged them both with an expectant look. "You guys have something to say to Sadie?"

Kyle mumbled an apology to Sadie, then extended his hand to Gabe, feeling like a total jackass. Gabe hesitated for a long moment, glaring at Kyle, but then he blew out a harsh breath and shook Kyle's hand.

Kyle was just opening his mouth to make good with Gabe, when his phone rang. Grateful for the interruption, he snatched his phone from his pocket and answered without even looking. "Agent Dawson."

He could hear voices, distant, indistinct. "Hello? This is Agent Dawson." Frowning, he pulled the phone back

and checked the display. *Holy shit. Abby.* She'd actually called him back. He'd totally pussed out when he'd
called earlier, not even having the balls to leave a voice
mail. But she'd called him anyway. That was a good
sign, right?

His stomach flipped end over end, and he forced himself to keep his cool when he cleared his throat and said,
"Hey, Abby."

"Abby?" Sadie echoed, trading looks with Joe, knowing well Kyle and Abby's history. Then Kyle saw her
silently ask, "Why's she calling?"

"Abbs?" Kyle said when she didn't answer. "You there?"

"Everything okay?" Tom asked.

Kyle held up a finger to indicate he needed a minute.
He took a couple of steps away and plugged his other
ear. His frown deepened as he strained to listen. Even
though he couldn't quite make out all of what the man
on the other end was saying, he recognized that particular tone. His blood ran cold and he had to fight back the
sudden panic that wormed under his skin.

"Abby's in trouble," he whispered urgently to his
brothers. Keeping his phone to his ear, he motioned for
them to follow him. "We gotta go."

"What data?" Abby rasped, although she had a feeling
she already knew the answer.

The man's gun dug deeper into her ribs, making her
wince, but his tone was calm when he said, "Come,
come. That's not how the game is played. I tell you to
give me the data, you hand it over. No one gets hurt.
You don't get to change the rules."

Game? He thinks holding a gun to my ribs is a freaking game?

He wasn't just a pro; he was a whack job.

"You think you're the only client I have?" she asked, her voice thankfully more defiant than she felt. "You're going to have to be more specific than that if you want me to play along."

"Tartarus."

Abby's eyes went wide. He was talking about Tartarus Security Services International, her brother-in-law's company. But she hadn't yet divulged any information to Hamilton about the connection between the investigation she'd conducted for him and how it tied back to her brother-in-law's private security firm. So how in the hell did the guy holding a gun to her ribs know about it? Unless maybe Hamilton had known all along…

In the distance, Abby heard the sound of approaching sirens. Praying to God it was the police sent in response to her 911 call, she decided to keep the intruder talking. Find out what she could until they arrived—and maybe provide a little evidence to whoever might be listening on the other end of her open phone line.

"I didn't investigate Tartarus," she said truthfully. "There's been a mistake."

He pressed the gun harder into her ribs, just hard enough to make her cry out, but more in surprise and fear than pain. "Tick-tock, tick-tock. Running out of time…"

"I don't have it!" Abby yelled. "I have no idea what the hell you're talking about!"

The sirens were growing louder. "Well, you'd better figure it out," he growled in her ear, his almost playful tone suddenly harsh and deadly.

Oh yeah. This guy is completely unhinged...

"And not a word about the data to the police," he said, mildly chastising now, "or I'll send your sister's head to you in a box. Do you understand the rules as I have explained them to you, Deputy Morrow? Nod for me if you do."

Abby nodded furiously.

"Good girl. I'll be in touch."

He shoved her away none too gently.

Abby stumbled forward, and the phone flew from her hand, tumbling out of her immediate reach. A heavy pounding on the door had her scrambling to her feet and racing to the front door. She didn't even bother looking through the peephole or at the security camera mounted by the door to see who it was—it had to be better than the thief who'd just held her at gunpoint a moment before—and threw open the door.

Her knees buckled with relief when she saw who it was. Strong arms lifted her up and held her close.

"It's alright, baby girl," Sheriff Mac Dawson drawled. "I gotcha now."

Chapter 4

KYLE'S HEART WAS IN HIS THROAT WHEN THEY arrived at Emma Maxwell's house, a quick call to dispatch having confirmed his fear—an emergency call had come in from Abby's sister's house with a report of an intruder. Two sheriff's vehicles and three Oakdale police cars were already parked out front. The door stood wide open, and two of the Oakdale officers walked the perimeter, shining their flashlights along the hedges.

"Abby!" Kyle cried as he jumped out of Gabe's department Tahoe, not even bothering to close the door behind him as he sprinted toward the house. "Abby!"

An Oakdale officer met him at the door, barring his entrance. "I'm sorry. You can't come in here."

Kyle had the urge to throat punch the guy, but instead he reached into his jeans' back pocket and produced his ID. "Agent Kyle Dawson," he said, flashing his badge. "I received a call from someone at this residence."

"It's okay, Mike," Gabe said, coming up behind him with Tom and Joe in tow. "He's our brother. Let him in."

Officer "Mike" did a double take at Kyle, then stepped aside. "Sure. Sorry. Come on in."

Kyle squeezed by before the guy was even out of the doorway, rushing into the dark house. *Why the hell aren't there any lights, by the way?*

His father was barking orders in the semidarkness. As

Kyle headed in the direction of his father's voice, he felt a brief spike of apprehension at the thought of walking headlong into the same room as the Old Man, but his concern for Abby overrode his instinct to turn around and walk away.

"Abby!" he called out again as he reached the entrance to what appeared to be the living room. A man in what looked like a security guard's uniform sat on a couch with an ice pack on his crown, apparently having taken a blow to the back of the head.

Frantic, Kyle looked for Abby, his gaze taking in the entire room at a glance. His throat went tight when he caught sight of her sitting on the couch, her shoulders slightly hunched, her gorgeous blond hair a tangled mess. Her gray T-shirt was rumpled with a small tear near the collar, and her white capris had a smudge of dirt on the knee, but she was in far better condition than he'd feared he would find her. Sitting next to her was her nephew, Tyler, whose wide blue eyes were very similar to Abby's as the two of them turned their attention to the doorway where Kyle stood.

For a long, heavy moment, Abby's gaze met Kyle's, her expression unreadable. And for a few agonizing seconds, Kyle thought maybe she was in shock and didn't recognize him. But then she launched to her feet and rushed toward him, a strangled sob escaping her as he moved forward to meet her.

And then she was throwing herself into his arms, squeezing him around the neck so hard he could hardly breathe. He gathered her close, holding her as his heart pounded with relief and joy at finding her alive. It was almost as if they'd never been apart. *Almost*. But then

Abby's hold on him suddenly loosened and she was pushing out of their embrace.

She swiped at her cheeks as if embarrassed by her tears and took a step back. "Sorry. I shouldn't have—I mean, I didn't realize…" Her words trailed off as a frown brought her fair brows together. "What are you doing here? How did you know?"

"You called me," Kyle explained, trying to recover his composure and not let on how much he'd enjoyed having her back in his arms again—even for just a few short moments—and how much it killed him to let her go. "I heard what was happening and got here as soon as I could."

She cocked her head to one side, clearly confused. "But…I thought you were in New Orleans."

"In case you failed to notice, this happens to be a crime scene," his father interrupted. "And while I appreciate the FBI's concern, I'm sure you have more important business to attend to than a humble little B&E."

Kyle tried his damnedest not to roll his eyes. He should've known the first encounter with Mac would be like this after the way the last one had ended. And he wasn't surprised one bit to hear his own angry words thrown back in his face. But it still pissed him off.

He sent an exasperated glance his dad's way, then turned his attention back to Abby. "Breaking and entering?"

An almost imperceptible flush rose to her cheeks. "Yes." *She's lying. Why?*

"Perhaps you misunderstood me," Mac said, his voice louder. "We currently do not have need of your services, *Agent* Dawson."

Kyle turned to finally peg the Old Man with an

exasperated look. His father hadn't changed a bit. Tall and powerfully built, Mac Dawson was just as imposing as he'd ever been and as full of piss and vinegar as Kyle remembered. And he was looking at his youngest son like he was an intruder, an outsider who had no business there.

Hell, maybe he was right. But Kyle had never given him the satisfaction of an easy victory, so why start today?

Kyle turned his attention back to Abby, choosing to ignore his father's pointed dismissal. "What happened, sweetheart?"

—◦◦◦—

Sweetheart.

Abby suppressed a shudder as that one word speared straight through the heart. When Kyle Dawson had suddenly appeared in the doorway of her sister's living room, she'd thought she was hallucinating. But there he was, coming to her when she most desperately longed for him, his black brows drawn together in a frown, the already angular planes of his face even harsher in his distress.

Kyle ducked down a little so he was at eye level with her, those intense sapphire-blue eyes showing the depth of his concern as he searched her gaze. "Abby?"

"I interrupted the intruder," she explained, her gaze flitting briefly toward the sheriff, who'd looked skeptical from the start and was giving her the stink-eye even now. She cleared her throat a couple of times, before adding, "We scuffled. He got away."

Kyle nodded, his eyes narrowed. "Was that before or after he cut the power to the house and managed to get by the alarm system?"

She should've known Kyle would see through her story. He seemed to have almost a sixth sense when it came to crime scenes. But the photo of Emma bound and gagged suddenly came to mind, her concern for Emma's safety preventing Abby from confiding in Kyle.

"Clearly, he'd done his homework and had been casing the place, watching for an opportunity to break in when the family was out of town," she said.

That at least wasn't a lie. The guy had been prepared. He'd known exactly what he was doing. And she'd hazard a guess that he'd also known Curtis was out of town and that Abby and Tyler were there alone.

Speaking of Curtis... Where the hell is he anyway?

Kyle gave her a knowing look. "Abby—"

"I'm sure Mac and the boys can handle it," she interrupted, inwardly cringing, knowing that the reference to his father was a low blow. But it had the desired effect.

"You heard the young lady," Sheriff Dawson interjected. "Gentlemen"—he motioned to Gabe and Tom—"please escort Agent Dawson from the premises."

Gabe took a step forward to obey his father's order, but Tom put a restraining hand on his arm and shook his head.

"You look like you could use a little air," Kyle said, gently but firmly taking hold of Abby's elbow and leading her toward the doorway. She glanced over her shoulder at Tyler, reluctant to leave him after what they'd been through, but she saw Joe sitting beside him, chatting quietly to put the boy at ease.

Still, as great as it was to see Kyle, she wasn't exactly eager to be alone with him again. Silence had a way of opening the door to some really uncomfortable questions that she wasn't exactly ready to answer. That didn't even include the total bullshit she was feeding everyone about what had really happened.

"Excuse me, Agent, but I have some additional questions for my deputy," Mac said, his tone even in spite of the anger that flashed in his eyes. "And I would thank you not to interfere with my investigation, young man."

Kyle lifted his free arm to his side and bent slightly at the waist, offering his father a mocking bow. "Wouldn't dream of interfering, *Sheriff*."

Before his father could offer another word, Kyle ushered Abby from the room and out the front door. Abby's heart began to race as he led her farther into the growing darkness beyond the headlights and flashing blue-and-reds on the various vehicles.

Once they were out of earshot of any of the other officers, Kyle finally released her and turned to face her, hands on his hips. "Spill it. And don't give me any bullshit about interrupting a robbery. I could hear some of what was going on. I know he was after something you have—or he *thinks* you have."

Abby turned her head away, staring into the darkness crowding in along the dense tree line that bordered the property. "I don't know what you're talking about. I told you what happened."

Kyle grasped her chin and forced her gaze back to his. "Abby, it's *me*. You could always talk to *me*. Let me help you."

How could he be so kind after all she'd put him through, so caring when *she* was the one who'd pushed him away?

Abby closed her eyes, focusing on the way her skin tingled beneath the gentle pressure of his fingertips. "I can't."

"Why? Because of Mac?" Kyle demanded. "Screw him. You called me. I came. This is between you and me."

She shook her head as much as his tender grasp would allow. "It has nothing to do with Mac."

"Then what?" he pushed. She could feel his entire body tensing as if he was steeling himself. And then his hands fell away from her. "Is it because of what happened between *us*?"

She opened her eyes and met his gaze, her hands reflexively coming up to rest on his chest. "Oh, Kyle…" God, the pain she saw in his eyes just then was killing her. "No. It has nothing to do with us. If anything…"

Her words trailed off as she considered her words, torn between revealing her true feelings and letting him continue to think he'd never meant anything to her. She absently fiddled with the button on his blue-and-black-plaid button-down, suddenly getting the insane urge to pop it open and get to the toned pecs she knew were beneath the material. She dragged her gaze up to his, settling for her typical avoidance maneuver. "It's complicated."

His brow lifted, indicating he was totally on to her. "Well, I figure if it was simple, you would've already come clean with Mac. So tell me something I don't know."

She turned away and strode a couple of paces. "Kyle, I just *can't*."

"Bullshit!" he snapped, charging after her. "You called me here, Abby. If you didn't want—"

Abby spun around to face him, her arms spread wide. "If I tell you, my sister will die!"

Kyle twitched at her sudden revelation. For a long moment, he stared at her in stunned silence before finally running his hands through his hair in a frustrated sweep. "Jesus." He then made as if to reach for her, but his hand dropped back to his side. "What the hell have you gotten yourself into?"

She waved away his question. "Don't worry about it. I'll handle it."

"You'll handle it," he repeated, hands on his hips. "Right."

She bristled at his lack of faith. "What? Do you think just because I'm a woman I can't bring down the bad guy and get my sister back?"

The look he gave her was a mixture of anger and disappointment. "You know me better than that," he countered. "You know damned well this has nothing to do with you being a woman. It has everything to do with you not having any experience in this area."

"I went through the academy just like everyone else," she reminded him, slapping her hands on her hips, mimicking his posture, and lifting her chin defiantly. "And if I recall correctly, I'm a better shot than *you*, Kyle Dawson. So don't you tell me that I can't hack it."

He took a quick step toward her. "You want to prove to me you can do this on your own? Then you tell me what's going on and convince me that you're not going to end up getting yourself—and your sister—killed. Otherwise, I march right back in there," he said, jabbing a finger toward the house, "and tell the Old Man that you're bullshitting him. We'll see how well he takes that little bit of news."

Abby crossed her arms with a huff and pressed her lips together in an angry line. As much as she hated to admit it—and she seriously *hated* to admit it—Kyle was right. She was out of her depth on this one. She needed help. And as much as the thought of depending on Kyle made her want to hyperventilate into a paper bag, she wasn't about to let their history interfere with getting Emma back safely.

"Fine," she relented. "But not here."

Just as they turned back toward the house, Abby's phone dinged with a text message notification, startling her. Her gaze flitted to Kyle's. "He said he would be in touch."

"Want me to read it?" he asked.

She shook her head and swallowed hard, preparing herself for whatever the text message might hold. Dreading what was coming, she reached into her back pocket and took out the phone, holding her breath as she brought up the message.

But there was nothing she could've done to prepare herself. There was no text. Just a picture of what she figured was probably a man, based on the fact that he wore a suit and tie, lying on a concrete floor in a dark pool of blood. But his identity was a mystery, his face having been completely demolished, beaten and broken until it was nothing more than a pulpy, bloody mess of bone and gore. Even so, there was enough that looked familiar—including the ugly, expensive tie—to assure her of his identity.

Her hand reflexively reached for Kyle and grasped the front of his shirt, which was probably the only thing that kept her standing.

His arm went around her waist, offering her support. "Abby? What is it? Your sister?"

Abby shook her head slowly. "No. I think I found my brother-in-law." Her hand shook so badly as she turned the phone around for Kyle to view that he had to take it from her to see the photo on the screen.

Kyle's eyes went wide. "Holy shit."

Abby covered her mouth as an involuntary sob burst forth. She was barely keeping it together as it was, and now this… She knew that if her emotions broke loose, there'd be no reining them back in. She'd devolve into a hysterical cliché.

"Abby, sweetheart," Kyle soothed, "you don't know that this is Curtis. This guy's such a mess, there's no way of knowing."

She shook her head. "Curtis was due back this evening, but he's hours late. This has to be him, Kyle. Why else would someone send the picture?" She bent forward at the waist, bracing her hands on her knees and forcing herself to take slow, deep breaths to keep from passing out.

Dear God…

How could this happen? Where the hell was Curtis's so-called "personal security specialist" while Curtis was being beaten to death? The whole point of his hiring that giant wall of muscle Arlo—the MMA fighter turned bodyguard who followed Curtis around like a two hundred and fifty pound shadow—was to keep anything like this from happening.

And what was she going to tell her nephew? She had to make up some excuse, some reason why his parents hadn't returned. She wouldn't share the devastating news that his father had been murdered until she had some answers.

As she fought to draw in gulps of air, Kyle studied the phone. "Figures," he spat. "Blocked number." He hit Redial, waiting, but then shook his head. "I guess it would've been too much to ask for the asshole to have the factory-default voice-mail message listing the phone number. Abby, sweetheart, do you think you could figure out where this number originated?"

"Uh, um…" Abby straightened and smoothed her hair back from her face. Her synapses began firing again and she nodded. "Yes. There's an app you can use. It's on my phone. I hadn't tried it yet."

He handed the phone back to her, and she quickly called up the app and ran it against the blocked number. Within seconds the number was revealed on the screen. "I don't recognize that area code, do you?"

Kyle cursed under his breath. "Yeah. I do. It's from New Orleans. What are you doing?"

Abby was typing the phone number into her Internet browser. "I know it's a cell phone, so I'm looking for what service he uses. Then I can get a search warrant and hopefully figure out what we need to know."

"But in order to get a search warrant, you're going to have to provide probable cause," Kyle pointed out. "And that means telling someone about your sister. You okay with that?"

Abby couldn't hold back a frustrated groan. "*Damn* it!" Her shoulders sagged. "We *have* to find this guy, Kyle."

He nodded, his black brows drawn down in a frown. "We'll find him, Abby. And we'll get Emma back. I swear it."

He spoke with such confidence Abby almost believed him.

Chapter 5

"DID YOU RESOLVE THE PROBLEM?"

Greg Fielding ground his back teeth and gripped his phone tighter, resisting the urge to tell his employer to go piss up a rope. Instead he said, "Not exactly. The police arrived before I could locate the data."

"Hmm."

That was it. No yelling. No chastisement. Just that single short, ambiguous sound. But Fielding wasn't an idiot. He'd fucked up. And his employer wasn't in the habit of forgiving those who failed him. Fielding had worked for "Mr. Smith" before and knew he was far more likely to end up with a bullet at the base of his skull, courtesy of one of the other hired help. If they could find him.

"She knows we have her sister," Fielding continued. "And I've made it clear what will happen if she doesn't deliver the data."

There was a slight pause before he heard, "And?"

Fielding's thoughts raced. *And* what? What the hell else did his employer want to hear? "And I'll be in contact to arrange a drop."

Another pause.

Prick.

The guy was a pompous, self-righteous pain in the ass that Fielding would've been more than happy to take out just for shits and giggles if he hadn't needed the fat paycheck that'd be coming his way once this job was over with. Mr. Smith was damned lucky he paid so well.

For that reason alone, Fielding checked an exasperated huff and continued, "Should I apprehend Emma Maxwell's son too?"

"No need," his employer assured him.

Fielding waited for the rest of the explanation, but none came. Whatever. He wasn't being paid to give a shit. Whatever game his boss was playing was his own business. Fielding had been hired to abduct Emma Maxwell and get some sort of data from her sister. The rest of the bullshit was somebody else's job to clean up.

"I'll be in touch as soon as I have the data," Fielding assured his employer.

"You have twenty-four hours, Mr. Fielding."

Fielding tossed his phone aside with a muttered curse and snatched his night-vision field glasses from the passenger seat of his Bronco. He'd bought the piece of shit a few days earlier from the buy-here, pay-here lot just for this trip. The smarmy salesman was more than happy to hand over the keys without any questions when Fielding gave him a stack of hundreds with a few extras thrown in to expedite the transaction.

The vehicle was just the kind he liked for his line of work—nondescript, no real distinguishing characteristics, and able to handle pretty much any terrain. Not that northern Indiana had much in the way of difficult topography. Mostly farm fields and countryside in this area, especially in the two little towns he'd visited thus far.

The bigger hazard was the Amish buggies that seemed to be everywhere. He'd damned near run one over on his way to Maxwell's house earlier that evening. He'd come over a slight hill only to see the little black buggy in the middle of his lane. When he jerked the wheel to avoid nailing it, he'd almost flipped the Bronco.

But the only flipping was the bird he sent the driver's way as he passed. If he hadn't already secured a nice comfy seat in hell with what he did for a living, he imagined that little gesture probably would've earned him a few more points toward upgrading to first class.

He grinned, reliving some of his greatest hits, but a sudden sting on his forearm jolted him from his musings. He swatted the mosquito with an angry growl just as a light appeared in the doorway of the house he was watching. He raised the field glasses to his eyes.

Abby Morrow was leaving the house where she'd dropped off the kid and was getting back into a Mustang with the dark-haired guy who'd driven them there. The boy wasn't on his list, but it didn't hurt knowing where he was holing up, just in case Abby needed a little more persuasion after all.

The house belonged to the smokin' hot girlfriend of some local deputy, so that certainly complicated things. Fielding wasn't a chickenshit, but he wasn't a moron either. Breaking into the home of a cop didn't exactly tip the odds in his favor. And catching a bullet just to snag some kid who would most likely be a total pain in the ass wasn't exactly high on his bucket list.

Anyway, considering the way Abby Morrow had reacted to the picture of her sister, odds were good she'd fold in no time. Just a little more pressure was all she needed. In his experience, a little urgency was always a good motivator.

It was weird having Abby sitting in the car next to him again. Kyle glanced into the rearview mirror at the empty backseat of the '67 Mustang his brothers had restored for him on the sly as a surprise college graduation present.

A smile curved his lips before he could check it.

The car had seen a lot of action since then, especially during the summer when he and Abby were together. They'd made out there on more than one occasion, so into each other, so hot and horny that they couldn't always make it home before they needed to get their hands on each other. The thought of Abby then—half-naked and panting, her tanned skin glistening with sweat as his fingers stroked her toward mindless bliss to hold her over until he could get her home and bury himself in that same slick heat—made his cock go rock hard.

He shifted in the driver's seat, trying to make himself a little more comfortable, and had to force his grip on the steering wheel to relax. He barely managed to suppress a groan of need. He hadn't been with anyone since Abby. It wasn't like he hadn't had the opportunity, but none of the other women who'd crossed his path could hold a candle to the one at his side.

He sent a furtive glance her way to see her staring straight ahead and chewing a little at her bottom lip in that way that drove him crazy. It was the sexiest damned thing he'd ever seen. Which did wonders for the raging erection threatening to burst through his zipper.

Shit.

In an effort to divert his thoughts to something less boner-inducing, he cleared his throat and asked, "Did you tell Tyler the truth?"

Abby started, clearly having been wrapped up in her own thoughts. She turned and stared at him for a moment as if she'd forgotten he was there. "That his mother's been kidnapped and his father's dead, you mean?" she asked finally. "No. I told him his mom and dad had both decided to stay out of town a few more days—not a huge stretch of the imagination since Emma's already delayed her return twice and Curtis's business trips often go longer than anticipated. And I gave him the same story I told your dad about what happened at the house. He knows I'm lying about it being a normal break-in. I could see it in his eyes."

"Tyler's a smart kid," Kyle confirmed.

She closed her eyes for a moment. "I know. I just…I hate leaving him alone right now."

"He's not alone, Abby," Kyle assured her. "He's with Joe and Sadie. They're people he knows and trusts. And Joe's not going to let anything happen to him."

She brushed a couple of tears from her cheek. "I know. I just feel guilty. I should be with him right now."

"Don't feel guilty," Kyle insisted. "You can't conduct this investigation with him in the room, Abby." He hesitated, carefully considering his words before adding, "We just don't know what we're going to find."

Abby took a shaky breath but nodded.

"We're going to find her, Abbs."

She sent such a grateful look his way that his heart about broke in two. He hoped to God he was right.

"I don't know what to do about Curtis," she said.

"Who do we report it to? I mean, I don't even know where that picture was taken."

"I don't know," Kyle admitted. "Unless we figure out who sent it and where it was taken, I'm not sure there's anything we *can* do beyond reporting him missing. We still can't be certain he's even the guy in the photo."

She heaved a sigh. "I hate being at this asshole's mercy."

"Well, soon he won't be holding all the cards," Kyle assured her.

She twisted in her seat to face him. "What do you mean by that?"

He ducked his head a little guiltily. "I told Joe what was going on."

"Without running that by me first?" she cried. "You know what'll happen if they find out we've involved the Sheriff's Department!"

"Abby," Kyle said, keeping his tone even, "we need help on this. Mac might've played along with your story, but he's not an idiot. Who do you think trained me how to assess a crime scene? Odds are good that he's going to be back there as soon as the sun's up, taking another look. If we're going to keep him off the scent, there needs to be some misdirection. Joe can keep him focused on the burglary angle while we pursue our leads. But I think you underestimate my dad. I sure as hell don't see eye to eye with the guy, but he's not going to do anything that would get Emma killed. If you were just straight with him—"

"No!" Abby interrupted. "I'm not telling anyone else about this until my sister is home safe and sound. What if it were one of your brothers?"

She had a point. There's nothing Kyle wouldn't do

for one of his brothers. Even as strained as his relationship was with Gabe, he'd still throw down against anyone who threatened to do him harm, consequences to himself be damned.

"Okay. Fine," he relented. "We'll play this your way." *For now*. "But, uh, you should know I also asked Joe to look into the phone number."

"Oh my God," Abby moaned. "Kyle…"

Good lord, I wish she was moaning that phrase in a totally different context…

"I trust Joe with my life," he reminded her. "He'll know what to say to Elle McCoy to get her to request the search warrant so we can see the cell phone records." When Abby gave him a doubting look, he added, "She's the deputy prosecutor, Abby. We had to go through her. I'm sure Joe will just use the ol' Dawson charm to convince her to keep things as quiet as possible."

"You're a bit out of the loop," Abby informed him. "Gabe's been trying to get into Elle's pants for years, and she keeps turning him down like a hot stove. I hate to tell you, Kyle, but she's immune to that 'ol' Dawson charm.'"

"Good thing I didn't send Gabe to do it then, eh?" he said, offering her a half-grin. But when that didn't lessen her concern, he told her solemnly, "We had to try. This guy's got us by the short and curlies, Abby. We need to get some kind of leg up on him."

Abby nodded. "Okay. You're right. I just—" A single sob shook her shoulders. She hissed a curse under her breath and pressed her lips together in an angry line.

God, it was breaking Kyle's heart to see her going through this. The fucker who was holding her sister had better hope Emma came home okay, or Kyle would tear the bastard limb from limb. That protective urge he'd always felt toward Abby surged with a vengeance, making his blood boil with anger. He had no right to the feeling; that was for damned sure. But it didn't stop him.

Not knowing what else to do, he reached over and grasped her hand, giving it a squeeze. What he *wanted* to do was pull over and drag her into his arms, hold her close, and kiss her lips until she melted into him and let him take away all the pain and sorrow for a few fleeting moments. But he had to settle for just holding her hand.

"We're gonna get Emma back," he said. "I promise. And we'll figure out if that was Curtis in the photo."

Her hand shifted a little in his grasp, and for a second he thought she was trying to withdraw from his touch. But, to his surprise, she twined her fingers with his, squeezing back. "I don't want to get you mixed up in all this, Kyle. I'm sure you have your own cases back in New Orleans to worry about."

In spite of her words, he didn't miss the note of hesitant hope in her voice.

He smoothed his thumb over her knuckles and shook his head. "I've been reassigned," he explained. "I'm in the office up here now. I haven't officially started yet—just moved my stuff into my office today." He frowned, catching the time on the clock. "Or *yesterday*, I guess. And I'm using a week of vacation time to get settled, so don't worry about me."

When he glanced Abby's way, her eyes were wide and her chest was heaving a little as if she was out of breath. "You…" Her words trailed off and she swallowed hard before continuing. "You've been reassigned? *Permanently?*"

Was that a note of hopefulness in her voice again? Was it possible that she was *happy* to have him back in the area? Kyle's stomach rolled with some tentative hope of his own. "Well, you know, it's never permanent. But, hey, who knows? I could get transferred again— maybe to Middle of Nowhere, Alaska, or something next time."

"Middle of Nowhere, Alaska?" she repeated with a chuckle.

He turned the full force of his grin on her. "Hey, what can I say? It's a glamorous life I lead."

Abby laughed a little harder than his joke warranted, and he was glad to see some of her tension dissipate. God, he wished he could help her out in that regard in a few other ways.

Well, hell. Here we go again... Way to go, genius.

He shifted in his seat once more, hoping she thought he was just antsy and wasn't on to the party in his pants.

He could feel the weight of her stare and glanced her way again but wasn't quite sure how to interpret her expression. "Abbs?"

"Why did you call me?" she asked.

He offered her a halfhearted smile. "I'd wanted to let you know I was back in the area and find out how you were doing."

"Yeah, well," she drawled, "guess you got the answer to *that* question. Welcome to the latest episode of *Morrow Family Dysfunction.*"

Kyle chuckled. "Have you *met* my family?"

She laughed a little at that. "Touché."

They rode in silence for several moments before either of them spoke again.

"Thank you," she said so softly he almost didn't catch it. "You don't have to do this…"

He squeezed her hand, wishing he could respond truthfully with, *Of course I do. I love you. I never stopped loving you.* But he settled for, "I know I don't. But I am. So where should we start?"

Good question.

She gently extracted her hand from his grasp and drew her legs up to her chest, stalling a moment as she collected her thoughts. "At the beginning, I guess." God, the old saying about hindsight being twenty-twenty certainly couldn't have been truer than in this case. "A few weeks ago, a man named Patrick Hamilton contacted me. Have you heard of him?"

Kyle shrugged. "Nah. Who is he?"

"He's the owner of a whole network of companies, including an investment firm called Hamilton Whitmore," she explained. "He suspected that one of his employees was involved in unethical activities, and wanted to hire me to investigate and provide any evidence I came across as to who it was and the transgressions being committed."

Kyle glanced at her. "Mac was cool with you freelancing?"

She squirmed a little, remembering how she'd pulled at the sheriff's heartstrings, explaining how the money from the job could help her mother. "He wasn't wild about me using county equipment for some big shot out of Detroit, but he finally agreed."

Abby could tell Kyle was frowning even though she only had a view of his profile. She knew that look well. His mind was already processing the few facts she'd provided, connecting the dots. "But if this guy Hamilton is such a big deal, why didn't he just hire someone there in Detroit?"

"I asked that same question," she admitted. "Hamilton said he preferred to keep the investigation out of the hands of anyone local for fear that the information would get back to his employee."

"Okay, I get that," Kyle admitted. "But why *you*? No offense. I just know that there are entire firms that specialize in the type of investigation Hamilton wanted. Why—or maybe more importantly, *how*—did he hear of you and the work you do for Fairfield County?"

"Asked that as well," she assured him. "I certainly know I'm not the only one who could've taken on this project. He said he heard about me after the Brannigan case hit the papers."

Kyle shook his head. "Not familiar with that one."

"Ted Brannigan was an executive at one of the big drug companies that I busted for child porn," she said. "Most of the news stories didn't mention my name— which is fine by me—but a few in the Midwest found out I was the investigator and put my name in the paper. Hamilton claimed that's where he first heard about me, and that then he had *me* investigated to determine if I was the real deal and equal to the task."

"And you were okay with all this?" Kyle pressed. "You didn't think Hamilton seemed a bit paranoid just to find out if one of his employees was taking long lunches and knocking boots with his admin?"

"Turns out he had reason to be paranoid."

He glanced her way, brows raised. "Yeah?"

She nodded. "There were several people who'd aroused his suspicion, all high-level employees. Every one of them had something to hide, some skeleton in the closet that probably wouldn't have surprised anyone. But none of it was what Hamilton was hoping I'd find on them."

"And…?" Kyle prompted.

"And so I expanded my search," she continued, "and followed some email trails down a rabbit hole."

Kyle connected a few dots of his own. "And you found what you were looking for."

"And then some." When he sent an expectant look her way, she said, "The guy he should've been worried about was Preston Whitmore—the son of Hamilton Whitmore's founding partner and Patrick Hamilton's godson."

"You think Hamilton knew his godson was dirty?"

She shrugged. "Hard to say. He honestly might've had no idea."

"Okay, playing devil's advocate here," Kyle told her. "If Hamilton knew about Whitmore, it could explain why he wanted to keep things quiet. Could be that the list of people he fingered were folks he had it in for anyway and wanted to sacrifice as the proverbial fall guys."

"Maybe," Abby agreed. "Or maybe he was just hoping someone else was really behind it and Preston was a pawn."

"So what all was this guy Whitmore into?"

Abby grunted. "What *wasn't* he into? He was making

dirty deals all over the city to line his own pockets. And he was on the take with at least one drug cartel, helping them launder money."

"No shit?"

"Oh, but that's not even the best part," she said, a bitter little chuckle bubbling up before she could stop it. "He was also doing business with Tartarus Security Services International."

"Wait," Kyle interjected. "Isn't that your brother-in-law's company?"

Abby tried to suppress a shudder, remembering the photo of "Curtis" she had received. She was certain the image would haunt her for years. "Yes."

Kyle cursed softly.

"As I was going through everything I could find on Whitmore, I came across deleted emails between him and my brother-in-law."

Abby still couldn't believe Whitmore was such an egotistical jerk that he actually sent all of his shady correspondence through his work email account. What a moron. Clearly, he figured that being the cofounder's son, he was immune from the firm's technology policy. Oh, how wrong he'd been... As far as she was concerned, he might as well have posted all his criminal activity updates on Facebook.

"What was your brother-in-law's relationship to Whitmore?" Kyle asked. "I mean, why would he need to be getting dirty with this guy? Curtis's company has private security operations all over the world. Hell, my brother Joe came across some of his guys in Afghanistan when he was there."

Abby swallowed. "The company has been plagued

by a whole slew of financial issues. Curtis used to go on about it after he got a few cocktails in him. As of about four years ago, Tartarus was on the verge of going under."

"So what changed?" Kyle asked as he turned into her neighborhood.

She sighed, trying to tamp down her humiliation at having to admit the truth. "He and Whitmore went into business together."

Kyle finally reached her driveway, pulling his car up to the garage door and turning off the engine before he asked, "Doing what?"

For a moment, Abby sat staring through the windshield, shame weighing down her tongue and making it difficult to speak the words. But then Kyle reached over and reclaimed her hand, giving her fingers a squeeze. "Abbs?"

When she turned to meet his gaze, his expression was so filled with concern that it caused her throat to tighten. But she answered, "Human trafficking."

Kyle's grasp went slack. "What?"

Now that she was getting the truth off her chest, the words came tumbling out. "Whitmore gave Curtis the funds to set up the first few facilities in Central and South America, Asia, a couple in Eastern Europe as well. Within a year, Curtis had made back the money plus enough to pull Tartarus back from the brink. Another year and they were raking it in hand over fist."

Kyle dragged a hand down his face. "Jesus."

"I know, right?" she replied. "I had no idea that human trafficking was so prevalent. I mean, these are women and *girls* being forced into the sex trade, domestic servitude… And in one of the email trades between Whitmore and Curtis there's mention of a client list."

This made Kyle's spine stiffen. "You have the list?"

She shook her head. "I haven't found that yet, but reading between the lines, some seriously big names stand to lose everything if it comes out that they've been ordering underage virgins for their carnal enjoyment."

Kyle ran a hand through his silky black hair, that stubborn cowlick just over his left brow making a thick lock fall over his forehead. Abby instinctively lifted her free hand to brush the hair away, but then let her hand drop back into her lap, hoping he hadn't noticed. Luckily, he seemed preoccupied with his own thoughts.

"You think they're blackmailing their client list," Kyle announced after a moment.

Abby nodded. "I think there could be an awful lot of people who have a grudge against my brother-in-law. I'd planned to step out of it and give everything to the feds to sort out, but then…"

"But then everything happened with Emma," he finished for her. When she nodded, he gave her the charming grin that turned her insides into molten lava. "Well, lucky you, you have a fed sitting right here."

She grinned a little in spite of herself. "Thanks, but I don't want to involve you any more than I already have. It's too dangerous."

His expression instantly became serious. "Exactly why you need someone who's got your back. Now, show me your findings. I want to see everything you've got."

Chapter 6

As early morning sunlight began to creep through the blinds in Abby's study, Kyle pushed back from the desk and stretched his arms, arching his aching back. He'd been sitting in that damned chair for hours, paging through the information she'd compiled.

God, she was brilliant. She might not be out in the field studying crime scenes and questioning suspects, but in just a few days she'd managed to sift through several years of incriminating evidence to bring a swift end to her brother-in-law's nefarious partnership with Preston Whitmore.

But obviously someone had beaten her to it when they'd apparently murdered Curtis Maxwell and texted Abby a photo of their handiwork.

He turned his attention to the overstuffed suede easy chair in the corner of the room where Abby was curled up asleep, having finally taken his advice to get a little rest. She'd tried valiantly to stay awake as he read through her reports, checking her phone every five minutes on the off chance that she might've missed the next text from her sister's abductor.

But when he caught her nodding off for the fourth time, she'd given in and retreated to the chair with strict orders to wake her when he finished or if she received further instructions—whichever came first.

But she looked so peaceful, so damned beautiful

that the last thing he wanted to do was drag her out of what he hoped were pleasant dreams and into the stark, heartbreaking reality that her dead brother-in-law was an asshole of the lowest order and that her sister was now being held captive because of it.

There'd be time to talk about everything and figure out a game plan after she'd caught some shut-eye and was thinking clearly again. And he could relate. His mind was mush. And his eyes were so grainy from lack of sleep that he wasn't sure he'd be able to pry them open again once he finally closed them.

He checked his watch. Half past the ass-crack of dawn. Awesome. Chances were that he'd be getting a call from Joe in a few hours to give him an update on the search warrant for the abductor's cell phone provider.

The fact that the number was from New Orleans had his spidey senses tingling in a big way. It was pretty damned coincidental, considering the case he'd just been booted from down in the Big Easy. Except he didn't believe in coincidences.

He scowled at Abby's laptop as he shut it down, mentally going back through all the info he'd read. He hadn't seen anything in the data linking Curtis and Whitmore to what had been going on in New Orleans, but he sure as hell wasn't going to discount anything just yet. In fact, until he could rule it out, he was going to presume that the human-trafficking operation he'd been working to bust and the one Abby's brother-in-law was running were somehow linked.

The question now was how much to share with Abby. If he divulged even *half* of the shit he'd been on to down in NOLA…

He shook his head, making the call and shoving his conscience aside for the moment. Abby'd be pissed as hell if she discovered he'd withheld information from her. But he'd have to risk it. There was no sense in making her worry even more about her sister. She was already teetering on the verge of a total meltdown. He didn't have the heart to tell her that there was no way the abductors would kill Emma. Not a pretty, weak woman like her. Although after they finished passing her around to clients, forcing her to ingest enough drugs to keep her compliant, Emma would probably *wish* she was dead.

He'd just have to make sure it never came to that.

He rubbed at his eyes again, the raspy, burning sensation on his eyelids reminding him he couldn't do shit without some sleep. He got up from the desk and went through the house, once more checking all the doors and windows, making sure they were locked and that the alarm was on. The alarm hadn't stopped Emma's abductor from breaking into her estate and getting the drop on Abby. But she hadn't expected it. And she hadn't had backup. It'd be different this time around if the bastard tried something. Kyle would make damned sure of that.

When he came back into the room, he started toward Abby's couch to crash for a couple of hours, but then he heard her moan softly and shift uncomfortably in her sleep. So instead he scooped her up in his arms, cradling her against his chest.

She murmured something unintelligible and turned into him, resting her head against his shoulder.

"It's alright, sweetheart," he whispered, pressing a kiss to her hair. "I'm here."

He carried her back to where he remembered her

bedroom to be. It was pretty much the same as he recalled, except that she had a new bedspread. She'd ditched the white one with the big purple flowers. This one was smoky lavender—almost gray—with black fili- gree embroidered at the bottom.

He grinned, remembering how he'd teased her about feeling like he was making love in a botanical garden every time he'd stayed over. But the fact that it was gone now tugged at his heart. Had she gotten rid of it because it reminded her too much of him?

He rolled his eyes at his own presumptiveness.

Uh-huh. Sure. She'd redecorated her bedroom because she'd had such a damned hard time getting over him…

Yeeaah, might want to rein in that ego, dude.

He gently set her on top of the comforter, then glanced around for something to drape over her and spotted a poofy, fluffy blanket folded over a wingback chair nearby.

As he arranged the blanket over her, she suddenly stirred, her eyes snapping open. She bolted upright with a gasp. "What time is it? Did he call? Text? Have we heard anything?"

Kyle shook his head and sat down on the edge of the bed. "Nothing yet. And it's early. Too early for anything to happen. Go back to sleep."

Her eyes went wide, as if in panic. "I can't, Kyle! I have to do *something*."

She threw the blanket off and started to get up, but he put a firm hand on her shoulder and pressed her back against the pillows. When her chest began to heave with rapid breaths, he eased his hold a little and let his hand skim down her arm.

"Sweetheart, there's nothing we can do right now. It's Saturday. Joe managed to get in touch with Elle last night, but by the time he reached her it was too late to call the judge. She was going to call about the warrant first thing this morning. But I'm pretty sure that by 'first thing' she didn't mean five thirty."

"Have *you* slept at all?" Abby asked, her voice breathy.

He shook his head, his lids suddenly weighing about two tons. "I was going to make sure you were comfortable and then go catch some shut-eye on your couch." He smoothed the hair away from her face, too tired to resist the urge. Then he bent and pressed a kiss to her forehead, letting his lips linger far longer than he should have. When he pulled back, he said, "So, are you comfy then?"

She swallowed hard, then nodded.

"Okay." Now way past being able to string two words together, he started to get to his feet, but to his utter astonishment, she grabbed his hand, keeping him there. Then, without a word, she shifted over, making room for him to lie down beside her.

Suddenly he was wide awake again.

In the back of his mind, the rational side of Kyle was hopping up and down screaming, *Bad idea! Bad idea!*

But Kyle toed off his shoes and stretched out beside her anyway. When she lifted the edge of the blanket, offering to share, he hesitated for the briefest moment, but then edged closer. They lay there side by side on their backs, their shoulders almost touching. Kyle could feel the tension in that tiny bit of space, an undercurrent of electricity that was making every nerve ending hum with awareness.

Abby cleared her throat. "Are *you* comfy?"

Kyle chuckled, grateful she'd spoken first, breaking the tense silence. "Not especially."

She returned his chuckle, then rolled onto her side, facing him, then moved his arm so that she could snuggle against his shoulder. "How's this?"

How was it? How *was* it? It was *perfect*. And sheer torture. Mr. Rational had now pulled out his megaphone and was screaming at the top of his lungs for Kyle not to be an idiot. Too bad being an idiot when it came to Abby was kinda his thing.

Kyle pulled her in closer and pressed another kiss to the top of her hair. "Much better."

Then he closed his eyes and tried to ignore the welcome weight of Abby's arm draped over his waist. And the scent of her hair. And how damned much he wanted her.

And as if Kyle's brain realized it needed to intervene before he did something colossally stupid, sleep suddenly claimed him.

———

What the hell was she doing?

She'd practically thrown herself at Kyle, inviting him to lie down next to her. Thank God he'd drifted off to sleep or who knows what would have happened.

She certainly knew what she'd *wanted* to happen. She'd wanted it to happen ever since he'd come rushing into her sister's house, yelling her name. The world was spinning out of control, but there Kyle stood at the center of it all, a pillar of strength when she needed him most.

She'd given him an out, had offered to let him bail. But he'd insisted on helping her get her sister back safely. Was it possible he still loved her? He clearly still cared. He'd curled her into his body, holding her. She wasn't a moron—she could feel the sexual tension between them, the desire that spiked in them both whenever they touched. Even if he no longer loved her, he still wanted her. Too bad they had lousy timing. The fact that he'd dozed off was no doubt a blessing, most likely saving them from a very awkward morning after.

Besides, she couldn't let herself be distracted right now. She needed to be focused if she was going to get her sister back. As soon as she'd heard his soft snore, the tension in her muscles had eased, allowing her to drift back to sleep as well.

And although her dreams thankfully consisted of remembrances of the summer she'd spent with Kyle and not of the horrible events of the day, they'd been far from restful. The time she and Kyle made love on her boat was most prominent among the images that replayed in her sleep—probably because of the number of times she'd dreamed of it in the last three years.

She'd anchored them in the secluded area that evening, hoping to flirt some more under the cover of growing darkness and maybe finally get up the nerve to kiss him. She'd never been particularly forward, but the knowledge that he was leaving town soon—and that this might be her last chance to finally act on the sexual tension between them—gave her the courage to make her desire for him known.

A kiss. Just one kiss. That's all she'd been hoping for that night. But when she dropped the anchor and turned around to make a goofy remark about being alone at last, she found him standing right behind her, the look in his eyes unmistakable. And then he was kissing her, his mouth hot and sensual. Her bikini top came off within seconds and his hand was on her breast, his thumb brushing over her hardened nipple and making her shudder.

Then they were stumbling back to the captain's chair, the T-tops offering a little privacy as he sat her down and got on his knees, pulling her to the edge of the seat so he could kiss her again, long and hard, and then move down to take one of her nipples into his mouth. She shuddered, close to release, so he moved to the other nipple, lavishing attention on that one as well. Then he was kissing a path down her stomach until he reached her bikini bottoms. He drew back a little, sending a heated glance up at her. When she nodded, practically begging him to go on, he obliged.

A finger ran along the edge of her bikini, making her breath come in gasps. And when he finally pulled the cloth aside and pressed his mouth against her, her cry echoed across the water. But Abby didn't care. Not one damned bit. Her only thought was for the mind-numbing bliss Kyle's tongue elicited. When she came, he chuckled, a deep rumble that vibrated against her. Which sent an aftershock through her that was almost as powerful as the orgasm that had just rocked her.

And with a groan of need, she pulled him up so that they were both standing. As her mouth sought his, she shoved his trunks over his hips, gratified by the strength and power of his erection as she took him in her hand. Then she was shoving him down onto the captain's chair, straddling him, sheathing him with her body, making them both moan…

Abby jolted awake, not surprised by the ache in her core or the dampness in her panties. Dreaming about their first time together always had that effect on her.

The sun was completely up now, and she could only guess at the hour. In spite of her sleep-addled brain, she was keenly aware of the hard planes of Kyle's stomach where her hand rested and the comforting weight of his arm curled lightly around her and his body pressed against hers.

At some point while they'd slept, they'd shifted into the tangle of arms and legs they'd so often enjoyed during their summer together. When she awoke to find their bodies had so easily fallen back into the familiar, her initial reaction was to pull away and put some distance between them. But then she felt the warmth of his arms wrapped around her, heard the steady rhythm of his heartbeat in her ear soothe her in a way she sorely needed at the moment, and sank into his embrace.

When she felt him draw in a long, deep breath sometime later, she knew he was rousing. That was always the first sign. A sad grin curved her lips, knowing that the contentment she'd been enjoying would soon come to an end.

"Hey there," he whispered, his deep voice a little raspy with the vestiges of sleep. "What time is it?"

She closed her eyes, her arm around his torso tightening ever so slightly. *Time to let you go*, she wanted to say. Instead, she raised her head and glanced at the bedside table. "Eight forty-five. We should probably get moving." With a sigh, she pushed up onto her elbow and started to pull out of his embrace as she announced, "I'll go make us some coffee."

But before she could move out of his hold, he grasped her nape and kept her from pulling away, his gaze searching hers intently, looking for…

What?

If it was anything akin to what Abby was looking for as she searched his, then she was in trouble. Serious trouble.

Because the longer she held his gaze, the more charged the air between them became and the harder her heart pounded. Her gaze dropped briefly to his lips, which was a mistake. God, those lips. She'd never forgotten their warmth, how they could be so tender one moment and harsh and demanding the next. And she longed to feel them against hers, just once more…

―――

For a moment, Kyle thought he was still dreaming. Abby was in his arms, curled into his body as she'd been so many times before. And when she'd started to draw away, he'd impulsively grasped the nape of her neck, planning to steal a kiss and tempt her to stay in bed for another half hour or more, but as the sleep clouding his judgment faded, he hesitated, reality crashing back down on him, reminding him that she was no longer his.

Yet as he met her gaze and felt her pulse thundering against the back of his fingers as they skimmed along the curve of her throat, he dared to hope she still felt the same attraction, the same undeniable magnetism that had existed between them before.

His gaze dropped to her full pink lips, so soft and enticing. As he watched, they parted on a little gasp, and his eyes snapped back up to hers. "Abby," he whispered, not sure what else to say, all the blood flow having abandoned his brain in favor of other, more insistent areas of his anatomy.

Then, to his astonishment, she leaned in, pressing a tender kiss to his mouth. He was so taken aback that for a moment he didn't even react. But then his arms went around her, and he was rolling her onto her back, his lips devouring, his tongue slipping between her teeth to tangle with hers. And when her hand came up to grasp the back of his head, her fingers twined in his hair, a groan of need rumbled up from the center of his gut.

Dear God, kissing her was as incredible as he remembered. Check that. It was *better* than he remembered. It was mind-blowing bliss. And he wanted more, *needed* more.

He released her mouth to press kisses along her jaw, her throat, her collarbone, pausing to lathe the hollow at the base of her neck with his tongue, eliciting a gasp. But before he could venture any lower, she was pulling his mouth back up to hers, kissing him hungrily, nipping at his bottom lip with her teeth, sucking on it gently in the way she knew drove him out of his mind.

His hand skimmed down her ribs, then slipped beneath the hem of her shirt. She gasped when his fingertips met her bare skin, breaking their kiss.

He pulled back just enough to peer down at her. "Should I stop?" he panted, the need that gripped him making it impossible to breathe. "Just say the word, Abby."

A range of emotions played over her lovely features in an instant. "Kyle, I…" Her words trailed off, but she didn't look away, her gaze traveling over his face. He started to pull back, to back off and give her some space, but her arm was still around his neck and now tightened ever so slightly, keeping him from moving away. "I'm so sorry," she told him softly, reaching up to brush the hair off his forehead. Her fingertips trailed down to his temple, along the curve of his jaw, and across his lips that still hovered so close to hers. "I never should have—"

A knock at Abby's front door startled them both. Kyle rolled away, lunging to his feet and holding a finger to his lips. Abby nodded and followed him down the hall, keeping close. Instead of approaching the front door, he crept into the sitting room and pulled back the blinds just enough to get a look at the driveway, sighing when he realized who it was.

He jerked his chin at Abby. "It's okay."

Abby gave him one last questioning glance before opening the door. He saw her features immediately smooth in relief when she saw who it was. "Hi, Elle. You want to come inside for a cup of coffee?"

"Thanks," he heard Elle reply. "But I can't stay."

Kyle strolled in from the sitting room to stand beside Abby, offering a smile to Fairfield County's deputy prosecutor. She was in cutoff shorts, a form-fitting T-shirt, and running shoes. With her red hair pulled back in a messy ponytail, she was even more gorgeous because of her disheveled appearance. No wonder his brother had his eye on her.

"Hey, Elle," Kyle said, extending a hand. "Good to see you again."

Elle glanced back and forth between him and Abby and tried unsuccessfully to smother a grin. "Hey, Kyle. Welcome home. Looks like I'm not the first to jump on the welcome wagon." She cleared her throat. "So to speak."

"Just helping Abby on a case," Kyle assured her, glancing at Abby and suddenly noticing her kiss-swollen lips and the beard burn he'd left on her cheeks. Clearly his bullshit denial to Elle's unasked questions just made him and Abby look even guiltier.

But who cared? So what if Elle knew that he and Abby had been well on the way to—*What?* He had no frigging clue what would've happened if Elle hadn't arrived. Would he and Abby have ended up naked together, making love with the frenzied passion that had so often consumed them? Hell if he knew. But he sure as shit would like to give it another go later and see where a few more hot and heavy kisses took them…

Elle's smile broadened. "Uh-huh," she said, laughter in her voice. She sent a none-to-subtle wink Abby's way, bringing an adorable flush to Abby's cheeks, then held up a piece of paper and wagged it at Kyle to take. "Here's your search warrant, lover boy. Joe's lucky I like him as much as I do, or I would've been very displeased to have my date interrupted last night. And can I just say how much Judge Pettigrew enjoyed me waking him up at seven this morning? Better make this one count."

Kyle glanced over the warrant, then gave her a terse nod. "Thanks, Elle. I owe you one."

"Yeah, you do," she agreed. She hopped down the steps, but at the final stair, she turned back to add, "And the first thing you can do to pay me back is tell your brother Gabe he's a jackass."

Kyle was taken aback by the sudden pronouncement. "Okaaaay," he drawled, looking askance at her. "I'm not disagreeing. Trust me. But what'd he do to piss *you* off?"

She put her hands on her hips, and this time her smile held no mirth. "Let's just say that the next time he nearly blows one of my cases because he can't stay away from a key witness's girlfriend, he'll have to swallow to scratch his balls."

Kyle's brows shot up.

Well, didn't that paint a picture?

He gave her a curt nod. "Jackass. Got it."

Elle lifted a hand in a wave as she turned to go, calling over her shoulder, "Have fun, kids! Don't *work* too hard!"

Kyle turned to quip to Abby about his brother's jacked-up methods for getting the pretty prosecutor's attention but saw she'd already disappeared. He frowned as he shut and locked the front door. "Abby?"

"In here!"

He went into her study and saw she was already on the phone, her laptop up and running, fingers tapping rapidly on the keyboard. She waved him in and motioned for him to hand over the search warrant.

Okay, then. Back to work. Guess they'd talk about what had happened between them later. He handed Abby the search warrant and crossed his arms over his chest, staying out of her way as she hunched over her keyboard, her brows furrowed in concentration.

Unfortunately, not being able to have an active role in the investigation at that moment allowed his mind to wander back to what had happened in Abby's bedroom just a few moments before. He'd felt the longing in her kiss just as she'd no doubt felt his. And yet she'd said she was sorry for it. Check that. She'd actually said she was "so sorry." What the hell had she been about to apologize for?

Oh yeah. He was definitely looking forward to that conversation later. They had a hell of a lot to discuss—that was for damned sure.

"Hi," he heard her say into the Bluetooth device in her ear, mercifully calling him away from his current train of thought. "This is Deputy Abigail Morrow…"

Chapter 7

"GOOD MORNING, SUNSHINE," FIELDING GREETED HIS pretty prisoner as he entered the little maintenance closet where he was keeping her. Emma Maxwell was stunning even with her hair matted with blood and her face covered in mascara smudges. He'd still do her. But he wasn't into forcing himself on a woman. He had scruples after all. And considering the look of fear and disgust she was giving him, he didn't feel a case of Stockholm syndrome coming on.

He'd originally kept her blindfolded, but that had made her scream like a fucking banshee, so he'd taken the blindfold off, deciding to risk her seeing his face in exchange for a little peace and quiet. Besides, he wasn't the kind of guy who stood out in a crowd. That's what made him so successful at his line of work. He blended in, becoming almost invisible in his ordinariness. Average height, average build, average looks, no distinguishing characteristics at all.

In twenty-five years he'd never once been ID'd. He sure as hell wasn't worried about some self-absorbed socialite being able to pick him out of a lineup—provided he was ever caught. But he wouldn't be. He was a master of the game. He'd never lost. Not once. And Emma Maxwell knew the score. She had proven to be a very compliant pawn. And she understood very well that, as a pawn, she was expendable—as regrettable as that might be.

He opened the bag of fast-food breakfast sandwiches he'd brought with him and took a deep breath, his stomach growling when he caught the mouthwatering scent of artery-clogging goodness. "Mmm," he said, leaning close to her ear. He wasn't surprised when she shrank away from him, trembling. "Smells good."

When he drew back, her trembling subsided ever so slightly as her gaze flicked down to the bag and then back up to his face. He might've even called it *pleading*.

"You hungry?" She didn't respond, but he heard her stomach rumble in response. "You behave yourself, and I just might be inclined to share a little. You want a bite?"

She swallowed around her gag and nodded just a little.

He grinned at her. "Well, alrighty then. I'm gonna take this gag off you, but you scream and I'll break your jaw." His smile widened—so as not to frighten her. "Then you'll be hungry *and* hurting. Are we clear?"

She nodded furiously, her eyes taking on a wild look.

Fielding pulled the gag off and gave her a stern look when a strangled little sob came out of her pretty mouth. "Remember, no screaming."

When she stared silently at him with those wide blue eyes, he unwrapped one of the sandwiches and held it up to her mouth. She cast one questioning look his way, hesitating, but then sunk her teeth into the sandwich, tearing off a sizable bite.

He smoothed a hand over her filthy hair as she wolfed down some more of the sandwich. "Easy now," he rebuked mildly. "Don't want to make yourself sick."

Her brows twitched together slightly while she sent a curious look his way. She was confused by his kindness, no doubt. Honestly, he didn't give a shit about *her*. It was just way too fucking early to be cleaning up puke, especially the puke of some rich bitch whose husband had apparently crossed the wrong people. Taking care of her to some degree, keeping her guessing and fearful was all just part of the game. It wouldn't do him a damned bit of good if she choked to death because then he'd have to forfeit. And that just wasn't an option.

So he forced what he hoped resembled a friendly smile in case that kind of shit would keep her from causing problems. "Now, be a good girl," he told her, "and after you eat maybe we'll give your sister a call."

—∞—

Abby shoved away from her desk with a frustrated groan. Two hours. She'd been on the phone with the cell company for two *freaking* hours trying to get the information she needed. When they'd given her grief about it being Saturday and not being able to get back to her until Monday at the earliest, it was all she could do not to totally lose it. As it was, she *might've* made some threats involving hot pokers up someone's ass. But she'd finally reached a supervisor who wasn't a complete douche bag and had the necessary authority to honor the search warrant Abby had faxed over.

And they'd given her a name: Peter Montgomery Fortinbras.

Trouble was, after a closer look, it turned out Mr. Fortinbras had died in service to his country on a beach in Normandy on June 6, 1944.

Abby rubbed her temples, trying to assuage the headache pounding there. God, the last thing she needed was a full-blown migraine interfering with her efforts to find her sister. Mapping the cell phone's locations every time the kidnapper made a call or sent a text hadn't helped either. According to that information, the fake Mr. Fortinbras hadn't left New Orleans in days.

"Still no luck." She sighed as Kyle came in with her rewarmed cup of coffee. "I don't know what else to do at this point except wait for him to call and give me the instructions for an exchange."

Kyle sat down on the edge of her desk. "The most important thing now is to just get Emma back. If you have to turn over the data, so be it. We'll continue to sort through the rest of the information later. You have a backup copy of everything, right?"

She nodded. "Of course."

"Then we'll give them what they want and get your sister back," he assured her. "And after she's safe, we can do whatever it takes to bring the bastards down."

"Promise me that they won't get away with this, Kyle," Abby said, her voice breaking under the strain of her emotions.

He lifted a hand and caressed her cheek lightly. "I swear it."

She held his gaze for a long moment, captivated by the determination and sincerity she saw there and was tempted to smile at the walking, talking contradiction that was Kyle Dawson. As much as he sought to distance himself from his family, Kyle was more like his father than he cared to admit. He was a Dawson through and through.

His desire to protect and serve extended well beyond those he personally cared about. She knew without a doubt that he was the kind of man who would lay down his life protecting a complete stranger as soon as he would for a loved one. And while his courage and self-lessness made her immensely proud of him and all he stood for and were among the reasons she'd fallen so crazy in love with him, they also made her wonder in which category his desire to help *her* was placed.

The way he'd kissed her that morning, the passion that had ignited in an instant—and no doubt would have consumed them had they not been interrupted—could've been nothing more than a product of the stress of the situation. *She* certainly would've been willing to throw caution to the wind to forget what was going on just for a moment.

Wasn't it true that people in high-stress situations often attached themselves to others who shared their experiences, misinterpreting the desire to spit in death's face as a true emotional connection?

Or was it just the pull of mutual desire between two consenting adults? Was he just taking advantage of an opportunity that presented itself? Because, let's be honest. He'd been a gentleman. She'd felt his surprise when she kissed him.

It'd been a bullshit move on her part when she'd been the one to break things off. She had absolutely no right to accept his help—or his tender caresses—without an explanation. He deserved better than that.

"Abby?" he asked, breaking into her thoughts. "You okay? What did the phone company say?"

"Dead end." She sighed. "The name on the account is an alias. The address is a fake. And according to GPS data, he hasn't left New Orleans in days. Clearly, the guy who sent me the text with the dead man's photo isn't the same one who broke into my sister's house."

Kyle frowned, appearing to be just as frustrated as she was. "What about *that* guy's phone number? Did you run it through?"

"Tried," she assured him. "He's using a carrier not supported by the app. I even tried a couple of other apps to see if they would unmask the number. If I can't get a number, I can't figure out his provider and get a warrant. We can keep trying, but unfortunately some of these carriers don't retain the data for more than a day or two. So depending on the carrier, we might already be too late to grab it. Of course, a guy like this is most likely using a prepaid burner phone anyway."

"So what now?" Kyle asked.

She cradled the cup of coffee in her hands, letting it warm her palms and take some of the chill out of her blood. "I guess we wait for him to call back."

As if on cue, her phone started to ring, the caller ID showing a blocked number.

"Put it on speaker," Kyle told her, jerking his chin toward the phone.

She nodded and took a deep breath before tapping the speaker icon on the screen. "This is Abby."

"Good morning, Deputy."

Kyle's gaze snapped to hers, asking a silent question. Abby nodded. This was definitely the guy who'd attacked her. "Where's my sister?" she demanded. "I want to talk to her."

"Of course."

Abby could tell that the guy was smiling.

There was a pause, a shuffle, and then a small, shaky voice whimpered, "Abby?"

Abby's hand flew up to stifle a sob of relief. "Are you

okay, Em?" she asked, forcing the tears from her voice. "Are you hurt?"

There was an uncertain sniffle. "I, uh, I hit my head in the car accident."

"Car accident?" Abby repeated, sending a frown Kyle's way. "What are you talking about?"

"I was coming home from Chicago and—"

Her words abruptly cut off, but Abby could still hear muffled, angry words. "Emma?" she said, lurching to her feet as if she could bolt to her sister's aid at a moment's notice. "Are you there?"

"I'm sorry," the man said, his voice infuriatingly calm. "Mrs. Maxwell is indisposed. She's rather rattled, as you can imagine."

"So help me, God," Abby seethed, "if you've hurt her—"

"Really, Deputy," he interrupted. "You're going to fall back on cop clichés? I figured you were more imaginative than that."

"Just tell me what you want in exchange for my sister," Abby said, fighting to keep her anger and frustration in check. Kyle moved to stand beside her and put an arm around her shoulders, bringing her in close, his presence lending her strength.

"You know what I want," the man informed her. "An even exchange. Your sister for the data in your possession."

Abby glanced up a Kyle. Could it really be that easy? Was the kidnapper seriously willing to turn Emma over without any fuss? Abby had to believe it. It was the only hope she had. "Fine," she agreed. "When and where?"

Chapter 8

"I DON'T LIKE THIS," KYLE MUTTERED AS ABBY DROVE her Camry down the pothole-ridden rural road. They were approaching an abandoned power station tucked back from the road and mostly obscured by weeds that had grown high in the uncultivated fields during the decades that the building had stood vacant.

He could see why the guy had chosen this location—it was secluded and deserted, making it easy to hide his activities from any potential witnesses. Kyle's skin began to prickle in warning, the ways this exchange could go south playing through his mind. So, yeah, he didn't like it. Didn't like it one damned bit.

He could tell by the way Abby gripped the steering wheel that she was just as anxious about the setup as he was. That said, he had to give her props for having a few conditions of her own for the exchange.

She'd agreed to hand over the flash drive containing all her findings, but the pass code to get past the encryption wouldn't be turned over until Emma was safely in the car and they were on their way. And she'd threatened that if the abductor tried to get by the encryption on his own, it would erase the data. Kyle had no frigging clue if that was even possible or if Abby was just bullshitting the guy, but it sounded plausible to him, so hopefully the bastard would buy it as well.

And if not, Kyle had his own contingency plan in

place. One that would've made Abby furious had she been
aware of it. When she'd gone to take a quick shower and
change her clothes, he'd taken the opportunity to make a
couple of phone calls. The first one was to his brother Joe.
And the next—as much as he hated to do it—was to his
brother Gabe. Joe had insisted that they have more than
one person on standby near the exchange site and had
reminded Kyle that their elder brother had a lot of surveillance experience, especially since he'd taken on the task
of investigating the local cop-hating extremists who were
growing more vocal and threatening in their activities.

Although Joe was too diplomatic to say it, Kyle had
a feeling that including Gabe was Joe's way of forcing
his brothers to come to a truce. Yeah, good luck with
that. As long as Gabe kept treating Kyle like he was the
devil incarnate, there was no chance in hell they'd be
knocking back a few beers together anytime soon. But
for all their differences, Kyle had to admit that the one
thing they *could* agree on was that *nobody* threatened
one of their own.

"There it is," Abby announced, jolting him from
his thoughts.

The dilapidated cinder-block buildings came into
view, most of their grime-covered windows broken.
The reservoir that had once fed the power station was
now almost completely dried up, leaving a great gaping
hole in the earth that had partially filled with trash
and tangled weeds. Chunks of concrete jutted up from
among the rubble, evidence that someone at some point
had attempted to bulldoze the ruins of the power plant.
But based on the state of the place, those efforts had
been abandoned long ago.

"Why do I suddenly feel like I'm in one of those cheesy horror movies?" Kyle muttered, that prickle of warning he'd been experiencing since setting up the exchange now squirming relentlessly beneath his skin. He shifted restlessly, his ass twitching with apprehension.

"There should be a maintenance building," Abby said, squinting through the windshield. She pointed at a squat building that sat on the outskirts of the campus. It was one of the few structures that didn't appear to be in complete disrepair. "There."

She came to a stop just out of the line of sight of anyone who might've been in the building and turned toward Kyle, her already fair skin a shade paler than usual, her delicate features drawn with anxiety.

"You'll stay close?" she asked.

"I won't let you out of my sight." He cast his gaze over the terrain and nodded toward another building nearby. "I'll be right there, covering you. Okay?"

She nodded, her lips pressed together in a grim line.

Abby looked so frightened that Kyle wanted to drag her into his arms and assure her that everything would be fine. But he wasn't entirely sure that his kiss would be welcome. Instead he settled for cupping her cheek and letting his thumb smooth over her skin for just a moment.

"I'll see you soon," he told her, forcing a grin.

She covered his hand with hers. "You'd better."

———

Abby watched Kyle steal away, silent as a wraith, to take up position. When he was in place, she put the car in gear and inched forward toward the maintenance shed, her heart hammering. When she was within about two hundred feet of the shed, her phone pinged with a text message notification. She glanced at the phone that lay on her thigh.

Close enough. Keep your hands on the wheel.

She immediately stopped and put the car in park, putting her hands at ten and two on the steering wheel. She trained her squinted gaze on the door to the maintenance shed while monitoring their surroundings in her peripheral vision for any approaching threats. The sun was at just the right angle to hit the dust and road grime on the windshield and obscure her view.

The door of the maintenance shed suddenly creaked open a crack, and Abby straightened, all of her senses immediately on high alert. The door continued to swing open at a maddeningly slow rate, but at last she saw movement from the shadows within.

A ragged sob burst from Abby's lungs when Emma finally took a tentative step into the sunlight, blinking against the brightness and bringing a hand up to shield her eyes. She looked horrible—her hair was dirty and matted, her clothes bedraggled and torn. There was a tear in her pantyhose at the knee and she was missing one of her black leather pumps. But at that moment she'd never been a more welcome sight.

Emma's face twisted with emotion when she saw Abby's car, and she took a few hurried steps forward before coming to an abrupt halt and sending a frightened look over her shoulder.

Abby seethed with anger at the man who even now held her sister captive. Every instinct was to launch out of the Camry, run to her sister, and rush her to the safety of the car, but Abby forced herself to remain where she was, gripping the steering wheel with white knuckles, waiting for her instructions. After what seemed like an eternity, her cell phone pinged with another text message.

Get out of the car.

She unlatched her seat belt instantly and threw open the door, grabbing her Glock from the compartment in the door as she got out, raising her weapon and aiming it at the door of the shed.

Her sister began to sob hysterically when she saw Abby and looked as though she might collapse with relief.

Abby's heart twisted with sorrow and outrage. That bastard was going to pay.

"Emma, sweetie, it's almost over," she called out. "Just do what he tells you, okay?"

Emma visibly worked to rein in her emotions and nodded, sending another glance over her shoulder.

"Come on, you bastard," Abby muttered. "What next? Just tell me already…"

Abby's phone suddenly rang, startling her. She answered without even looking at the number. "What now?"

"I will ignore your rude greeting for the sake of our business relationship."

Abby frowned and glanced at the display screen. "Hamilton?"

"You were expecting someone else?" he drawled.

"As a matter of fact, I'm waiting for your goon to give me the exchange instructions," she snapped. "But don't worry, I'll be chatting with *you* later, you son of a bitch."

She hung up before he could respond. The phone rang again in an instant. This time Abby looked at the number. It was blocked. "Tell me where to leave the flash drive," she said without preamble.

"There's a cinder block about halfway between your car and the shed. Leave it there and take your sister. Then you will text me the encryption key." Abby started to hang up, but before she had the chance he added, "And, Deputy, if you have failed to uphold your end of the bargain, if the data isn't there, if the encryption key is a fake, it won't be just your sister in my crosshairs."

Not bothering to acknowledge the threat, Abby ended the call and shoved the phone into the back pocket of her jeans. She strode forward without hesitation, her gun still raised and at the ready. When she reached the cinder block, she pulled the flash drive out of her front pocket and held it aloft, turning slightly to make sure the abductor saw it before squatting down to place it on the block.

As she stood, she motioned for her sister. Emma ran forward, throwing her arms around Abby's neck with such force that Abby stumbled back a few steps. She gave her sister a quick, one-armed squeeze, keeping her eyes on the shed. "It's okay, Em. It's over. Now let's get you home." She felt Emma nod and released her. "Go ahead. Go get in the car."

Abby slowly backed toward her Camry, her gun still trained on the maintenance shed, but there was no movement. When she heard the car door slam and knew Emma was safely inside, she hopped into the driver's seat and set her gun on her lap before throwing the car into reverse and peeling out, the car's tires sending up clouds of dust and gravel in her haste to get her sister away from the scene.

She heard Emma whimper quietly in the passenger seat and slowed slightly, not wanting to terrify her sister any more than she already had been. When Abby was far enough away that the weeds once more obscured her view of the shed, she whipped the car around so that it was facing the opposite direction and put it into park.

She grabbed her phone and typed in the encryption key as promised, but her thumb hovered over the text button for a moment, debating, wondering if Emma's abductor would make good on his threat if she failed to keep her end of the bargain. Was she willing to risk that? She still had two backup copies of the data. She could still expose these bastards for what they'd done.

Abby cursed under her breath and tapped the screen, sending the encryption password and praying she'd made the right call.

A split second later, the back door of the Camry opened and Kyle dove inside, startling a screech from Emma.

Abby reached for her, sliding a hand down her arm. "Shhh, sweetie, it's okay!" she assured her sister. "It's okay. It's just Kyle. You're okay. You're safe." Then she turned in her seat to look at Kyle. "Did you see him?"

He shook his head. "No. The guy's a ghost. I went into the shed after him the minute you took off, but he was already gone. Don't ask me how the hell he got out without me seeing him. The only other entrance to the damned place was padlocked." He ran a hand down his face, scrubbing at his stubble. "There's plenty of evidence that he'd been holding her there, but I didn't find any sign of *him*. I couldn't even find any trace of which direction he'd gone. No tire tracks, no markings of any kind."

"He left before you got there," Emma said, her voice shaking. "He left a radio in the shed with me, to give me instructions."

"Damn it!" Abby hissed, smacking the steering wheel in her frustration.

"We'll call it in on the way to the hospital and get a team out here to process the crime scene and sweep the woods," Kyle promised. When she huffed angrily, he reminded her, "We don't have the equipment or resources to track this guy down right now, Abby. But Emma's safe—and we need to keep her that way. Let's just get her to the hospital, and we'll sort out the rest."

Abby gave him a curt nod and fastened her seat belt, then slammed the car into gear and punched down on the accelerator, not wasting any more time in getting the hell out of there. She reached down to stow her gun, but her sister placed a filthy hand on top of hers.

"Please," Emma said, her voice thin and trembling. "Keep it there."

Abby sent a smile her sister's way and nodded, but as soon she turned her eyes back to the road, she clenched her jaw, her fury making her blood boil. She lifted her gaze to the rearview mirror, catching Kyle's for a moment and seeing the same steely resolve she was feeling. Without a word, he reached out and briefly placed his hand on her shoulder, giving it a comforting squeeze. Her heart swelled as a storm of emotions washed over her, gratitude for his strength and support chief among them. Tears choked her, but she swallowed them back, needing to maintain her brave front for Emma's sake.

She glanced at her sister. Emma was curled up in the seat in a fetal position, her eyes wide and unfocused as she stared at nothing in particular, the trauma from her ordeal written in the creases in her beautiful face.

Abby's grip tightened on the steering wheel as fury once more surged through her veins.

Oh yeah. She couldn't *wait* to have that chat with Hamilton.

Chapter 9

Kyle paced restlessly in the hallway outside Emma's hospital room, waiting for Abby to emerge and share information on her sister's condition. The woman had looked like hell and had clearly been in shock when they made the exchange. The sight of Emma or any other woman in that condition, so wan and forlorn, would've been enough to make Kyle seethe with rage, but the fact that she was Abby's sister made him want to tear that fucker limb from limb.

And it pissed him off to no end that the son of a bitch had slipped away without a trace. As soon as Abby had gone into the hospital room with her sister, Kyle had called his brother Joe to see if they'd had any better luck in apprehending Emma's abductor. They hadn't. They'd been in position, planning to catch the guy if he tried to run, but they'd never even caught a *glimpse* of him.

Where the hell had he gone? How had he gotten by all of them?

His brothers were going to check out the shed and the surrounding woods before the investigative team showed. With any luck, they'd find something that would give them a lead. They needed something— *anything*—to go on.

Recalling the pain and guilt—yes, *guilt*—in Abby's eyes when she'd met his gaze in the rearview mirror made his chest ache. Abby blamed herself for what happened to her sister, which was bullshit. Yeah, so she'd taken on this contract, but how the hell could she have known what she'd find? Or that her own brother-in-law would be involved? If anyone was to blame, it was that pompous asshole for putting his family in jeopardy just to make a buck.

Kyle balled his hands into fists at his sides, wishing he could get his hands on Curtis Maxwell and have a little chat about protecting the woman and son he was supposed to love. Of course, if that guy in the picture Abby had received really *was* Maxwell, then someone else had had a point of their own to make—and a far more emphatic point at that.

His brows drew together in a frown as Kyle mulled over the facts as he knew them so far so that he could relate them to his brothers when they arrived at the hospital. But something just wasn't adding up. Chief among his concerns was who the hell had sent that picture from New Orleans. If Maxwell and his buddy Whitmore were in league with the human-trafficking ring that Kyle had been on to down south, their reach was far greater than probably anyone realized.

He abruptly quit pacing, dropped into one of the stiff vinyl-covered chairs that dotted the long hallway, and leaned his head back against the wall. He needed to bring Abby in on the investigation he'd started in New Orleans and get another look at the data she'd discovered. As soon as she handed it over to the feds, he'd be out of it. The idea of those assholes hurting more innocent people, destroying more lives with their perversity, rankled at him all the way down to his bones.

With a frustrated groan, he pushed up from the chair and resumed his agitated strides.

"Hey!"

The familiar sound of his brother's voice brought Kyle's head up. He'd expected to only see Joe and maybe Gabe, but his stomach sank when he saw their father marching toward him, a dark scowl making him look more ominous than ever.

Great. Here we go…

"You guys okay?" Joe demanded.

Kyle briefly glanced toward his father, then nodded. "Yeah, we're good. The doctors are checking out Emma now. Abby's in there with her. Did you guys find anything?"

Gabe shook his head. "We didn't find shit. Maybe the investigative team will uncover something we missed."

"Well, I think when Abby comes out, we all need to have a good long sit-down," Mac informed him.

Kyle bristled at his father's tone. They'd been planning to go to the sheriff after assuring themselves that Emma was okay. But the Old Man's goddamned condescending tone and his typical way of talking to Kyle like he was a fucking twelve-year-old raised Kyle's hackles in an instant.

"Abby's been through one hell of an ordeal," he snapped. "You might try a little compassion for once."

"Compassion?" Mac echoed. "What the hell are you trying to say, boy?"

Joe sent a pleading look Kyle's way. "C'mon, man. Not here."

"No, Joseph," Mac said, waving a hand at his son. "Your brother clearly has something to say to me, so he might as well get it off his chest."

Now it was Gabe's turn to try to intervene. He ducked his chin a little and said quietly, "Dad, maybe we should save this conversation for—"

"Go on, *Agent* Dawson," Mac said, ignoring Gabe. "You got something to say, get on with it."

Kyle shook his head, not bothering to hide his disgust. "Whatever. This is bullshit. I'm not doing this with you here." He started to go around his father, muttering, "You don't get to be the center of attention today, *Sheriff.*"

Mac grabbed Kyle's arm, keeping him where he was. "Just what the hell is that supposed to mean?"

Kyle lifted his gaze to his father in open defiance. "It means this is Abby's case. You don't get to barge in and save the day and get your name in the papers."

He heard one of his brothers curse under his breath but didn't turn to see which one it was. Hell, it might've been both of them.

Mac's eyes narrowed, and he studied Kyle for a moment. "You think I do this for the recognition? You think I do *any* of what I do for my own glory?"

"Well, don't you?" Kyle shot back, wrenching his arm from Mac's grasp.

"This is not the time or place for this conversation, Kyle," Joe hissed, peering up and down the hallway.

Kyle acknowledged Joe's warning with a glance. He sure as hell hadn't intended to dredge up old issues that'd been lying dormant, building pressure just below the surface all these years. But now that a fissure had appeared in his resolve, there was no way to keep the hurt and anger from erupting. "Since we were kids, all you've ever done is talk about the Dawson history, the Dawson legacy, how our family was the law in Fairfield

County even before it *was* a county. It was always about carrying on the family tradition and doing right by our family name."

"There's nothing wrong with being proud of where we came from," Mac reminded him.

"No, there's not," Kyle hissed. He took a menacing step forward in open challenge and jabbed his finger into his father's chest. "But when you let your pride and vanity get in the way of caring for your dying wife, you need to reexamine your priorities!"

"Jesus, Kyle!" Gabe spat. "What the hell are you talking about?"

Mac actually jerked at Kyle's accusation, his normally stoic face twisting with emotion as he took a step back. "How dare you."

Kyle continued to advance, on a roll now that he'd started. "Where were you all those nights when Mom was going through chemo? When she was zoned out on pain medication and calling out your name?"

Mac looked visibly stricken, his face drawn. "You mother was the most important thing in the world to me."

"Yeah right," Kyle scoffed. "She was so important to you that you abandoned her to spend more time on the job."

Kyle didn't quite know what hit him until he saw Mac's furious face looming over him. Then the pain in his jaw came on full force. But then Mac's rage subsided and a look of profound sorrow came over him. "If this is how you see what happened, then it's no wonder you hate me."

As Joe helped Kyle to his feet, Mac turned to Gabe. "You tell Abby I came by," he muttered. "And when she's ready to talk to me, bring her to the station so we can get this sorted out."

Gabe nodded, still looking a little dumbfounded by what had just occurred. The three men watched their father lumber down the hall, his broad shoulders hunched forward.

"You're a fucking idiot," Gabe muttered as soon as Mac was out of earshot. Then he turned his own angry gaze on Kyle. "Do you think you're the only one who was devastated by Mom's death?"

Kyle flinched at his brother's question. "Of course not," he said. "I just don't understand how Dad could be so cold about it. He just sat there at her funeral, didn't show any emotion at all. And then he walked away from us and left us to deal with everything on our own."

Gabe shook his head. "Someday you should try to get to know the Old Man. Because you don't know shit."

"I know he abandoned us," Kyle shot back. "Just like he abandoned her."

Gabe turned on his heel to leave but paused, turning back to his younger brother. "You know why he was working all those hours, Kyle?" he asked. "So we could pay Mom's medical bills. They'd already gone through their savings, retirement, and our college funds. They'd even taken out a second mortgage on the house. He was trying to save her life, you dick."

"I didn't know," Kyle murmured, suddenly feeling like the world's biggest asshole. All the years he'd blamed their father for abandoning their mother when she'd needed him most, and Mac had just been doing his damnedest to save the woman he loved, a last-ditch effort to find the miracle cure that would keep her with them. And he'd failed. Nothing he'd done had made a difference. Knowing his father and his stubborn belief that failure was not an option, Kyle realized the weight of this particular failure must've been crushing.

"Of course you didn't know," Joe said, running a hand over his dark brown high-and-tight hair. "You were thirteen. Mom and Dad didn't want you to worry about anything more than you already were."

Kyle glanced back and forth between his brothers. "Why didn't any of you guys tell me what was going on?"

Gabe managed a sad smile, his chin trembling a little to Kyle's utter astonishment. "Because you're our baby brother," he managed. "Dad's not the only one who's always tried to protect you."

As Kyle watched Gabe walk away, he began to feel a little light-headed. It was as if everything he'd built his world on had suddenly shifted. All the rage and resentment that had fueled him, had guided his decisions for going on twenty years, had been based on the misplaced anger of a grief-stricken teenager who'd been kept in the dark by the family who loved him.

At that moment the door to Emma's hospital room opened, and Kyle turned to see Abby standing in the doorway. Her face had never been a more welcome sight. He desperately wanted to gather her into his arms, bury his face in her golden hair, and let her sweet love envelop him and heal all the places where his soul felt broken.

—∿∿—

Kyle looked like hell. And Joe didn't look a whole lot better. What the hell had happened out in the hallway? She'd heard their voices—Kyle's in particular—raised in anger. She'd been expecting to see Gabe and Mac standing outside the hospital room as well and found herself glancing up and down the hall.

"How's Emma?" Kyle asked.

"Um…" She frowned. "She's going to be okay. No physical injuries besides the contusion on her head. Apparently, a car ran the limo off the road about ten miles from her house, and she struck her head when the car went into a ditch."

"What happened to the driver?" Joe asked.

Abby shook her head. "Emma wasn't sure. She said she blacked out and woke up in the maintenance shed."

"We need to check to see if there was an accident called in for a car fitting the limo's description," Kyle said to his brother. "If not, could you get a car out there to take a look?"

Joe gave Kyle a terse nod and immediately got on his phone, calling in to the Sheriff's Department.

Abby narrowed her eyes at Kyle, studying his dazed and distracted expression. "You okay?" she asked softly, coming to him and placing a hand on his chest before she realized what she was doing.

He nodded and shrugged dismissively. "Yeah, sure. I'm good. Just had a lovely conversation with Mac. Always a good time."

She'd never asked Kyle what had happened to strain his relationship with his father, and he'd never volunteered the information. But she had a feeling that when she saw Mac next and explained how she'd lied to him and taken on her sister's abductor, she'd probably learn firsthand. Mac had become a surrogate father, the man she turned to for advice, for support. He was gruff and emotionally closed off, sure, but he was a good mentor, a good man. Which made the rift between Mac and his son all the more baffling to her.

Joe pocketed his phone as he came back toward them. "As luck would have it, a guy called in a possible accident earlier this morning. Dispatch sent someone out a couple hours ago and found the driver dead behind the wheel, single gunshot wound to the head."

Abby's gaze snapped to Kyle's. "I need to talk to Mac, tell him what's been going on."

And wouldn't that just be a load of fun?

She tried not to think about how furious Sheriff Dawson would be when he learned the truth. Abby could hear him now, his booming voice filling the room, disappointment and betrayal in his eyes.

Kyle traded a look with his brother, but then he nodded. "All right. We shouldn't leave Emma alone though."

"You guys go ahead," Joe told him. "Sadie's going to bring Tyler to see his mom as soon as the doctors give the all clear. I'll stay here and keep an eye on the room in the meantime. When you're at the office, ask Tom to send a deputy to come and relieve me tonight."

Abby felt such a rush of relief and gratitude that she threw her arms around Joe's neck and hugged him tightly, then pressed a kiss to his cheek. "Thanks."

"No worries," he assured her. "You're family, Abby." When her eyes widened, he added after a covert glance at his brother, "We take care of our deputies."

Her heart sank a little at the clarification, even though she had no right to think he'd meant anything more. Still, she wasn't displeased when Kyle reached for her hand and kept her close as they left the hospital. Or when he continued to hold her hand as he drove her car to the Sheriff's Department.

"You want to tell me what happened in the hallway?" she finally asked softly, calling him out of his thoughts.

He inhaled and let the breath out on a sharp sigh. "Mac and I had a long overdue chat."

She studied him for a moment. "Should I ask how it went?"

He laughed in a short, bitter burst. "Probably not." They sat in silence for a long moment before Kyle spoke again. "When my mom died, I was angry, lost. She'd been the glue that held our family together, and after she was gone…" He shook his head. "It just fell apart. Tom and Gabe were already grown, were going to college, starting their law enforcement careers. They had that to keep them going. And Joe, well, he was in high school and would go off on his own or with Sadie all the time."

The sorrow he still bore from the loss was almost a palpable presence in the car. "What about you?"

He shrugged, then sent a halfhearted grin her way. "I got into trouble mostly. I was grounded more often than not, which did wonders for my relationship with my dad. After a while, I think he just gave up. Or at least it seemed that way to an angry teenager with a chip on his shoulder. In some warped way, I think I blamed him for Mom's death, thought of him and not the cancer as the enemy. At least that gave me something tangible to hate."

"I'm so sorry," she whispered, hating to see him reliving such pain but touched beyond measure that he was sharing this with her. "I was around the same age when my dad was murdered. I know what you had to be going through. I wish I'd known you then."

He grunted. "No you don't. I was a total asshole." He released her hand to scrub at the stubble on his jaw. "Hell, I guess I'm not a whole lot better than that now."

Abby frowned in confusion. "What are you talking about? You're one of the best men I've ever known."

He turned to look at her for a moment, confusion creasing his brow. Then he looked away, turning his attention back to the road. He cleared his throat a couple of times, the easiness between them suddenly turning awkward.

Of course he had to be perplexed! She could only imagine what he was thinking. If she'd thought he was such an amazing guy, why the hell had she rejected him so suddenly that summer? Why had she walked away from what they had, from his love?

"Kyle…" she began, her words trailing off as she fiddled with her cuticles. "This morning—"

"We're here," he announced unnecessarily, cutting her off.

Abby took the hint. She wished like hell that they could pick up where they'd left off and pretend she'd never been such an indescribable idiot. But that part of her life was over. She'd missed her chance at happiness with Kyle and had to accept the fact. Besides, there were far more important things to deal with right now. Discussing a broken heart was probably pretty low on the list. Still, she sat in the car for a moment after he got out, her hands in her lap.

When her car door suddenly opened, her gaze snapped up to see Kyle holding the door open. He extended his hand and helped her from the car. "You did well," he assured her softly, apparently mistaking the reason for her inner turmoil. He gently cupped her cheek, his warm palm soothing her ruffled spirit in so many ways. "And I'll be right there with you when you talk to Mac about what happened."

She turned into his palm a little and closed her eyes for the span of a breath before forcing her thoughts back to what had happened to her sister. "He's still out there—the man who took her. We can't let Hamilton or his hired goon get away with this."

"I made you a promise, Abby," Kyle reminded her. "I'm going to keep it."

Dear God, what have I done by letting him go?

She'd walked away from the love of her life, the man who'd made her feel more than anyone ever had before or since. Instead of embracing the love he'd offered, she'd thrown it back in his face, declared she could never love him, had intentionally broken his heart, thinking it would save him heartache in the long run.

And the really shitty thing about it? It'd all been a lie. A lie so heinous it had broken her own heart to utter it.

But she knew if she'd confessed that she was head over heels in love with him he never would've left to pursue his dreams. And eventually he would've grown to resent her for holding him back. She'd grown up in a household filled with that kind of bitterness, and there was no way she'd live like that again.

Of course, that didn't keep her from wanting to kiss him so badly at that moment that she began to tremble with the intensity of that desire. So when he took her face in both his hands for one heart-stopping moment Abby thought he was going to kiss her again. When he tilted her head down and pressed a kiss to her forehead, her stomach sank with disappointment. Not that she minded the chaste kiss; it was sweet and comforting. But she longed to feel his lips on hers once more.

She couldn't help the tiny sigh of disappointment that escaped when he released her and took a step back. But she squared her shoulders and followed him toward the door of headquarters. And when he turned back to wait for her, she accepted his extended hand, knowing she had no right to expect anything more from him than that.

Chapter 10

KYLE'S GAZE FLICKED TO THE CLOCK ON THE WALL OF his father's office, the seconds seeming to tick by a year at a time. Abby had gone through the entire story for Mac and Tom from start to finish, up to and including their rendezvous with Emma's abductor at the power station to make the exchange. Mac had listened without interruption, his expression unreadable, never once betraying what was going on inside his head.

Tom was the only one to show any response, alternately shaking his head and rubbing a hand along the back of his neck where Kyle knew his brother's stress always seemed to take up residence.

When Abby finally finished talking, Mac just continued to stare in stony silence. But Tom certainly had a few choice words.

"What in *the hell* were you two thinking?" he demanded. "I expect this kind of renegade bullshit from Kyle, but *you*, Abby? I don't give a rat's ass what the guy said—you don't enter into a situation like that without backup! You both could've been killed!"

Kyle squirmed a little. "We didn't go without backup," he mumbled, sending a guilty glance Abby's way. "Joe and Gabe were there as well."

"*What?*" Abby cried out over Tom's juicy curse. "Why didn't you tell me?"

"Because I knew you'd be against it," Kyle admitted.

"The guy told you to come alone. It had taken some convincing for you to even allow me to come, so I knew you wouldn't go for having my brothers along for the ride. But Tom's right. There was no way I was going to let us walk into a dangerous situation like that without someone I trusted backing us up."

"And what if he'd found out?" Abby insisted. "What if he'd seen one of them? Then what, Kyle? He could've killed Emma!"

"I wasn't worried about Emma!" he shot back, the words coming out before he could stop them. When Abby's face blanched, he said in a rush, "I'm sorry, Abby. That's not what I meant. What I should've said was—"

"Save it," Abby interrupted, her voice catching. The look of betrayal in her eyes was so obvious, Kyle was relieved when she turned her attention to Mac and Tom. "I'm sorry for misleading you, but you have to understand my position. I had to do what was necessary to get Emma back safely. Now that she's out of danger, I'm happy to turn over all the evidence I have."

"The first thing we need to do is talk to Emma," Tom told her. "See if she can tell us anything more about her abductor, maybe give us a description. And I'll contact the police in Detroit to see if they can bring Hamilton in for us to question."

"I'm going with you," Abby informed him.

"The hell you are."

Everyone's gazes snapped to Mac who'd finally spoken. "You're officially off this case, Deputy Morrow."

Abby gaped at Kyle's dad, but Kyle wasn't overly surprised. "But Mac—*Sheriff*," Abby amended, "you need my expertise. You still don't have any idea who abducted Emma. And I'm the one who has the relationship with Hamilton. I should be the one to question him."

"It's precisely because of your relationship with the suspect that you're off the case, young lady," Mac replied, his tone even, matter-of-fact.

"And what about my brother-in-law's possible murder?" Abby pressed. "Who's going to look into that? Are you going to follow up on it at all?"

"We have no body," Kyle reminded her, answering for his father. "There's technically no murder unless we have a body."

"You said yourself you can't be one hundred percent certain that it's Curtis Maxwell in the picture," Mac pointed out. "And you can't tell me where or when it was taken. You just know that the person who sent it— apparently himself a dead man—was in New Orleans at the time. All we can do is treat this as a missing person's case and follow up on Maxwell's actual whereabouts. I'll put one of the deputies from Investigations on it."

"Technically, it's my jurisdiction," Kyle pointed out, careful to keep his tone nonconfrontational. When his father's eyes flared in challenge, Kyle added a deferential "*sir.*"

"Pardon me, young man?" Mac drawled, leaning back in his chair and regarding his son with an expression Kyle knew all too well from his teen years.

It meant his dad was going to listen silently, nod as if he was considering carefully, and then shut him down without hearing another word on the matter. But that wouldn't be the end of it if they fell into their usual routine. The conversation would devolve into a no-holds-barred screaming match within minutes—seconds if they were both in the mood for a throw down.

Kyle took a deep breath and let it out slowly, deciding to change tactics in a move that went against years of rebellion against parental authority—and, hell, pretty much *all* authority. He cleared his throat a couple of times, then said, "With all due respect, Sheriff"—God, the words burned his throat like acid, but he continued on—"technically, this one falls under federal jurisdiction, especially as Curtis Maxwell's disappearance could've transpired on foreign soil. With your permission, I'd like to pursue the leads on Patrick Hamilton's involvement in the abduction of Emma Maxwell and the disappearance of Curtis Maxwell and his bodyguard."

Mac and Tom stared at Kyle like he'd just sprouted a dick on his forehead, neither of them responding.

The silence was more than Kyle could take, so he went on, "Of course, I'd appreciate your assistance, if you can spare people, particularly Deputy Morrow because her expertise and unique knowledge of the case make her indispensable."

"Tom, Abby," Mac said, his gaze trained on Kyle as he spoke, "could you give us the room, please?"

Abby and Tom left the room without a word, Abby sending an anxious glance Kyle's way as she eased the office door closed behind her.

As soon as they left, Mac's eyes narrowed. "What exactly are you up to, boy?"

Kyle shook his head, frowning. "What do you mean?"

Mac folded his hands across his abdomen. "You know exactly what I mean. I raised you, young man. I know every trick in the book. Just what the hell are you trying to pull? You trying to make me look like an idiot? Trying to impress Abby? Win her back by humiliating me?"

Kyle's stomach sank. This sure as hell wasn't going the way he'd intended. "No, sir. I'm trying to work together. That's all."

Mac grunted. "Well, Agent Dawson—"

"It's *Kyle*," he interrupted, no longer able to put up with the condescension. "I have a name."

Mac jerked back a little. "Sorry?"

Kyle shook his head. "It's always 'boy' or 'young man' or 'Agent Dawson' with you," he pointed out, shoving up from the chair and striding toward the door. "Well, I have a name, Dad." He paused, hand on the doorknob and turned back toward his father, vaguely noting that he'd called him "Dad" for the first time since he was thirteen years old.

"I'm well aware of that fact," Mac barked. "I'm the one who gave it to you. My brother was one of the bravest men I've ever known. And since he didn't leave behind any of his own sons when he was gunned down by some drugged-up bastard, I thought one of *my* sons would be worthy to carry his name."

Kyle stared at his father for a long moment, the implication in Mac's words crystal clear. So much for trying to make amends. He made a sound that was something between a grunt and a bitter laugh, then shook his head. "Yeah," he said, pulling open the door. "Well, sorry to disappoint."

Several heads snapped up at the sound of Mac's office door slamming, including Abby's. When she came toward him, her brows furrowed with unasked

questions, Kyle waved her away and strode straight to
his brother where he sat on the corner of an unoccupied
desk, arms crossed as he waited.

"I tried," Kyle said without preamble, lifting his arms
in resignation. "But he's never going to see me as anything except a total fuckup. I'm done, Tom. If he wants
to get into a pissing match with the feds over this case,
he can be my guest. But in the meantime, I'm tracking
down these leads and doing my damnedest to bring these
assholes to justice. You can either help me or get the hell
out of my way."

Tom regarded his brother with his typical, unflap-
pable gaze. "You're an obstinate, hotheaded pain in the
ass, Kyle."

Kyle eyed his brother. "So…you'll help me then?"

Tom shrugged. "Of course."

Kyle hadn't said a word to her on the drive back to her
house to get his car. Not a single word. She wasn't sure
if he was lost in thought or pissed off at her for some
reason. Which only served to piss *her* off more than she
already was. What the hell had he been thinking when
he went behind her back and pulled Gabe and Joe in on
the exchange for Emma? Why hadn't he just told her
what he'd planned?

When she pulled into her driveway, she couldn't take
it anymore. "So what now?" she demanded, slamming
the car into park.

Kyle didn't look at her when he said, "I'm going back
to my apartment to shower and change. Then I guess
I'll grab a few things, head back this way, and crash at

Joe's or Tom's for a few days while I help you on the case." He finally cast a guarded look her way. "What about you?"

She frowned at him. "What do you mean?"

"Well, I figured you'd want to get your sister settled when she's released tomorrow," he said with a shrug. "Does she have somewhere safe she and Tyler can stay for a while?"

"With the security measures Curtis had installed at their house, I would've thought *that* was the safest place for them. But considering what happened, that's clearly no longer an option." She frowned, trying to think of a viable alternative. "I guess they can go up to the cabin for a few days, but I'd feel a lot better if someone was guarding them."

Kyle nodded. "Agreed. I'll talk to Tom, see if he can spare someone." He offered her a grin, clearly trying to make amends. "I'd check with *my* office, but I haven't even met my new boss yet. Kind of early to start asking for favors."

She didn't fall for that cocky grin of his. Well, not *really*. Maybe her stomach went all fluttery a little— but she was still pissed and refused to return his smile. "Don't worry about it. I'll go with them. I think Mac will understand if I use a couple of vacation days to take care of my family. If he needs me on a case, he can call my cell."

Kyle sighed. "Abby—"

"So you should probably get going," she interrupted. She caught a glimpse of his disappointed look just before she got out of the car, grabbing her sidearm and slamming the door behind her. She didn't even glance behind her as she made her way up the front steps. But she came to an abrupt halt when she saw the front door.

The door was closed and there was no evidence that the lock had been tampered with, but there was something…off. She couldn't even place what it was. She just had a feeling in her gut.

"Abby?"

She cursed under her breath as she spun around. She gave Kyle a pointed look, then jerked her chin toward the door.

He pulled his gun from the back of his waistband and stepped to one side of the door, motioning for her to take up position on the other side. Abby twisted the doorknob, finding it was unlocked, just as she'd suspected.

Kyle entered first, clearing the entryway and moving deeper into the house. Abby heard his juicy curse and her stomach sank, knowing what she was going to encounter even before she made it to her study.

So she wasn't entirely surprised when she saw the room had been tossed, every drawer in her desk emptied onto the floor, every paper from her filing cabinet scattered across the floor, pictures torn off the walls, her overstuffed chair shredded and the stuffing strewn among the other debris.

"Stay here," Kyle said gently, briefly grasping her arm as he passed by. "I'll check the rest of the house."

Abby nodded absently, but she had a feeling the rest of the house would be fine. Whoever had broken in had gotten what they came for. Her laptop was gone from her desk. She hurried to the closet, pulling open the door that was already ajar and hoping like hell the third copy of the data was still in her fireproof safe.

When she saw the door to the safe standing open, she didn't even bother looking inside. She knew the second flash drive was gone. With a dejected sigh, she slumped against the door frame and slowly slid down until she was sitting on the floor with her knees pulled up to her chest.

She was still sitting there a moment later when she heard Kyle calling from the hallway. "Abby?"

"In here." She lifted her eyes to his when he came into the room. "They took my laptop and the backup drive I had in my safe."

"What about your server, the backups there?" Kyle asked.

If she hadn't been so dejected she would've been touched by how much he remembered about her life. She'd never known anyone else who'd been even remotely interested in the technical aspects of her job. But he'd asked. And she'd given him the grand tour, bouncing around like a little girl showing off her newest toy.

Unfortunately, most of those toys were gone now. "Stolen."

Kyle's shoulders sagged. "Do you have another copy?"

She shook her head. "No. That was it. I'd have to redo all the reports, go back through the data to compile the results. It could be done, but it'll take a while. Hamilton would need to send me another copy of everything. And he's not likely to do that, is he? He holds all the cards here."

He eased down next to her. "Then get some things together. You can come back to my place. There's gotta be something you can do, something you can restore somewhere, right? You can use my laptop. I'll help you, if you want." His lips hitched up in one corner. "It'll be just like old times."

Her stomach somersaulted at the idea of going back to Kyle's apartment. She averted her eyes, remembering all too well the few times he'd helped her work on cases so she could finish early and spend more time in his bed. Unfortunately, they'd rarely made it through her work before they'd ended up there anyway.

"That's sweet, Kyle, but there's nothing to restore. Nothing came through email, so I don't even have that to fall back on."

There was a pause, then Kyle cleared his throat a couple of times. And his voice was a little deeper than normal, husky even, when he said, "You could come back to my place anyway."

Abby's entire body went taut with tension, her heart suddenly hammering. "I need to go check on Emma," she evaded, "and make sure Tyler's okay. Then—" Her phone rang, mercifully cutting off her excuses. She snatched it from her pocket. "Deputy Morrow."

"Greetings, Deputy. I believe we have some unfinished business."

Abby's blood boiled. "You got what you wanted, you son of a bitch!" she spat. "Why the hell are you calling me, Hamilton?"

Kyle's brows shot up and he motioned for Abby to let him listen in. She tilted the phone away from her ear so he could hear the conversation.

"You have yet to deliver the information I requested," Hamilton replied. "As soon as you deliver your reports, that will conclude our business relationship. But until then—"

"You have a lot of nerve," she seethed. "You kidnapped my sister to extort the data when I stalled, had your goons break into my house to steal the other copies, and now you have the audacity to call and pretend you have no idea what's happened? And what the hell did you do to my brother-in-law? Where is he? Was that him in the picture you sent?"

"Deputy Morrow," Hamilton replied, his voice infuriatingly calm, "I believe there has been some mistake. I assure you, had I been behind any of the heinous activities you describe, the last thing I would do is call you to gloat and incriminate myself."

"You wouldn't be the first criminal to try to use misdirection to cover your tracks," she pointed out.

Hamilton sighed. "Deputy Morrow—Abigail—for your sake, I almost wish that were the case. I think perhaps you should tell me what exactly you found that has put you and those you care about in jeopardy. And as I imagine you are already attempting to call me in for questioning, I will come to you as a show of cooperation and good faith." There was a slight pause, then, "Shall we say ten o'clock tomorrow morning at the Fairfield County Sheriff's Department?"

Abby glanced at Kyle. He gave a curt nod. "Fine," she snapped. "Don't be late, Hamilton."

When the line disconnected, Abby slumped against the doorjamb. "Do you think he's telling the truth?"

"Guess we'll find out tomorrow." Kyle got to his feet and scrubbed at the stubble on his chin. "So, you're sure you don't want to come with me to my apartment? I don't like the idea of you staying here on your own right now."

Abby surveyed the destruction in her study and suddenly felt defeated, *deflated*. And she realized the last place she wanted to be was there at her house. But she was going to have to be there when she called and reported the break-in and Tom sent someone over to file the report. And she hadn't been lying when she'd said she needed to check on Emma and Tyler.

"You'd better go ahead," she said on a sigh. "I'll deal with things here."

He eyed her warily. "Abby…"

"I'll be fine," she assured him. When he still hesitated, she said, "The guy at Emma's got the drop on me because he caught me off guard, Kyle. I'll be okay here for the ten minutes it'll take for one of the guys to show up and take the report after I call it in."

"Fine." He nodded but the look in his eyes betrayed his disappointment. "But I'm still not happy about it. I'll give you a call when I'm headed back. You're not staying here tonight alone."

She tried valiantly to ignore how her stomach twisted nervously at the thought of him staying another night with her. Trying to maintain some outward composure in spite of her insides Muppet-flailing on her, she led Kyle to the front door where they both hesitated, suddenly awkward.

Kyle shoved his hands into his pockets, his eyes on the ground. "I'm sorry about earlier, Abby. I should've talked to you before bringing my brothers in on the exchange. I had no right to make that call."

She crossed her arms over her chest. "You're right." When his head remained lowered but his gaze snapped up to regard her through those long dark lashes of his, she couldn't help a grin—or the wave of heated desire that washed over her. Her voice was a little raspy when she said, "I'll see you soon."

He held her gaze for a moment longer, letting the charge between them build until Abby's skin began to tingle, longing for his touch. Then he gave her an abrupt nod, threw open the door, and was down the steps, striding hastily toward his car, before Abby could do more than shiver at his sudden absence.

She stood in the doorway, watching him pull out of the driveway, already missing his presence in her house. As soon as his car was on the street, she pulled out her phone and dialed Tom's direct line. While she waited for Tom to pick up, she mentally calculated how long it would be before Kyle returned.

Chapter 11

KYLE HAD BEEN WAGING AN INTERNAL DEBATE WITH himself for most of the drive to his apartment—the need for information warring against the prospect of eating a healthy helping of crow with a chaser of humble pie. Humility had never really been his thing, and having to apologize to those he'd pissed off when the offense was still so recent, so raw, made his gut churn with disgust.

But by the time he'd showered, dressed, and thrown together a few days' worth of clothes, he knew he didn't have any other option. He had to find out if there was a possible connection between Abby's case and the one he'd been working down in New Orleans. And that meant going to the source.

As he was leaving his apartment, he grabbed the party-size bag of peanut M&M's from one of the boxes he still hadn't unpacked and mentally prepared for the humiliation he was about to put himself through. He tore open the bag and popped a handful of the sweet and salty goodness into his mouth, then fired up his Mustang.

A few minutes down the road, after he'd stalled as long as he could, he heaved a resigned sigh and dialed the number.

The phone only rang twice before Kyle heard, "Dave Peterman."

Kyle cleared his throat, but his voice still sounded tight when he said, "Hey, Peterman, it's Kyle Dawson. I was—"

The phone beeped rapidly, the line disconnecting. Kyle pulled the phone away from his ear and stared at it with a frown, trying to determine if he'd lost signal. When he saw it was at full strength, he tried again.

"What the hell do you want?" Peterman demanded this time without preamble.

"Don't hang up!" Kyle said in a rush. "I need your help."

Peterman grunted. "You have a helluva lot of nerve calling and asking *me* for help, Dawson. Right now, I wouldn't piss on you if you were on fire."

Kyle's brows shot up. *Well, damn. Maybe this* wasn't *such a good idea...*

Now to make with the eating of the crow. "I was a dick," Kyle announced. "I admit it. And you're right— you're the last person I should be asking for help. Trust me, if someone I cared about wasn't in danger, I guarantee I wouldn't be calling."

There was a long, heavy pause while Peterman apparently mulled things over.

"Please," Kyle said, forcing the word from his tongue, even though it pained him. "Just hear me out and then you can either help me or tell me to fuck off."

Peterman sighed. "You have ten minutes to convince me to give a shit. Go."

"Do you still have Harlan Rhodes in custody?" Kyle asked, cutting right to the chase.

He could tell Peterman was frowning when he said, "Yeah, he's not honoring the terms of the deal, so he's serving his time for the parole violation. Not sure if we can get anything else to stick before we have to release him again—which is any day now. Why?"

"I need to find out if he's ever heard of Patrick Hamilton, Preston Whitmore, or Curtis Maxwell," Kyle explained.

"You're not on the Rhodes case anymore," Peterman warned him. "You need to let it go."

Kyle bristled. The fact that he'd been kicked off the case after putting so much blood and sweat into it still burned his ass. But he needed Peterman's help if he wanted answers. "I'm not working the Rhodes case. I'm on to something here in the Midwest and think it might have ties to the operation we were working. If I'm right, you'll want this information as well. It'll just make your own case stronger."

There was another long pause and then, "I'm listening."

Kyle quickly brought Peterman up to speed on Abby's investigation and what she'd uncovered so far.

"You have the data now?" Peterman asked, his tone far more focused and sharp now that he saw the same possibilities Kyle did. "Could you send it to me for our guys to take a look?"

"No," Kyle said on a sigh. "All the copies she had were stolen."

Peterman cursed under his breath. "This guy Hamilton—if he really isn't involved, maybe he could send her the data again."

Kyle nodded. "Maybe. We'll see what that smug fucker has to say tomorrow morning. But even if he can get another copy of the data, it would take Abby some time to recompile everything and connect all the dots."

"Doesn't matter to me if it takes a month of Sundays as long as we get it," Peterman assured him. "And if it's about needing to devote more resources to the project, just send the raw data along with a few notes from her on what we should look for." There was another pause, then, "You know what this means if you're right about the connection between the two cases, right?"

"Yeah," Kyle said. "It means this thing is even bigger than any of us imagined. I want these assholes, Dave. I don't ever want to find another—" He bit back his words, his throat suddenly tight at the remembrance of the kind of atrocities against humanity that made him physically ill. He cleared his throat, forcing himself to pull it together. "We have to take them down."

"I know." If Kyle hadn't known any better, he would've thought Peterman was actually showing him some compassion. "We'll get 'em. Just send me that data when your girlfriend gets another copy, and we'll get our guys right on it."

"Will do," Kyle assured him, not bothering to correct him about Abby's relationship to him. Hell, he wasn't sure what to call her either. "Give me a call after you talk to Rhodes."

"And, uh, Kyle?" Peterman added. "About everything that happened down here…"

"No worries, man."

Kyle felt like a huge weight had been lifted off his shoulders after talking with Peterman and getting confirmation from a colleague about what he'd already suspected—the fact that Abby's corporate investigation had uncovered a human-trafficking operation similar to the one he'd been investigating in New Orleans was just a little too coincidental. He'd worried that maybe he'd been so obsessed with the case in New

Orleans that he was now suspecting connections that
weren't there.

Now he just needed to see if Hamilton was willing to
back his claim of innocence and produce another copy
of the data for Abby.

He dialed her number to let her know he was on his
way, but the phone merely beeped in his ear in protest.
Frowning, he glanced down.

No signal.

He groaned. Seriously? He'd just been *on* the frigging phone!

Fucking hell.

Had to love the effect the wide, open fields and
sparse population had on his cell phone signal—here
one minute, gone the next. He'd have to wait until he
was closer to give her a call.

He shifted restlessly in his seat, wishing he'd insisted
that she come with him on his trek to his apartment. The
thought of having to wait yet another hour before being
able to hear her voice again was enough to make him
twitch with impatience. But it was a lot more than that.
He wanted her with an intensity that was staggering.
And unless he was mistaken, she wanted him too.

Kyle pressed his foot down a little harder on the
accelerator, urging his Mustang forward, eager to get
back to Abby and give his new hypothesis a try.

———— *✴✴✴* ————

The sky was growing purple as twilight settled over the
horizon by the time Abby pulled into the hospital parking lot with a couple of bags from the local burger joint
she knew her nephew loved. She'd dealt with the police

report for the break-in at her home and had assured Tom numerous times that, yes, she'd be just fine, and yes, his brother would be back soon so she wouldn't be alone. Then she'd spent some time picking up what she could of the mess before finally saying, "Screw it!" and leaving it for later.

At least having things to deal with had kept her from dwelling too much on the events of the last two days and what awaited her, Emma, and Tyler. She'd been putting off another visit to the hospital as long as she could and had no more excuses.

Still, her stomach began to churn, sending her digging through her purse for a couple of Tums as she approached her sister's hospital room door. "Hey, Bradford," she said, forcing a smile for Deputy Adam Bradford when his gaze snapped up from the John Gilstrap novel he'd been reading.

"Hey, Abby," he said with a jerk of his chin, his hazel eyes crinkling in the corners when he returned her smile.

She'd always liked Bradford. He was a good guy and had an even, easygoing temperament that made him one of Tom's most trusted deputies. She was glad to see he was the one who'd been assigned to look out for Emma.

"Hungry?" She reached into the bag and withdrew a burger, offering it to him.

He shrugged. "Sure. I could eat. Thanks."

"No problem. I appreciate you watching over my sister." Her gaze darted toward the closed door. "Everything going okay?"

"Been quiet since I got here," he said. "Tyler hung out with me here in the hall for a while when Mrs. Maxwell took a nap. He's a good kid."

This time Abby's smile was genuine even though she felt suddenly tired. "Thanks."

He gave her a terse nod and returned his attention to his novel.

Abby took a deep breath, then knocked quietly and pushed open the door. Tyler was sitting next to his mom on the hospital bed, happily chatting with her about something on his phone, and Emma was smiling, actually engaged in what he was saying.

Abby stopped dead in her tracks, a sudden surge of emotions making it hard for her to breathe. Emma and Tyler both glanced up with a smile for her when they realized she'd entered the room.

"Hi, Aunt Abby!" Tyler chirped. "I was just showing Mom how to play *Angry Birds*. Can you believe she's never played it before?"

Abby glanced at Emma, then back at Tyler. "No way! I thought everyone had played that game at least once."

Emma smoothed her son's hair, her lips trembling a little as she pressed a kiss to the top of his head. "I think there are a lot of things I've missed out on, sweet boy. But not anymore."

Abby swallowed the tears constricting her throat and held up the bag of burgers. "Hey! Anyone hungry? I brought your favorite, Ty."

The boy's eyes lit up. "Sweet! Did you bring one for Mom? She doesn't eat anything but salads and stuff."

Emma held out a hand to take the bag. "Are you kidding me?" she said. "I'm starving! We might have to send your Aunt Abby out for seconds. What do you say?"

He laughed. "Or maybe *thirds*!"

Emma laughed with her son and rooted through the

bag, handing him a burger and taking out one for herself. "Abbs?" she asked, holding up the bag. "Are you going to have one?"

Abby waved it away, completely overwhelmed by the change in her sister. "Nah, you two go ahead. I just wanted to stop in and see how you were doing."

Emma swallowed a bite of her double cheeseburger with everything and gave her sister a meaningful look. "I'm okay. At least, I will be."

Abby sat on the edge of Emma's bed on the other side from Tyler and patted her sister's leg. "You need anything, I'm here," Abby reminded her. "You know that, right?"

Emma nodded, her blue eyes going bright with unshed tears. She suddenly laughed and sniffed when Tyler stopped mid-chew to frown at her in concern. "Whew!" She chuckled. "These onions are getting to me! Strong, aren't they?"

His frown instantly morphed into a smile. "But that's why they're so good!"

"Well, hey," Abby said on a sigh. "I will let you two enjoy your dinner. I'll come back a little later to pick up Tyler."

"No!" Emma cried. Then she cleared her throat and took a deep breath, looking a little embarrassed by the note of desperation in her voice. "I mean, I've asked the nurses if he could stay here with me. They're going to set up a bed for him in here."

Abby nodded. "Well, um, okay then. I guess I'll just bring a change of clothes for both of you and pick you up tomorrow. I figured I'd take you to the cabin to recuperate for a few days."

"What about school?" Tyler asked.

Abby shrugged. "I'll give them a call for you. Okay, monkey? Explain your mom needs you for a couple of days. I'm sure it'll be fine."

"Cool!"

Abby got to her feet and gave each of them a hug and a kiss, reluctant to leave them but wanting to give Emma time with Tyler.

"Deputy Bradford is still just outside your room," she assured them, "so if you need anything, just let him know. Or give me a call and I'll be back here in a flash."

"Have you heard from Curtis?" Emma asked before Abby could step away. "I tried to call him, but it went straight to voice mail."

Abby stiffened. "Um, no. I haven't heard from him." She knew she should tell her sister about the picture and what she feared had happened to her husband to prepare her for the worst. But not in front of Tyler. And not until she'd spoken to Hamilton to get some answers. "How about I keep trying to get in touch with him for you?"

Emma must have sensed something in Abby's voice because her smile faded. She nodded. "Okay. Maybe Tyler and I will just watch some movies tonight and give the phone a rest."

Abby nodded slightly. "Probably a good idea."

Emma blew out a shaky sigh but then steeled herself, squaring her shoulders in a display of strength Abby had never before seen from her older sister. "Well, I'm sure we'll hear something soon."

Abby slipped from the room then, leaving her sister and nephew to enjoy their dinner together, and had a quick conversation with Deputy Bradford, making sure he understood the situation. When her phone rang, startling her, she flushed and lifted a hand in good-bye to her colleague as she answered.

"Hey, beautiful," Kyle said when Abby answered. "Have you eaten yet?"

"No," she said, sighing. "I just picked up something for Emma and Tyler. How about you?"

"Just peanut M&M's," he told her. "I should be there in about an hour. Meet me at Mulaney's?"

She hesitated. "I don't know… I feel like I should get back home and deal with everything there, see if I can find something, *anything*, that will lead us to this guy."

"Abby," Kyle said, "there's nothing more you can do tonight. We've filed a missing persons report on your brother-in-law. We've brought the Old Man and my brothers in on this. We're meeting Hamilton in the morning to question him. Now you need to take care of *yourself* if you're going to be of use to Emma and Tyler—and that means eating and sleeping from time to time."

She smiled. "You're one to talk. Last time I checked you *lived* on peanut M&M's, pizza, and coffee."

"It's a date then," he said, the word sending a ridiculously girlie flutter through Abby's stomach. "I'll meet you at Mulaney's in an hour."

—∿∿—

Fielding had driven for a couple of hours and was more than a little irritated when he arrived at the new high-rise office building that belonged to Mr. Smith and discovered the construction site was not nearly as secluded as he normally liked for conducting business. Although the standard chain-link fence surrounded the steel and concrete structure to keep out curious passersby, there was little else in the way of security.

Amateurs.

He grunted as he parked his car a block away and headed back to the construction site, sticking to the shadows as much as possible and keeping his pace casual. As usual, he blended in with the smattering of people who still peppered the sidewalks now that rush hour had ended, their heads down, eyes on the sidewalk.

As instructed, Fielding went around to a gravel lot where a few cars were still parked and found the green Taurus that had been left there and got in. He flipped down the visor and caught the keys as they fell. The car started up with a quiet rumble, and a moment later he was pulling out onto the street and winding along the circuitous, nonsensical route that his employer had insisted upon.

It was completely unnecessary. No one was following him. Fielding would've known. He had almost a sixth sense when it came to shit like that. If someone took notice of him in a crowd, he sensed it in an instant.

Just as he'd felt that Abigail Morrow hadn't been alone earlier.

He'd sensed it the moment he heard the car coming up the gravel path leading to the maintenance shack. But the feeling had been with him even before that. Someone—maybe more than one someone—had been watching the place for at least an hour before she arrived. He'd felt the weight of their gazes on him.

The bitch had brought backup, had broken the one rule he'd set for the exchange. If this one had been personal, he would've been seriously pissed—and that pretty little deputy would've paid for her transgression. But whatever. He should've known that Abby Morrow would have an ace up her sleeve. She was far too clever. But he'd evaded them easily enough, slipping out of the shed long before they'd gotten there and taking up position in another building for when this little game of theirs played out.

Fortunately, Emma Maxwell had proved to be such a compliant captive, totally buying in to the fact that he'd be watching and assessing how well she played by the rules. If she given even the *slightest* hint that he was not in the shed, he would have put a bullet between her eyes. He wished all his playthings could be so good.

He'd waited until the other two men had come and gone, giving them time to be on their merry way before he came out of his hiding spot. There'd be more coming, looking for evidence. They wouldn't find any. They never did. He never lost.

And really, when it came down to it, he had no skin in this game so he could afford to let the other players bend the rules a little. After all, it could be amusing to see how they tried to beat him at his own game. But this time he was only in it for a paycheck. And as soon as he turned over the flash drive to his employer he'd be a million dollars richer. Not a bad payout for a couple days' worth of headache.

He was still wearing a smug grin when he pulled into the parking lot of a boarded-up convenience store that was covered in graffiti and gang tags, the sidewalk cracked and crumbling from years of disuse. He had to admit, his employer had selected the drop location well.

There was a vacant lot on one side, the site of another business at some point, but now only the concrete foundation remained. On the other side had been another business that was now just a burned-out shell. Whether the fire had brought an end to the business or was the result of an arsonist who couldn't resist the empty building, he couldn't tell. And he didn't give two shits. He just wanted his money.

As instructed, he pulled around to the back to park next to a rusted-out dumpster. The moment he got out of the car, something skittered from within the shadows.

Rats.

Charming.

He grunted with disgust. For being a rich asshole who wore ridiculously overpriced suits, Mr. Smith had a surprisingly intimate knowledge of this particularly seedy neighborhood.

Fielding checked his watch, confirming that *he* was right on time. His irritation at being kept waiting made the muscle in his jaw twitch. He was never late. Not ever. That was one of the reasons he had a steady flow of jobs. The arrogant bastards who hired him to do their dirty work knew he could be depended on to be punctual.

Clearly, the same could not be said for his employer.

Twenty minutes later, a silver Lincoln finally pulled into the lot and parked so that its headlights were pointed directly in Fielding's face, briefly blinding him and keeping the driver in shadow as he got out of the car.

"Good evening, Mr. Fielding."

"Fuck you," Fielding shot back. "You're late."

He couldn't be sure, but he thought he could see the guy smirking. "I was unavoidably detained."

Yeah right.

Fielding had seen guys like this before. They'd stabbed so many people in the back to get where they were that they had to be constantly looking over their shoulders. So they pulled shit like this all the time to show the other guy who was still in control. It was a power play of the most transparent variety.

Well, Mr. Smith could think what he wanted. Fielding knew the truth.

"Do you have my money?" he demanded.

"Of course." The man reached into the car and pulled out what looked like a small briefcase. Then with a casual flick of his wrist, like a million dollars was just pocket change, he tossed the case. It hit the pavement and slid, coming to a stop about midway between him and Fielding.

Fielding reached into the front pocket of his jeans and pulled out the flash drive, holding it up pinched between his forefinger and thumb. He made to pitch it toward his employer, but the man held up a hand.

"No need."

Fielding gaped at the man standing in the shadows. There wasn't much that surprised him. Not really. But he had to admit, this time he was seriously fucking dumbfounded. "You don't want the data?"

Mr. Smith leaned against his car, one hand nonchalantly tucked in his suit pants pocket. "I know what it says. I just didn't want that bitch to share it with anyone."

Fielding narrowed his eyes. Either the guy was incredibly cunning or incredibly stupid. "You think she didn't make another copy?"

The man chuckled. "Do you think you're the only one

I have working for me? While she was dealing with her
sister's abduction, I had someone else steal her laptop,
server, and a flash drive she foolishly hid in her safe."

Fielding grunted. "What makes you think she didn't
save it to the cloud?"

The man's laughter was so derisive it made Fielding
silently seethe with rage. Who the fuck did this guy
think he was? "Oh, Mr. Fielding," Smith drawled, "she
wouldn't save it to the cloud. That's not her style."

"How the hell would you know?" Fielding demanded,
curious now.

"Do you think this is the first time I've dealt with
something of this nature?" his employer replied. "She's
not the first to investigate me. And I've yet to be wrong."

Now Fielding was just getting pissed. "But—"

"Before you even suggest that perhaps she's already
turned over the report," the man interrupted, "I can
assure you she hasn't. I had another acquaintance of
mine hack into her email to keep an eye on things the
moment I learned of her investigation. There's been no
correspondence about the investigation."

Fielding suddenly found himself rooting for the
pretty little deputy, hoping like hell she would take
down this asshole. Not because he gave a damn about
any of the bullshit going on—he just wanted this prick to
get bitch slapped. "I've read all about her," he reminded
his employer. "She's good. She can probably recreate
those reports in no time if she gets the source information from her client."

The man opened his car door. "Yes, well, that would
take a little time, I imagine. And time is something
Deputy Morrow is lacking."

"What the hell is that supposed to mean?" Fielding demanded.

Fielding could see the asshole's smug smirk even in shadow. "Come now, Fielding. You're a professional. You know there's really only one way to keep secrets secret."

He knew all too well. Which was the reason he never asked for real names or many details when dealing with his employers. They were all "Mr. Smith" or "Mr. Jones" or some other alias that kept them unknown to him. The less he knew about them, the less likely he was to catch a bullet for his trouble. Hell, he probably shouldn't have asked as many questions as he just did. But his employer clearly wasn't concerned about getting caught.

Fielding watched the guy pull away as casually as he'd arrived, as if he wasn't plotting to commit murder. His own hands weren't without stain. God knows he'd done his fair share of killing. But not one of his marks hadn't deserved it. Abby Morrow was different. Her only crime was being good at her job. It was a damned shame.

He shook his head as he strolled to where the briefcase containing his money lay on the ground. He snatched it up but waited until he was back in the car to open the case and peer inside. A smile curved his lips as he took in the neatly stacked bundles of bills, picked one up, and fanned through it. He grabbed another couple of stacks and flipped through them as well, then counted the number of stacks, making sure his employer had held up his end of the bargain.

A million dollars, just as he'd agreed.

As Fielding pulled out of the parking lot and headed back to his hotel, he couldn't help but wonder how the asshole planned to off Abby Morrow. Would it be something bold, something to warn away any future attempts by the person or organization or whoever the hell had been investigating him?

He almost laughed. *Yeah right.* That slimy cocksucker didn't have the balls to go head-to-head with anyone. That's why he paid people like Fielding to do it for him. Nah, he figured it would probably look like an accident. Or maybe a random act of violence, a senseless shooting by some sick bastard who "the system" had failed.

He actually felt sorry for Deputy Morrow. It didn't seem fair, even to him, that someone that ball-rocking gorgeous should bite it without even having a fighting chance. Where was the sport in that? She should at least have the *option* of trying to save her own sweet ass.

Fielding grinned as a thought suddenly came to him. He didn't have another job scheduled for a few days. Maybe he'd stick around and see how this thing played out. Or, maybe, since he was feeling so generous with a million dollars sitting on the seat next to him, he'd even see what he could do to even those odds.

Chapter 12

WHEN KYLE ENTERED MULANEY'S, HE FINALLY FELT like he was home. The county's oldest pub had been the favorite watering hole for the Dawsons since Pete Mulaney, the original owner and proprietor, had offered a young lawman named Silas Dawson a place to stay even though the man had just come to town and hadn't a penny to his name. So the Dawsons still seemed to feel it was their duty to keep an eye on the place in repayment for the kindness.

At least, you'd think that was the case, given how often the local population of Dawsons and all their cousins and friends hung out at the pub after work on any given day. And apparently today was no exception.

His brothers sat around a table in the center of the room, their smiles and laughter filling his chest with warmth. Sadie sat next to Joe, leaning into his embrace, his arm draped around her, hugging her close. And next to Sadie was Abby, her cheeks flushed from laughing, her eyes bright and sparkling with a happiness he hadn't seen since he'd returned.

The sight of her now—beautiful and glowing, the stress and concern that had plagued her having at least temporarily vanished—made Kyle want to kiss the hell out of her right there in front of God and everybody. But before he could take a single step, she happened to glance up and see him standing near the door. Her smile grew, alighting in her eyes. In an instant, she was on her feet and coming toward him.

God, she was striking—lean and athletic and sexy as hell without even realizing it, without even trying. With each step she took, his cock got harder. He swallowed and shifted a little, trying to covertly adjust himself, but then she was within inches of him, her smile beaming, eyes dancing with amusement.

"I didn't think you'd ever get here," she said. "I was about to send out a search party."

He winked at her, trying to hide the fact that his balls were throbbing. "Counting the seconds until I returned?"

She rolled her eyes, but he didn't miss the way her cheeks flushed. "You wish."

"Let me say hey to my brothers, and we'll go grab a table," he said, chuckling.

She grimaced a little. "Sadie and Joe asked if they could join us, and then Tom and Gabe showed up… And I think Elle McCoy is coming as well. I hope that's okay."

What the hell was he supposed to say? That the last thing he wanted to do was hang out with his family and friends? That if he didn't get her alone soon and find out where things stood between them, his balls would be a permanent shade of blue?

So he shrugged. "Yeah, of course."

"You two gonna go bump uglies or have a beer?" Gabe called out, apparently already halfway to shit-faced if the volume of his voice was any indication.

Kyle shared a glance with Abby, then gestured for her to take the lead. "I *did* promise you dinner," he told her. Then as she turned to go, he leaned in and said so that only she could hear, "But dessert's totally your call."

He felt her stiffen, and her eyes were wide when she cast an uncertain glance his way as if wondering if she'd understood the innuendo correctly. He winked, confirming she had. When her gaze snapped forward again, her cheeks were crimson, drawing a knowing smirk from his brother Joe, who raised his beer slightly in salute, then discreetly turned his attention back to Sadie.

Kyle jerked his chin at the party as they reached the table. "Looks like you guys got a jump on me," he said, pulling out Abby's chair for her. "What's everyone drinking? The usual—Sam Adams?"

"None for me," Sadie demurred with forced nonchalance. "Just water."

Kyle's eyes narrowed, his investigative sixth sense suddenly on alert. From the discreet glance she sent Joe's way, Kyle figured she probably wasn't just abstaining because she was designated driver that night. "Hey, Joey," he said. "Why don't you help me carry the beers?"

Joe took a swig from his bottle and then dropped a kiss on Sadie's hair before following Kyle to the bar where the current proprietor, Charlotte Mulaney, was tending bar with an efficiency and friendliness that kept business booming. But just in case she had to set friendliness aside to crack some heads, Charlotte kept her great-great-granddad's shillelagh hanging on the wall as a reminder that she wouldn't take any shit.

"Well, as I live and breathe!" Charlotte cried when she saw Kyle approach the bar. She tossed aside her bar towel and opened her arms wide. "Get over here, baby boy!"

Kyle couldn't help grinning as he leaned across the bar top to give her an awkward hug. "Hey, Charlotte. Good to see you again. You haven't changed a bit."

She slapped playfully at his shoulder, her hazel eyes twinkling. "Liar."

"Are you kidding me?" Kyle retorted. "You're gorgeous."

And he wasn't exaggerating. At sixty, Charlotte Mulaney's hair was still as fiery red as it had been when she was eighteen and turning all the boys' heads. It was common knowledge that she'd been the chief rival for Mac Dawson's affections back in the day, until it became clear that Mac was looking for a serene, quiet, sweet sort of woman to marry. And, well, Charlotte Mulaney was about as outspoken and headstrong as they came and wasn't about to change her ways for any man, no matter how much she loved him.

She laughed and winked at Joe. "I think someone's got his beer goggles on early." Then without missing a beat, she said to Kyle, "When'd you get back to town, honey? Have you seen your daddy yet?"

Kyle cleared his throat. "Yeah, you could say that. I got back a couple days ago. Mac was… Well, you know how he is."

She sighed. "Mac Dawson is a stubborn ass. But he's a good man, and he loves you. Just remember that." Then Charlotte's famous grin returned. "So what can I get you boys?"

Kyle returned her grin. "Five Sams and a water."

Just as Charlotte turned to fill his order, a huge party of college coeds came up to the bar, giggling and chatting, thumbs flying as they texted and then shared whatever was so amusing. Charlotte sent a pleading look his way. "Mind if I go ahead and get these gals taken care of?"

Kyle spread his hands. "Take your time."

When Charlotte went to help the coeds, Kyle leaned his elbows on the bar top and laced his fingers together, staring ahead at the row of bottles along the back of the bar. "So, when's Sadie due?"

Joe sputtered on the swig of beer he'd just taken and cast a wide-eyed glance at his brother. "How'd you know?"

Kyle gave Joe a wry look. "Seriously? You're asking *me* this? I know you, Joe. And I know Sadie. Plus, she looks…"—he cast an assessing glance over his shoulder—"different. And, don't think I'm a total ass-hole for noticing, but her boobs look bigger." He added quickly, "No offense, man."

"Shit, are you kidding me?" Joe muttered. "They're fucking amazing. I didn't know that happened this early."

"How far along is she?" Kyle asked.

Joe took another swig of his beer, finishing it off. "Ten weeks. I went to the doctor with her the other day." He shook his head. "It's incredible. I mean, I love Sadie more than life. I don't even know how to put that kind of love into words. She's everything to me. *Every*thing. But when I heard that tiny heartbeat… I don't know. I feel like nothing in my life meant anything until now. Like nothing I've accomplished even comes close to what Sadie and I have created together."

Kyle grasped his brother's shoulder and squeezed it before slapping him lightly on the back. "I'm happy for you, big brother. Congratulations."

Joe ran a hand down his face. "It's crazy. Who thought I'd be the first one of us to be a dad?" The moment the words came out, Joe's expression suddenly looked contrite, and he quickly added, "Shit, man. I'm sorry."

Kyle frowned at him, wondering why in the hell Joe

would feel sorry about anything where Kyle was concerned. "What are you apologizing for?" He chuckled.
"I'm not in any hurry to have kids. I'll leave that to you
and Sadie. I figured it would be Tom who'd jump on
that grenade first, but…"

"Guess he and Carly ran out of time," Joe finished
for him.

Kyle nodded. "Yeah. Guess so. But hey—mazel tov
to you and Sadie."

Joe still looked confused by Kyle's reaction—or lack
thereof—but he grinned and rolled his eyes. "We're
Catholic, moron."

"Speaking of that… What's next?" Kyle asked,
catching a glimpse of one of the coeds snapping a photo
of Gabe with her cell phone and giggling behind her
hand when she showed the picture to her friend. "You
two getting married?"

"I want to," Joe admitted, picking at the label on
his beer bottle. "We talked about it, but she said she
didn't want me to marry her just because she's pregnant
and reminded me that it's not 1950. On the other hand,
she's worried how the school will react about having an
unwed mother on staff. The thing is, I was going to ask
her anyway. I've already bought a ring."

"You tell her that?"

Joe nodded. "Yeah. Well, the part about planning to
ask anyway. I haven't told her about the ring. I want to
actually propose, make it special for her. I've never pic-
tured any other woman as my wife, Kyle. It's always been
Sadie—since we were kids. I don't want to blow this."

"Don't worry about it," Kyle assured him. "It'll all
work out. You two were meant for each other. I mean,

shit—if *you two* can't make it, there's no hope for the rest of us poor bastards."

Joe chuckled. "Thanks."

"And you know you can talk to me, right?" Kyle said. "I may be your little brother, but I know a thing or two." He grinned. "Maybe I can tell you about the birds and the bees, explain how this happened."

Joe punched his arm. "Asshole," he said with a laugh. "You don't know *shit*, trust me."

Kyle twitched a little at his brother's cynical tone. "What's that supposed to mean?"

"If you had a clue, you sure as hell wouldn't be here hanging out with *us* tonight," Joe informed him.

Kyle raised his brows when Joe jerked his chin at Sadie and Abby as the two women chatted and shared a plate of fries. He heaved a sigh. "I don't know, man. I'm not sure where things stand there."

"Here you go, boys," Charlotte said, startling them from their thoughts as she set the bottles on the bar. "And this is the last one for Gabe. I'm officially cutting him off. He's been hitting it hard since he walked in tonight. Something weighing on him?"

Joe slid a glance his way, making Kyle wonder if he was going to mention the incident at the hospital, but instead he said, "One of the cases he's been working almost got tossed out. He's taking it pretty hard."

"That happens sometimes," Kyle reminded him. "It sucks, but there's nothing we can do about it."

Joe gave him a sad smile. "Yeah, but usually it's because of some technicality or lack of evidence. This one's all on him."

Kyle immediately thought of the comment Elle had

made about Gabe's inability to keep it in his pants and cursed under his breath. Then muttered, "Damn it, Gabe."

"And you know the real pisser?" Joe continued. "It's the Chris Andrews case."

Kyle's stomach dropped. He didn't need Joe to tell him who Chris Andrews was. Gabe and Chris had been best friends growing up, inseparable. Until an anticop fanatic walked into the diner where Gabe and Chris had been eating lunch and opened fire, killing Gabe's closest friend.

"Ah, shit," Kyle said. "No wonder he's in full-on self-destruct mode."

"He'll be alright," Charlotte assured them. "He's a Dawson. You boys always come through in the end." When Kyle gave her a doubtful look, she gave him a cockeyed grin. "I seem to recall having a number of conversations just like this one with your daddy over the years. Still do."

Kyle's brows shot up, and not for the first time, he wondered about the nature of Mac's relationship to Charlotte. He had no doubts that his dad was always faithful to his wife during their marriage, but he also knew that Mac had spent a lot of time at this bar over the years, especially after their mother had died. And apparently he still did.

But before Kyle could ask any probing questions, Charlotte winked and jerked her head toward the tables behind them. "Now you better get back to those lovely ladies of yours, boys." She leaned across the bar and patted Kyle's cheek affectionately. "And don't you be a stranger, honey."

As soon as Charlotte rushed off to tend to another patron, Joe gathered up his share of the drinks, then pegged Kyle with a meaningful glance. "Charlotte's right about one thing," he said. When Kyle frowned in confusion, Joe continued, "We Dawsons are far too proud and stubborn for our own good. I waited so long to tell Sadie how I felt about her that I almost died before I had the chance. What we do, Kyle, going out there every day and putting our lives on the line…there's no guarantee any of us are coming home when the day's over. If you're still in love with Abby, tell her."

Abby was trying her damnedest to enjoy her dinner and pay attention to the chatter at the table. Elle McCoy had arrived, fresh from convicting one of the biggest meth dealers in the state and even livelier than usual. But Abby didn't miss Elle's occasional irritated glances toward where Gabe was flirting mercilessly with a group of giggly coeds or Gabe's heated gaze as he looked at Elle when he thought no one else was paying attention. The two always seemed to be at odds, but Abby would've had to be an idiot not to sense the sexual tension between them when they were in the same room. Too bad they were both too stubborn to admit how they felt for each other.

And, God, she could certainly relate.

Kyle had been strangely withdrawn and distracted since he and Joe returned from the bar, barely sparing her a glance as he split his attention between his brothers and Sadie and the bartender, Charlotte. If she didn't know better, Abby would think he was purposely avoiding talking with her. And yet when he'd arrived, he'd flirted with her, implying that their night could end in a hot, sweaty tangle if she was onboard. And the more she sat there, witnessing the heated looks that passed between Joe and Sadie, the more she began to ache for Kyle's touch.

Beneath the table, his knee was touching hers, but she couldn't tell if it was because he wanted the contact or because they were so crowded around the table that there was no alternative. But even *that* slight contact was making her squirm restlessly, longing for more.

"And then that bastard has the *balls* to tell me that I should be barefoot in the kitchen baking him pies!" Elle laughed, drawing Abby out of her brooding.

"He obviously doesn't know you at all, baby girl," Charlotte teased, arriving just then with a plate of nachos for the group.

"No kidding," Elle drawled, sharing an amused look with her aunt. "My pies would land him in the hospital—or maybe a coffin."

"So," Charlotte said as she set the platter of nachos in the center of the table, "aside from the prodigal son returning and throwing Fairfield County into total chaos, what have I missed?"

They all traded glances before turning their gazes to Abby, as if asking permission to share what had happened over the last couple of days. All of these people were her closest friends, more family to her than her own blood relations. And yet suddenly she felt cornered, claustrophobic. The coeds who'd been giggling an hour ago were now rowdy. The jukebox was blaring Bon Jovi so loudly her head was beginning to ache. The chatter of the pub's regulars, normally a welcome buzz of activity and congeniality, suddenly seemed shrill and grating.

Grimacing, she pushed back from the table. "You know, it's been a crazy couple of days. I think I'm going to head home."

Kyle was on his feet in an instant. He pulled her chair out for her as she rose, then said to the rest of the gang, "I'm going to take Abby home. Charlotte, we'll come back tomorrow morning for Abby's car."

Charlotte nodded, looking a little confused. "Sure thing. I'm sorry, Abby, honey. I didn't mean to upset you."

"No, no!" Abby said, waving away her words. "Really. I'm just tired."

Joe jerked his chin. "You guys be careful. Call us if you need anything."

"One of you guys driving Gabe home?" Kyle asked, nodding toward where Gabe was leaning against the wall chatting up the pretty blond who'd taken his picture earlier.

Elle glanced over her shoulder. "Looks like he might already have a ride for the night," she drawled, not doing a very good job of hiding the hurt in her voice. Her smile was forced when she turned back to Abby. "But if not, we've got him."

Abby quickly made her good-byes and headed for the door, not even bothering to wait for Kyle in her haste to get out of the pub. But when she reached to push open the door, he got to it first and was holding it open for her, his brows furrowed in a concerned frown.

"You okay?" he asked as she rushed outside, taking in great gulps of night air.

She closed her eyes for a moment and took a deep breath, then let it out slowly. "Yeah," she assured him. "I just didn't want to relive everything right then. And

it just felt too close inside all of a sudden. I'm sorry to
rush out of there like that."

He tenderly slid his hand up and down her arm.
"Don't worry about it. Let's just get you home."

As she turned toward his Mustang, he placed his hand
lightly on the small of her back, gently leading her forward. "You know, if you'd like to go back and hang out
with them, I can take a cab," she offered. "I know you
have a lot of catching up to do. I don't want you cutting
your night short because I needed to get out of there."

"No way," he said, the pressure on the small of her
back increasing slightly. "I'm not going to let you stay at
your house on your own. We've already covered that."

She swallowed hard, her mouth suddenly dry, and
nodded. "Okay."

His hand slid around to grasp her waist, and he pulled
her closer, drawing her to a stop as they reached his
Mustang. "If you'd rather I not stay, we'll find you a hotel
room. It's no problem. I'll just crash at my brother's."

"No," she said, shaking her head ever so slightly,
unable to tear her eyes away from the intensity of his
gaze. "I want you to stay."

His frown eased at her words, but the heat of his gaze
intensified. She saw his throat move as he swallowed. And
then his gaze flicked down to her lips briefly. But it was
enough to make her heart pound and her breath quicken.

"We should go," she managed, vaguely noting the
sound of thunder rumbling as a spring storm moved in.

He nodded, leaning close to grasp the door handle
behind her, bringing them so close she could feel the
heat of his body. Her breath caught in a quiet gasp, but
he must've heard it because he paused, his hand on the

handle, his head hanging down while he seemed to consider his next move. Her heart pounded, every nerve in her body on alert as she waited to see what he would do next.

The moment seemed to stretch out for eternity, the charge building between them and echoing that of the night air, tense from the storm that threatened to break at any moment.

Her body began to tremble with the intensity of the tension and her efforts to rein in her desire to turn into Kyle's embrace, to feel his lips on hers, his hands on her skin. She shuddered, images of them in a naked tangle filling her mind.

Apparently mistaking her shiver for trepidation, Kyle suddenly stepped back, putting space between them, and at last opened the door.

Abby cast a regretful glance his way before getting in. She flinched when he closed the door, and again when he got in and slammed his own. Kyle silently started the Mustang, the deep growl of the engine drowning out another roll of thunder.

They rode in silence. Every now and then, Abby could sense Kyle's gaze on her—just a glance away from the road as the rain began to fall. She studied the steady trickles of water as the rain hit the windshield and slid down the glass slowly like a lover's touch, only to be knocked away by the brutal slash of the wiper blades.

Is that how she'd been with Kyle? Inviting his touch only to rebuff him? Sending mixed messages about her feelings for him when they were really quite simple?

When Kyle pulled into her driveway, he turned off the engine and sat for a moment, staring straight ahead.

Finally, he turned toward her, his jaw tight. "I'm going to go check things out inside," he told her, his voice strangely gravelly and rough. "Stay here."

Before she could respond, he was throwing open the car door and sprinting up the steps to her house. Fear spiked in her veins when he entered the house without any trouble and for a moment she thought the door was unlocked once again, but then she remembered he'd never returned the key she'd given him when they were dating. The knowledge that he still kept the key on his key chain made her heart pound for another reason entirely when he returned a few minutes later.

The rain was coming down in sheets now, the storm raging in full force, drenching Kyle as he came toward the car, soaking his hair and plastering his shirt against the solid muscle of his chest. He raked a hand through his black hair, sweeping it back from his eyes in a careless move that was one of the sexiest things Abby had ever seen.

Before he even reached the car, she threw open the door and got out, slamming the door behind her as he stalked closer. He halted mere inches from her, his gaze intent on her face as if trying to read her.

"Why did you still have my key?" she asked, her breath coming in gasps at the nearness of him.

He looked at her with such unabashed desire that it paralyzed her. "Why did you never ask for it back?"

Thunder cracked and lightning split the darkness. As if that was the signal Kyle had been waiting for, he grasped her nape and his lips found hers in a savage kiss, his mouth plundering hers in pure, raw need.

Abby gasped as he pressed her back against the

car, spreading her legs with his knee so he could settle between her thighs.

She clutched his muscled back, rolling her hips against him, letting him know that she was *so* onboard with where his thoughts were headed. When he broke that savage kiss to nip at the curve of her throat, she cried out, already teetering on the edge of release. The rain pelted her face, the erotic caress of the droplets adding to her pleasure.

"Kyle," she panted as he found his way to her earlobe, his tongue teasing the sensitive skin there. "*Please.*"

Chapter 13

WAS SHE ASKING HIM TO STOP BEFORE THINGS WENT too far? Or was she pleading with him to give her the release that was rushing up on her swiftly? Kyle wasn't quite sure, but that single word brought his head up in an instant.

He pulled back and smoothed her hair away from her brow, marveling at the way the raindrops clung to her golden lashes. His hands framed her face, holding her tenderly as he peered down at her. His thumb smoothed over her bottom lip. He desperately wanted to feel their warmth again but needed reassurance that his kiss was welcome.

Abby's eyes closed at his touch, and her hands came up to cover his. Then she turned to press a kiss to the center of his palm, sending a jolt of sensation through every nerve in his body.

When she opened her eyes and held his gaze, the desire he saw there was so intense that he half expected to see steam rising around them in the stormy air. When she grasped his hand and led him toward the house, his heart began to pound as they slowly ascended the porch steps.

When they reached the door, she turned to search his gaze. Something in his expression must have amused her because her delectable mouth turned up at one corner and her lids lowered slightly, giving him a look so sultry that he couldn't help himself.

This time the kiss was slow and languid as they

drifted inside. He swung the door shut with his foot and blindly fumbled with the lock and deadbolt until they slid into place. They stood in her entryway, dripping water on her floor as the kiss deepened, his hands gently cradling her face.

Her arms went around his waist, bringing him in closer, holding him against her. Then her hands were tugging at his shirt, untucking it, the attempt made more difficult by the water weighing down the material. And then she was shoving the shirt up his torso.

He broke their kiss long enough to take a step away to grab the back of his shirt and haul it over his head, dropping it on the floor. Then his arms were around her, dragging her back into his embrace so he could once again know the bliss of her kiss.

"I want you, Abby," he muttered against her lips, his hands grabbing her ass and pressing her against him so there was no mistaking his intentions. She moaned deep in her throat, the sound sending a thrill along the length of his spine. He ravaged her lips again briefly, breaking the kiss abruptly and leaving them both panting.

When he pulled back to look into her eyes, he saw hunger, raw and primal. She licked her lips as if she might devour him. Then she grasped the hem of her shirt and swept it over her head and tossed it aside to join his on the floor. "If you want me," she said, her voice low and sexy as she reached behind her and unclasped the white, lacy bra she wore, "then take me."

Her bra slipped from her shoulders, baring the perfect swells of her breasts, her nipples already erect and begging for his touch.

Kyle didn't need to be told twice. He closed the

distance between them in one swift stride, his head dipping to take one of those sweet little buds in his mouth as his arms went around her waist.

She gasped as he suckled her hard, his teeth lightly grazing her nipple. Her head fell back, her fingers tangled in his hair as he ravaged her. She moaned again when he switched to the other breast, the sound of her need eliciting an echoing groan from deep in his gut.

His hand moved between them, slipping under her waistband until he reached her sex. The moment the pad of his middle finger touched the sensitive skin there, she cried out, her entire body going tense.

Holy shit.

She was already coming. Her body tensed and spasmed as waves of ecstasy washed over her. Her hips began to move rhythmically, urging him on. He slid his hand down further, slipping into the slick, swollen folds, warm and wanting.

"Jesus, Abby," he breathed, raising his head to watch the effects of his caresses. "You're so wet." He slid a finger inside her and felt her muscles grasping him, clenching as another release shook her. God, he could caress her like this all night, just to watch the way her orgasms played out over her beautiful face.

As the shudder of her release began to slow, he withdrew his hand to unbutton her pants. Drenched from the rain, they clung to her. Kneeling at her feet, Kyle peeled them down her legs. He pulled off her shoes and lifted each foot, freeing her of her jeans.

But with her sex now at eye level, he couldn't resist. Her knees buckled when his tongue flicked the hypersensitive bud of nerves and she cried out again, her fingers fisting in his hair as he stroked her with his tongue.

"Oh God," she panted, her hips rolling against his mouth. "I can't… I'm going to…"

She couldn't even finish the sentence, a fact that made Kyle's male ego swell with pride and his balls ache with desperate need for his own release. But he wasn't done pleasuring her, not even close.

He eased her down onto the hardwood floor of her entryway, then spread her thighs wide, drinking in the sight of her with hungry eyes. *Goddamn* she was beautiful. He pressed his mouth to her sex once more, chuckling when her body bowed off the floor. And as his tongue teased her clit, stroking and flicking until she moaned, he slipped his finger inside her again, then another, moving slowly at first, the tempo increasing until he was ramming her with rapid, harsh strokes. Her entire body was writhing, her breath coming in harsh gasps.

"Oh God," she panted again. "I'm coming. Don't stop. Don't—"

Her words broke off in a cry of release that echoed through the house.

Kyle withdrew then, pressing kisses to her hip, her belly, and the valley between her breasts and finally reaching her lips. She grasped his neck and kissed him savagely. When she broke the kiss, he rolled away and to his feet, toeing out of his shoes as he fumbled at his belt with hands that shook with his desire to bury himself in her.

Abby rose to her knees and took over, undoing his belt and the fly on his jeans, pulling them over his hips and down the length of his legs. When his erection sprang free, she took him into her mouth, sucking hard as she pulled back slowly.

He cursed under his breath, afraid another move like that would send him careening into mindless oblivion. He pulled her to her feet and pressed her against the wall in one swift motion. Then he lifted her leg, hooking his arm behind her knee, and thrust into her.

~~~

Abby clutched Kyle's shoulders, clinging to him as each powerful thrust pounded into her. God, she'd missed the feel of him, the way he filled her. She loved his masculine power, how he made love to her without holding back or treating her like some delicate flower. She loved how he moved, the power of the orgasms he wrung from her, the heat of his breath on her neck when his head dropped into the curve of her throat as he was getting close to his own release.

Her lids snapped open on a gasp. "Shit," she panted. "Kyle, we forgot—"

But he was already pulling out of her with a groan and a juicy curse at her reminder, snatching up his jeans and pulling his wallet out of his back pocket, fumbling for the foil packet inside. A few seconds later, he was unrolling the condom over his shaft. But for some reason he paused, not immediately coming back to her.

"Kyle?" she asked, coming to him instead. "If you've changed your mind…"

His fingers came up to caress the curve of her jaw. "Never," he whispered. "I just needed a minute to look at you."

Heat bloomed in Abby's cheeks at the look in his

eyes, the love she saw shining there. She didn't deserve that look, not after what she'd put him through when she'd broken his heart. But she welcomed it nonetheless. And hoped he could see the truth of her heart—even if she wasn't quite ready to give voice to it.

He must've seen *something* encouraging in her gaze, because he bent to press his lips to hers for a kiss so tender that Abby's throat grew tight with emotion. When he lifted his head, she took his hand and led him from the entryway to her living room where she playfully pushed him down onto the sofa.

A grin curved his lips as she moved to straddle him, guiding him once more into her body. This time they moved together slowly, savoring the friction where they were joined. Kyle's head fell back against the cushions, his eyes closed as he grasped her hips, guiding her up and down along his shaft.

"My God, I've missed being inside you," he murmured.

Abby leaned forward, pressing her breasts against his chest as she kissed him, the slight shift in her position intensifying her pleasure. Not wanting to come too soon, she drew away. When he opened his eyes, a slight frown of confusion creasing his brow, she met his gaze with a grin and brought her hands up to cup her own breasts, kneading them, pinching and rolling her nipples as he watched with hungry eyes.

She could feel him growing even harder insider her— as impossible as that seemed—and he sucked in a sharp breath when she rolled her hips in the way she knew he liked. When his tempo increased, his muscles growing tense, she leaned forward again, grasping the back of the couch as she rode him, letting the release she'd delayed rush up on her. This time as her orgasm shook her, she didn't hold back.

She screamed his name when light exploded in her head. His arms went around her torso, grasping her tightly as he continued to thrust. Then he shouted as his body bowed and his own orgasm overtook him.

When he fell back spent against the cushions, Abby collapsed against him, her body still pulsing with aftershocks. His fingertips trailed lazily up and down her spine, making her shiver.

"Sweet Jesus," he whispered on a sigh. When she didn't lift her head or pull away, he added, "Abby? You okay?"

At this, she finally did lift her head to peer down into his beloved face for a long moment, then pressed a lingering kiss to his lips. "I'm fine," she murmured against his mouth. "Better than fine. I'm fantastic." She pulled back enough to trace the chiseled planes of his features for a moment, then rolled off him, allowing him to get up and remove the condom. He didn't say a word as he tied it off and left the room to dispose of it.

When he returned, he was still naked, and she certainly wasn't sorry he'd left his clothes in her entryway. She'd always loved to watch him move, had always been fascinated by the way his toned muscles bulged and flexed.

He sat down on the couch next to her and slipped an arm around her, pulling her against his side. She curled into him, draping her arm over his torso and a leg over his thigh.

"I'm so sorry for how things happened before," she said softly, lifting her face and meeting his gaze as he peered down at her.

"You didn't love me anymore," he reminded her, the hurt in his eyes belying his casual tone. "There's nothing to apologize for."

For several long moments, they sat in silence, just holding one another. Then Kyle took a deep breath and let it out on a long sigh. "What's happening between us, Abby?" he asked. "Is this just sex, or do you think you might be able to love me again?"

Abby's heart ached at his words. If she was kind, she would've told him it was just sex, that they were just two consenting adults.

But her heart was too full at the moment to speak anything but the truth. "Love you *again*?" she repeated, pulling away just enough to meet his gaze. When he turned his head away, she laid a hand on his cheek and forced him to look at her. And with her eyes burning with tears of regret, she finally confessed what had been weighing on her for years. "Kyle, it'd be impossible for me to love you *again* because I never *stopped*."

—⁓—

Kyle blinked at Abby in dismay, not quite sure he understood her. "You said you didn't love me. When you broke things off, you told me you never had."

Abby averted her gaze, burying her face in his chest and clutching him tighter. "Could we talk about this later?" she asked, an edge to her voice.

For a second, he thought the sharpness in her tone was anger at him for reminding her of what had happened back then. But then he decided it sounded more like sorrow, anguish even. And he suddenly realized that he hadn't been the only one hurting these last three years. She'd apparently been just as heartbroken about how things had ended as he had. He'd never guessed that all this time she'd been hurting too.

The center of his chest ached at the thought. But that was over. They were together now, in each other's arms. If he had his way, he'd never let her go again. Joe was right. Life was too short to dick around and not at least tell her how he felt.

"I still love you, Abby," he whispered. "There's been no one since you."

The words brought her head up, her eyes searching his as if to test the veracity of his declaration. Her lips curved into a soft, oddly sad smile. His brows came together in confusion at her reaction, but when he opened his mouth to press her on the matter, she pressed her fingers to his lips, stopping his words.

"There's been no one else for me either," she assured him. "My heart wouldn't allow it."

Then she rose to her feet with that gracefulness he so admired and extended her hand to him. Standing there like that in the darkness, she called to him like a siren to a sailor lost at sea, and it was impossible for him to resist her.

As Kyle stood and took her hand, letting her lead him down the hall to her bedroom, he decided to stow his questions for later. Right now, all he wanted to think about was the woman walking ahead of him, her hips swaying hypnotically.

~~~

They'd just crossed the threshold into her bedroom when Kyle's grasp on her hand tightened and he pulled her to an abrupt halt. Abby threw a glance over her shoulder to see what was wrong, but before she could voice her question, he was jerking her into his arms and capturing her mouth in another savage kiss.

She pressed the length of her body into his, reveling in the warmth of his skin against hers. His hands smoothed down her back and over her bottom, then back up along her ribs and up under her arms until he reached her shoulders. He broke their kiss and eased her away from him, arching her back just enough that he could bend to take her nipple into his mouth.

Abby moaned, that familiar ache of need at her core pulsing with her desire to feel him inside her again. But the warmth of his tongue, the gentle scrape of his teeth, the coarseness of his stubble on her skin were pleasurable distractions.

As he left her breasts to press kisses along her collarbone to her throat, he carefully walked her backward toward her bed. The hard length of his erection thrust between her thighs, making her shudder with anticipation of the joining that would soon have her screaming his name.

When she bumped against her mattress and they could go no farther, he captured her face with his hands and took her mouth in a deep kiss, his tongue plunging rhythmically, tangling with hers. Abby let her head fall back, surrendering completely, content to go on kissing him like this forever in spite of the ache of need that had turned from a low, smoldering flame to raging heat.

As if understanding her desperate need, he suddenly broke their kiss and gave her a gentle shove. She cried out in surprise as she fell back onto the mattress, then giggled at the playful, sexy smile that curved his sensual mouth. But his smile faded, replaced by that heated gaze she knew was the precursor to mind-blowing rapture.

When he wedged himself between her legs and grasped her hips, roughly pulling her to the edge of the mattress and thrusting into her without warning, she sent up a wordless mewl of pleasure. And when he began to move his hips in long, measured thrusts, Abby arched off the bed with a moan, clutching the coverlet in her fists.

"God, yes," she gasped, her breath ragged as another release sped upon her. "Yes!"

Kyle groaned in response and when she met his gaze, she could see him straining to hold on, waiting to ensure that she'd found her release. His jaw was clenched so tight that the muscle near his ear twitched.

As her muscles began to contract around him, he suddenly withdrew and dropped to his knees, burying his face between her thighs and using his tongue to bring her over the edge. She cried out as her body shuddered, writhing against his mouth, and still he drove her on.

When she could no longer stand the intensity of the pleasure, she gasped his name, gently pulling his head up. He obeyed and instantly turned to her bedside table, jerking open the drawer and heaving a relieved sigh as he snatched up the box of condoms she kept there. Seconds later, he was sliding one over his shaft and then slipping into her again.

Abby rose up on her elbows and scooted back farther on the mattress. Never breaking his stride, he followed, easing his body down on hers, supporting himself on his elbows as his tempo increased.

His head dropped into the curve of her neck, his

breath hot on her skin, making her shiver as goose bumps prickled her flesh. She wrapped her arms and legs around him, clutching him close as his body tensed. The groan that rose up from deep within his chest made her shiver, and her body pulsed with his, a smaller aftershock of her earlier release.

When he collapsed, spent, she cradled him tenderly, smoothing his back and shoulders, pressing kisses to his hair, letting the love they shared at that moment seep into the marrow of her bones, filling her with the kind of joy she had only found in his arms and praying that when she finally found the courage to explain to him why she'd pushed him away three years ago, he would be able to forgive her. God knows she had yet to forgive herself.

Chapter 14

IT WAS JUST AFTER THREE IN THE MORNING WHEN Fielding spotted the guy creeping along the privacy fence that enclosed Abby Morrow's backyard. The man's dark clothes helping him blend into the shadows and become almost invisible, especially with the rain coming down in sheets, the howling wind blowing it sideways and obscuring his view. If not for Fielding's trained eye and years of experience *being* the man dressed in black and creeping along fence lines, he doubted he would've spotted him.

It was a shitty night to be on a job. The guy had to be pissed and cursing his decision to take the hit on Abby Morrow right about now. Fielding almost hated to take the fucker out. The guy's day was about to go from bad to worse.

There were lines that shouldn't be crossed. Planning to kill someone when you'd already gotten what you needed out of them was a bullshit waste of resources and created unnecessary risks. And if you *did* have to tie up loose ends, you should at least show a little creativity and forethought, for fuck's sake.

Yeah, well, this lame assassin would be in for a surprise if that pretty little deputy's boyfriend got wind of the intrusion before the hit could go off. The guy moved like he knew what he was doing. Odds were good that the jackass moving toward the front door didn't even know Abby wasn't alone.

There'd been no recon, no surveillance. And clearly the guy had no imagination, no finesse.

Fielding shook his head.

He'd almost be doing this loser a favor by doing him in before he got caught and had to suffer the indignity of having all his mistakes on a job laid bare in a very public trial. Even if the guy got off by some miracle, he'd never work again.

Fielding heaved a long-suffering sigh and pushed open the door of his SUV almost silently—not that the guy could've heard it anyway over the window-rattling rumble of thunder.

He hunched over and flipped up his collar to keep the rain from going down the back of his jacket. His gaze darted up and down the wooded street, checking for approaching headlights, then to the nearest houses, which were all dark, their occupants no doubt fast asleep. Gotta love a sleepy small town. Made his job a hell of a lot easier.

The hired gun was just pulling open the screen door to go to work on the deadbolt of the heavy wooden door when Fielding raced silently up the front steps. Without pause, he wrapped his arm around the guy's head and twisted in one swift motion.

The guy sagged in his arms. He hadn't even realized Fielding was there.

Pathetic.

Fielding glanced around again. Satisfied that no one had seen any of what had just gone down, he hefted the man up over his shoulder. He strode swiftly to his waiting vehicle and opened the rear door, then cast one more glance up and down the street before pitching the guy inside.

As he slid in behind the wheel and started up the SUV
he grinned, enjoying the game Mr. Smith didn't even
know he was playing. Fielding had eliminated the threat
for now. When his employer realized his hit man had
failed, he'd send someone else. But Fielding had done his
good deed, had evened the odds a little. And for tonight,
Deputy Morrow and her boyfriend could rest easy.

Or not.

If the little show they'd put on earlier was any indication, they were probably still screwing each other's
brains out. *Damn.* He'd pulled up to the neighbor's
house just a few minutes before they'd arrived home.
Talk about perfect timing.

He'd slid down in his seat when he saw the headlights
approaching and had a front-row seat for the heated make-
out session there in the driveway. For a minute there he
thought they might actually go at it right there against the
car. But to his disappointment, they'd headed inside.

As he pulled away, Fielding chuckled, wondering
if he should send a thank-you note to the deputy for
providing a little entertainment while he waited for her
would-be assassin to show. And maybe suggest she
invest in some curtains for the windows on either side
of her front door…

The next morning, Abby stood naked in front of the
mirror in her bathroom, dragging a comb through her
hair that was still damp from the long, sultry shower
she and Kyle had shared a few minutes earlier. They'd
had good intentions, planning on just kissing and caressing, but that had soon led to one seriously hot make-out

session. Although they'd both experienced their release in the shower, she ached to feel Kyle inside her again, to join their bodies in that blissful tangle of arms and legs and tongues.

She'd never been able to get enough of him. And now that he'd confessed he'd never stopped loving her, her guilt over pushing him away before was so crushing that she only found reprieve from it when he was in her arms, cradled by her body. And she was offering him all of her—heart, body, and soul.

As if sensing her need, Kyle came up behind her and wrapped his arms around her waist and pressed a kiss to the side of her throat. She tilted her head to the side to grant him greater access to her neck. And when his hand came up to cup her breast, she closed her eyes and leaned into him with a contented sigh.

"My God, I could make love to you all day long and never get enough of you," he murmured near her ear. As if to prove his point, his other hand drifted down between her legs to caress the folds that were already swollen and aching again for his touch.

Grinning, she moved her hips, pressing her backside against his groin. "The feeling's mutual."

He groaned and shifted to press his growing erection between her legs, thrusting his hips, teasing her with the gentle friction. "Should we go back to your bed?"

She let her head drop back against his chest, loving the way he could be so fiercely passionate a lover one moment and so tender and gentle the next. "We have to leave soon," she said, not surprised that her voice was breathless when his fingers were driving her mad. "We stayed in bed too long."

His deep chuckle vibrated against her back. "No such thing." He pressed a kiss to her shoulder, then nipped at it gently with his teeth. "Let Hamilton wait. You're much sexier company."

She knew she should've insisted, but it was impossible to think clearly when he was stroking her so expertly. "Oh God," she gasped as she felt another orgasm building. She moaned, pressing back against him, wanting more of him, *needing* more of him, *all* of him.

Apparently, that was all the encouragement Kyle needed.

With his free hand, Kyle opened the vanity drawer, blindly feeling around for the condom he'd brought with him to the bathroom that morning, just in case. He'd always been safe with his lovers. Always. But with Abby it was hard as hell to stick to his own rules. After that reckless night on the boat their first time together, he'd vowed to be less of a sex-crazed dolt. And yet there'd been at least one other time that they'd thrown caution to the wind that summer.

And now he'd almost done it again the night before. Thank God she'd brought him to his senses before he'd come inside her and potentially put her at risk of an unwanted pregnancy. It wasn't like with Joe and Sadie who'd been in love with each other most of their lives and had been together for a year now and were looking forward to spending the rest of their lives together. His future with Abby was just beginning to take form and was in no way certain.

He damned near shouted in triumph when he found

the condom and slammed the drawer shut. A moment later he was tearing open the package with his teeth and slipping it on.

He pressed Abby forward until she was bent over the vanity, braced on her elbows, then nudged her legs apart and thrust into her from behind as he continued to caress her clit.

Christ, she is beautiful.

Watching in the mirror as passion played across Abby's face had Kyle clamping down on his back teeth to keep his shit together. Her eyes were closed, her lips parted as she panted, her hair hanging over her shoulder, her breasts swaying with each thrust.

She was the sexiest woman he'd ever seen, had taken his breath away the first time he saw her. She'd walked into the academy that day, looking nervous as hell but somehow fearless at the same time. It was that combination of courage and vulnerability that did him in.

And the fact that she'd opened herself to him in every way was the greatest gift he could ask for. Even now, she gave herself over to their lovemaking, accepting him so willingly and without reservation, making his chest go tight with emotion.

As her muscles began to contract and her body raced toward release, he clenched his jaw tighter, forcing himself not to give in. But then she was shattering apart, and he followed right along with her with a shout, pitching forward and bracing himself against the edge of the vanity counter.

As his rhythm began to slow, he cursed inwardly at his selfishness. He'd wanted to last longer, give her the pleasure she deserved instead of a quickie in the bathroom, for chrissake.

With one arm braced on the counter, the other wrapped around her waist, supporting her, his body curled over hers as they waited to catch their breath, he kissed her shoulder again. Slowly he withdrew, a groan escaping him before he could check it. But then she turned around to face him, sliding her hands up his chest. He drew her back into her arms and brushed his lips to hers in a brief kiss. "Should I have stopped?"

She gave him a wicked grin. "Oh no. I think if you had stopped I would've been forced to employ extreme measures."

"Is that so?" He was grinning when he kissed her again. "And what kind of extreme measures did you have in mind?"

She giggled and slipped from his arms, throwing an arch look over her shoulder as she headed for the door. "Well, I guess you'll just have to wait until tonight to find out."

Kyle watched her sashay out of the bathroom and muttered a reverent curse, wondering just how long he'd have to wait to find out what was going through that gorgeous mind of hers.

Chapter 15

ABBY WAS GRATEFUL THAT KYLE'S FINGERS WERE twined with hers as they entered the Sheriff's Department to face Hamilton. Her knees were shaky, her entire body trembling with barely restrained anger at what that son of a bitch had put her sister through. He was damned lucky they were meeting in a public place—which is probably why he'd volunteered that instead of a private meeting.

Hamilton was no idiot; that was clear. She'd have to be on her guard. And he'd have to work damned hard to prove his innocence because she wasn't buying it for a second.

"Hey, you got a visitor, Abby," one of the deputies at the front desk informed her as soon as she entered the building. "He's in room five."

Kyle gave Abby's hand a reassuring squeeze, apparently sensing her nerves. "Have you ever done this before?" he asked her softly as they made their way toward the meeting room.

She shook her head. "Not like this. The only time I've ever questioned anyone was in dealing with victims or witnesses—never a suspect."

"Well, we aren't sure which he is yet," Kyle reminded her. "Just stay calm and let him talk. If he's guilty, the more he talks the better. More of a chance he'll trip himself up with his own lies."

She nodded, her heart pounding as the little plastic sign that jutted out from the wall beside the door marking the room "In Use" came into view. "Thanks," she said, pulling him to a halt just outside the door. "For everything. Really. I appreciate you being here with me."

He smoothed the back of her hand with his thumb and smiled, the gaze he gave her heating her blood and giving her courage. "Always. Remember that."

Although the knowledge of his unwavering support meant the world to her, his devotion pricked her conscience, and she wondered just how supportive he'd be when he found out about the secret she'd been keeping from him. Would he look at her so lovingly when he knew the truth?

Abby shoved her own concerns aside and took a deep breath, exhaling sharply and steeling herself. She opened the meeting room door and strode inside, her head held high, her expression intentionally hard, not bothering to hide her suspicion.

But the moment her gaze met that of Patrick Hamilton, she had a hard time keeping her mouth from dropping open to gape at him. She wasn't sure what she'd been expecting, but certainly not the devastatingly handsome, debonair man still this side of sixty who had either hit the gene pool jackpot or paid a lot of money to retain the appearance of youthfulness. Sitting there in the meeting room, which was more like a conference room than one of the dingy, gray concrete rooms so often depicted on television cop shows, Hamilton looked more like George Clooney than a nefarious criminal.

But Abby knew better than anyone that looks could be deceiving.

Hamilton stood when they entered and buttoned the jacket of his impeccably tailored suit as he said, "Deputy Morrow. A pleasure to finally meet you in person." He then turned his steel gray gaze toward Kyle and extended a hand. "Patrick Hamilton."

Kyle eyed him warily but shook his hand. "Agent Kyle Dawson, FBI."

Hamilton's brows lifted. "FBI?" He then turned his attention back to Abby and gestured to her to sit at the conference table as if he'd called *her* there to chat. "Won't you sit down? I'm eager to hear what you've found and why you are so suspicious of my involvement that you felt it necessary to call in the FBI."

For a split second, Abby thought about refusing his offer to sit and remaining standing to make it clear that *she* was the one in control of the situation, not Hamilton. But she had a feeling that no matter how she played things, the man wasn't used to deferring to anyone and knew how to maintain control even when giving the illusion otherwise.

So she walked around to the other side of the conference table and took a seat across from him, creating a barrier between them so that he didn't for one second think that they were on the same side—literally or figuratively.

"Thank you for coming down this morning, Mr. Hamilton," Kyle said, sliding back the chair next to Abby's in just the right way to make the wooden legs screech as they scraped the floor.

Hamilton flinched almost imperceptibly. "I'd say it was my pleasure, Agent Dawson, but I am concerned about what precipitated Deputy Morrow's accusations."

Abby wanted to lunge across the table and grab

Hamilton by the lapels of his designer suit and give him a good shake. Instead, she leaned back in her chair and met his even gaze as she'd witnessed Mac Dawson do on numerous occasions. "It seems that one of your employees was indeed involved in unethical activities, Mr. Hamilton. In fact, they were not just unethical but *illegal*."

Hamilton didn't bat an eye. "So it was as I suspected. Insider trading."

"No," she said, shaking her head. "Affairs, stealing supplies, and using company Internet to browse porn—definitely. But I didn't find any evidence of insider trading."

Hamilton's eyes narrowed slightly. "If not that, then what?"

"What do you know about your godson's involvement with a private security firm called Tartarus Security Services International?"

He shook his head. "Nothing at all."

Abby had to work to keep the angry tremor out of her voice when she hissed, "Well, the man you sent to kidnap my sister and then break into her house to assault me to get the data certainly knew all about it."

"As I said before, Deputy," Hamilton drawled, his demeanor completely unfazed, "I have no idea what you're talking about. I didn't hire anyone to kidnap your sister or assault you. What exactly did you find that this man wanted so badly?"

She glanced at Kyle, silently asking if he thought she should share her findings. When he gave her an almost imperceptible nod, she explained, "Your godson is involved in a rather extensive money-laundering operation, Mr. Hamilton."

For the first time, Hamilton actually looked taken aback. "Pardon me?"

"That's the least of your concerns," Kyle told him.

Hamilton shook his head, his confusion evident in his eyes. "There must be some mistake. Preston is his father's right hand. Mine as well. I have no children of my own, no nieces or nephews. Everything will be left to Preston when I pass. He'll be one of the wealthiest men in the country. Why would he want to jeopardize that by dealing with criminals?"

Abby eyed Hamilton for a long moment. Either he was truly baffled or he was an incredible actor. "Maybe he didn't want to wait that long," she suggested.

Hamilton looked away, suddenly very interested in a scratch on the cherrywood conference table. After mulling over her words for a moment, he shook his head. "No, he wouldn't have any need of money. He's already inherited millions from his grandparents and has a ridiculous salary that his father insisted upon."

Abby leaned forward and put her forearms on the table, clasping her hands together and taking an entirely different attitude. "Mr. Hamilton, maybe it wasn't about the money at first. And maybe he didn't intend to get into things this deep. I'll grant you that. Perhaps he planned to do just one job as a favor to the wrong person, but then he found it all too alluring. Maybe having powerful people in his pocket who owed him a favor was just too intoxicating. But I'm guessing if you looked into his finances you'd see he's greatly overspending even his ridiculous salary. You must know the lavish parties he throws, the kinds of friends he has, the celebrities and the old-moneyed elite who live hard and fast and who all tend to have particular...*habits*."

Hamilton looked shocked at her insinuation. But she wasn't saying anything that wasn't common knowledge. All Hamilton had to do was glance at the tabloids and he'd know the kind of company his godson kept— drugged-out starlets and washed-up pop stars who only continued to get invited to the best parties because of the crazy cash they were willing to throw around and the spectacular "party favors" they had access to because of their stardom—whether past or present.

She was being kind in letting Hamilton think his godson's dirty dealings were just for the money. But the fact was, Preston Whitmore had a habit of bragging to some of his cronies about who he'd slept with and the amount of cocaine they'd blown through—literally—at one of his parties in Chicago. And for a man who clearly lacked scruples, it was hardly surprising that he had no qualms about sleeping with a woman who was completely stoned out of her mind. Class act all the way around.

Hamilton took a deep breath and exhaled on a sigh, his silver brows drawing together in a frown. "I was something of a wunderkind in the industry when I met my business partner. Even then, Preston was a headstrong teenager, had a talent for falling in with the wrong people. But even though I'm only twenty years Preston's senior, his father hoped that if he made me Preston's godfather, I'd be a positive influence." He met Abby's gaze. "But you're telling me very clearly that I have failed not just Preston but his father as well."

Abby felt a momentary stab of pity for the man across

from her. "You can't help someone who doesn't want to be helped. Some people just…" Abby let her words trail off, her pity turning to irritation that she suddenly felt *sorry* for Hamilton when she still wasn't convinced of his innocence.

"Some people just…?" Hamilton prompted.

Abby regarded him with a harsh look. "Some people just believe they are above reproach, Mr. Hamilton. They think they can do what they want to whom they want and they will be exempt from the consequences."

Hamilton lifted a single brow. "You think I plan to ask you not to prosecute my godson?"

"Do you?" Kyle interjected. "It wouldn't be the first time someone like you tried to buy your way out of trouble."

"Someone like me?" Hamilton echoed with a grin. "No offense, Agent Dawson, but you don't know a damned thing about me."

Kyle spread his hands. "Fair enough. But Abby does. And she doesn't trust you. How do we know you weren't involved in this money laundering or other activities as well?"

Hamilton's gaze flicked toward Abby. "What other activities? There's more?"

"Let's get back to what you know about Tartarus," Abby said.

"I've already told you that I'm not familiar with that company," he replied, his calm slipping slightly.

"Tartarus is a private security firm with operations all over the world," Abby explained. "While investigating, I discovered that Whitmore was doing business with Curtis Maxwell, the owner of the security firm." When Hamilton failed to react to her brother-in-law's name or Whitmore's association with him, Abby continued, "They're using Tartarus as a front for an extensive—and extremely lucrative—human-trafficking operation."

Hamilton went visibly pale but then red began to creep up his neck and into his face, reminding Abby of the cartoons she watched as a girl when the character eats peppers that are too hot and steam starts shooting out his ears before the top of his head blows off.

"Why did you keep this from me until now?" Hamilton asked.

"I wasn't sure of your innocence," Abby admitted without hesitation.

"And now?"

She shook her head. "Still not."

"And yet you've told me all of this," he pointed out. "You've shown your hand."

"To watch your reaction to everything," Abby told him. "To see if you'd slip up on anything."

Hamilton's eyes narrowed. "You were fishing for more information. What else do you need to know?"

"Where my brother-in-law is." Abby pulled out her phone and found the picture of Curtis that she'd received and slid it across the table.

Hamilton caught it without taking his gaze off her. He blinked twice, then looked down at the phone. He twitched slightly when he saw the graphic image. "Who is this?"

"I think it might be my brother-in-law," Abby told him. "Curtis Maxwell."

Hamilton's brows shot up. "The man who owns Tartarus? The man with whom Preston is in league?"

Abby gave him a slight nod. "He's missing."

"Have you been in New Orleans recently, Mr. Hamilton?" Kyle asked.

Hamilton frowned at him. "No. Why?"

"We were able to trace the number back to New Orleans," Kyle explained.

"Could it have been a forwarded photo?" Hamilton questioned.

Abby shook her head. "The phone company records show no incoming media on the phone. Only outgoing."

Hamilton's scowl grew. "You're certain of all of this?" Hamilton ground out between clenched teeth.

Abby nodded. "Yes."

"There's no chance you could've misinterpreted any of your findings?" he replied. "And you have proof?"

Abby worked to keep her expression from giving her away. "We're in the process of getting a subpoena for the data you provided me during my freelance investigation. I would suggest you cooperate—for your sake and Preston's."

"That will not be possible," Hamilton interrupted, waving away Kyle's words.

Abby's chest tightened. "I beg your pardon?"

Hamilton rose to his feet, apparently signaling the end of the interview. "I assure you, Deputy Morrow, I do not condone my godson's activities any more than you do your brother-in-law's. But as much as I would like to help you, I'm afraid there are certain things that should be handled privately."

Abby's stomach sank. "What do you mean?"

"I can't imagine that you or your sister would like to be dragged through a very public trial any more than my company would," he explained. "You understand."

"You understand you're interfering with an investigation?" Kyle shot back.

"A regrettable fact," Hamilton agreed as he strode casually toward the door. "But as you have yet to prove that a crime has been committed, I imagine you'd be hard-pressed to prove that I'm interfering with *any*thing."

"As soon as we have the court order, you'll be required to provide the data," Abby insisted. "You realize that, don't you? You won't have a choice."

Hamilton nodded, pursing his lips as if considering her threat. "True," he agreed. "If you had a subpoena you could force me to comply and arrest me should I refuse—well, you could try anyway." Here he turned and offered them a chilling smile. "As you say, some individuals are immune to punishment. And I have many friends."

Abby tried to keep her body from sagging, but something of her frustration and disappointment must've showed in her face because Hamilton gave her a sympathetic look.

"I assure you, Preston will be dealt with," he vowed. "And if I discover the whereabouts of your brother-in-law, my dear, I will of course share that information with you."

"Mr. Hamilton," Kyle called out as Hamilton opened the door to leave, "did Preston know that you'd asked Abby to investigate some of the employees?"

Hamilton nodded. "Of course. He and his father were both aware. I had informed them of my suspicions about certain employees at dinner one evening. It was Donovan, Preston's father, who suggested we hire an investigator privately instead of going to the police." He gave Abby a pointed look. "It was Preston who mentioned the Brannigan case to me and suggested you as the person we should hire, Deputy."

Chapter 16

"WHY WOULD WHITMORE SPECIFICALLY REQUEST ME to do the investigation?" Abby mused aloud for what had to be the hundredth time.

And for what had to be hundredth time, Kyle replied, "I have no idea." He sighed. "Maybe he never thought you'd find anything. Maybe he didn't realize that his email could be detected. Hell, I don't know. Maybe he's an arrogant prick like his godfather. I really can't begin to guess."

It was true. He had no clue why that asshole would give Hamilton Abby's name. If he knew about the Brannigan case as purported, he had to know how good she was. It didn't make any damned sense. If the guy was guilty, why wouldn't he try to misdirect the investigation instead of assist it?

Kyle shook his head. Whitmore was like a serial killer returning to the scene of the crime to witness the aftermath with his own eyes. Which didn't seem to fit in this case. He was daring Abby to turn him in, to turn her own *family* in.

Kyle straightened at the wheel of his Mustang as they turned into the hospital parking lot. "Maybe Whitmore was banking on the fact that you wouldn't turn in your sister's husband," he suggested. But before she could respond, he cursed under his breath. "Never mind. That's a bullshit option. He had no way of knowing what kind of relationship you had with your brother-in-law. Hell, for all he knew, you could've hated Curtis."

Abby glanced at him out of the corner of her eye, looking decidedly uncomfortable. "That might not be such a bad thought, actually."

Kyle pulled into a parking spot and turned off the engine before turning in his seat to peg her with an expectant look. "What do you mean?"

"My mother was a model and an actress, remember?" She ran a hand through her hair, the golden tresses sliding through her fingers.

Kyle tried to focus on what she was saying instead of thoughts of running his fingers through that gorgeous hair the night before while she gasped his name. He frowned with forced concentration. "Yeah, so?"

"She and Dad had hated each other for years before he was murdered," she told him. "But no one ever knew that. We grew up learning how to put on a good show. Mom's role of grieving widow after Dad's murder would've won her an Oscar if anyone had known how she really felt."

Kyle reached over and took her hand in his, bringing it to his lips. "I'm sorry, sweetheart. That's not a great environment to grow up in."

"No, it wasn't." After a heavy sigh, she continued. "And unfortunately, I guess Emma and I took up where Mom left off."

Kyle shook his head slightly, confused. "How so?"

"Do you have any idea how many questions about my mom I got from curious teachers and concerned friends over the years?" she asked. "To hear us tell it, Mom was doing great. We rented furniture for parties because she'd had to liquidate most of what we had just to pay off all the debt Dad left her with. She filed for bankruptcy eventually—but only after she had nothing left."

"I'm sorry," Kyle told her, caressing her hand with his thumb. "I didn't know."

"Yeah, well, no one did," she said with a bitter laugh. "Certainly not Curtis when he proposed to Emma. He thought he was getting one hell of a windfall by marrying an heiress. And their marriage turned out just as bad as our parents'." She let her head fall back against her seat. "For a long time, I swore I'd never get married, never let myself get trapped like that—or trap someone else into a marriage he'd just regret later."

Kyle frowned, wondering what the hell she was talking about, wondering if maybe she was trying to tell him something. "Abby, you know I meant it when I told you I loved you that summer, right?"

She turned her gaze down to their clasped hands and nodded. But she didn't raise her eyes to meet his, curiously avoiding looking at him. He gently took hold of her chin and turned her head toward him.

"Then why did you push me away?" he pressed. "You say you never stopped loving me, which means you loved me then. So why lie? What were you so afraid of?"

She slipped her hand from his grasp. "Does it matter? Isn't it enough to know that I love you *now*?"

He dropped back against his seat, warring with himself. Part of him was still pissed that she'd lied to him—for what reason, he couldn't fathom—but part of him didn't want to press her too hard. Shit, she'd been through a hell of a lot in the last few days. The last thing she needed was him acting like an asshole.

Besides, *did* it matter?

His still-mending broken heart told him it did. She owed him an explanation for the hurt she'd caused when she pushed him away. But he ran a hand through his hair and blew out a harsh sigh. "Fine. But I want to talk more about this at some point. Could we at last agree to do that sooner rather than later?"

She nodded, visibly relieved. "Thank you for not pushing on this right now."

"Come on." He jerked his chin toward the hospital, switching the subject before he changed his mind. "Let's go see your sister. I'm sure she's eager to get the hell out of this place."

―――――∞∞∞―――――

"So you need anything else?"

Abby offered a smile in response to the deputy who'd been standing guard at her sister's hospital room since the night before. "Thanks, Bradford," she said as Emma and Tyler came out of the house with their overnight bags. Bradford had insisted on following them back to Emma's house while she and Tyler picked up a few things for their trip to the cabin. "But I think we can take it from here. Kyle's going to follow us to the cabin and make sure we get settled."

Bradford's head bobbed slightly, but his gaze was on Emma. He rushed toward her as she attempted to lift her suitcase into the back of her Lincoln Navigator. "Here, let me get that for you, Mrs. Maxwell."

When Emma gave the handsome deputy a shy smile, complete with a pretty blush, Abby tried hard not to roll her eyes. Her sister had been kidnapped on the way

home from visiting her *lover,* and her *husband* was
still missing, and yet she was flirting with her freaking
bodyguard, for crying out loud! Maybe Emma hadn't
changed so much after all...or maybe she was just
enjoying a little genuine kindness from a man without
ulterior motives. But still...

"Are we ready to go?" Abby snapped, earning a confused look from her sister. She ignored the question in
Emma's eyes and turned to her nephew. "Hop in, Ty."

Kyle came up behind her, placing a hand on the small
of her back to lead her away from the others, then leaned
in a little to murmur, "Everything okay?"

She gave a terse nod and crossed her arms over her
chest. "Yeah, I'm just..." She huffed. "Never mind. I
guess some things never change, no matter how much
you want to believe they have."

He pressed a kiss to her temple. "Want to talk about
it later?"

She felt her scowl soften. She was so glad to have
him back in her life. She'd missed his calming presence,
the way he could soothe her with just a touch, a word, a
look, a smile. She couldn't help but wonder if it wasn't
pure selfishness that had made her agree to his plan to
follow them to the cabin. She had to admit, if it'd been
anyone else she would've taken it as a lack of confidence in her ability to protect her sister and nephew. But
when he'd offered, instead of being offended, she'd felt
warmth start in the center of her chest and then radiate
through her body, filling her with gratitude and love in
equal measure.

And now she felt a twinge of guilt. The cabin was a few
hours away on crappy roads. The man had his own life, a

new apartment, a new job. He probably had all kinds of things he should be taking care of. "You sure you want to follow us up there?" she asked. "It's a bit of a drive. I'd understand if you'd want to bail. I mean, you haven't even had the chance to get settled since moving here."

"It can wait." He pressed his forehead to hers. "You're all that matters right now."

Abby wrapped her arms around his waist and rested her cheek against his chest, enjoying the warmth of his arms around her for a moment before finally sighing and pulling out of his embrace. "You know how to get there?"

He nodded, keeping his hands at her waist so she couldn't pull away completely. "I'll be right behind you."

Abby tilted her chin up to receive his kiss. It was just a tender brush of his lips against hers, but it was enough for heat to spread through her body and make her shiver at the intensity of it.

When she opened her eyes and saw his cocky, self-satisfied smile, he winked. "See you soon."

Abby was still grinning when she got behind the wheel of her sister's Navigator and started it up.

"So you and Kyle are back together?" Emma asked softly, casting a glance over her shoulder into the backseat.

Abby followed the direction of her sister's glance in the rearview mirror and saw that Tyler already had his earbuds in, his attention focused on the game he was playing on his phone. "Something like that," she admitted as she headed down the driveway toward the main road. "We haven't actually talked about it. It all just kind of fell back into place."

Abby could feel the weight of Emma's gaze without needing to look her way. Clearly her sister had something more she wanted to say but was holding back. Abby waited, wondering if she was going to come out with it.

After several miles of heavy silence, Emma finally cleared her throat and asked softly, "Have you told him?"

At this, Abby did turn her attention briefly to her sister, not entirely surprised at the question. Even though she and Emma had chosen different paths, had made very different decisions in their lives, and hadn't been especially close for the last decade or so, they were still sisters. There wasn't a whole lot she could hide from Emma. At least not for long.

The fact that her sister knew the circumstances surrounding Abby's decision to break things off with Kyle, that she understood why Abby had done what she had, was such a relief that all the emotions she thought she'd buried came rushing back in one wave of sorrow and heartache, bringing tears to her eyes before she could stop them.

She swiped angrily at her eyes before Tyler could notice and shook her head. "No," she admitted. "It didn't seem like the right time. When everything is over with this case, when we're sure you and Tyler are safe, then I'll focus on fixing what I screwed up."

"It wasn't just you, honey," Emma reminded her. "You can't get into that kind of situation on your own. And you didn't screw up anything, Abby. You did what you thought was best for everyone."

Abby took a deep, shaky breath, letting it out slowly. "That's what I thought too," she said. "But I don't know now… I loved him so much, Emma. And I've never stopped. If I had any doubts before, the last couple of days have removed them."

Emma reached over and placed a hand on Abby's thigh with a comforting pat. "Then you definitely need to tell him everything. If he loves you as much as you love him, it'll be okay."

They fell into silence again, each lost in her own thoughts. It was some time later before Emma sent another glance over her shoulder at Tyler, then turned back to face forward, staring straight ahead when she asked, "Something has happened to Curtis, hasn't it?"

Abby's stomach plummeted, wishing she had a better answer for her sister. "I don't know for sure," she said softly.

Emma nodded slowly. "I thought so. The way you were acting in the hospital… Curtis is a lousy husband. You've certainly witnessed that over the years, but I cared for him once. And he's Tyler's father. But there are things he's been involved in, Abby, things I've never told you about… I always worried something might happen to him."

Abby's head snapped toward her sister, her brows raised. "What do you know about what he's been involved in, Em?" she asked in a fierce whisper, checking the rearview mirror to make sure Tyler wasn't listening in.

Emma threw her a sardonic look. "He's not the only one who found our marriage lacking," she admitted. "In fact, he encouraged me to…" She paused, weighing her words. "Let's just say, I didn't become friendly with my Chicago acquaintance on my own. It was *arranged*."

Abby's stomach rolled at what she was hearing. "Do you mean"—she lowered her voice—"Curtis lent you out? For money?"

Emma flushed crimson, confirming Abby's fear before she gave a slight nod. "I didn't realize it at first. But by the time Travis accidentally let something slip about his arrangement with Curtis, I didn't even care. At least, that's what I told myself. Travis was incredibly generous to me, and I enjoyed our time together. It was certainly better than anything I'd had with Curtis in recent memory. But it made me wonder what else he might be involved in, what other people he might be taking advantage of, people who'd trusted him."

Abby blew out a harsh breath. "Jesus, Emma. How long have you known?"

Emma shrugged. "A few months. I found out right before I left for France."

A sudden thought occurred to Abby, sending a quiver down her spine. "Did Curtis know you found out what was going on?" she demanded quietly.

Emma laughed in a short, bitter burst. "Of course!" she said, her chin going up a notch defiantly. Her bravado lessened when she realized how loudly she'd spoken. Lowering her voice again, she said, "I confronted him before I left for my spa trip. Told him I knew exactly what he was up to and that he'd be sorry. I contacted a divorce lawyer while I was gone."

Abby's stomach was doing somersaults as she tried to process what her sister was telling her. "Did he know you were going to divorce him?"

Emma nodded. "He was furious, but that was more based on fear of losing the assets in my name than from losing me and Tyler, I'm sure."

A divorce like theirs would've made local headlines, maybe national. Lawyers would have to dig into their finances, including those of Curtis's business. If Abby could uncover all the illegal activities Curtis and Whitmore were involved in, a very nasty and public divorce would've certainly exposed at least some of it—maybe all of it—even if Abby hadn't uncovered the truth in her investigation.

And now Curtis was most likely dead.

"Anyway," Emma said with a shrug, "I broke things off with Travis when I was in Chicago. I told him I didn't think it would be right to continue our acquaintance, all things considered."

Abby's brows twitched together in a frown. "How did he take it?"

Emma smiled but Abby didn't miss the fact that her chin trembled when she said, "Fine. He wasn't upset at all."

Obviously, the man had meant something to her sister. Even if they'd had just a sexual affair, the fact that he'd failed to be upset at her ending things clearly hurt Emma.

Abby reached over and squeezed her sister's hand. "You deserve better, Emma. You always have. You know that, don't you?"

Emma sniffed and shrugged. "Yeah. Of course."

"I mean it," Abby insisted.

Emma sighed. "I'm not a twentysomething anymore, Abby. And I've never been beautiful. Not like you."

Abby gaped at the elder sister she'd always found stunning, wondering how she could not realize how gorgeous she was. "Who told you that you aren't beautiful? You're even more amazing now than you were in your twenties, Em. I'm not lying. Trust me, you turn heads

whenever you walk into a room. Deputy Bradford certainly couldn't get enough of an eyeful."

Emma's lips curled into a quiet smile at the mention
of Abby's colleague. "He's a very kind man. I'm sure
he would've been as attentive to anyone in his charge."

Abby couldn't argue there. But she'd seen the way
Adam looked at her sister. He was a goner. But now
wasn't the time to press the issue. Emma was going to
need time to heal, time to discover that she had a great
deal to offer a man worthy of her love. Abby had a feeling that her sister's lack of confidence and self-value was
thanks in large part to her husband's calculated cruelty.

"Just know that I'm here for you, Em," she said.
"We'll get through this together. Just like we have
everything else, okay?"

She squeezed her sister's hand again and offered
her an encouraging smile while on the inside her guts
were twisting with rage at the man who'd treated her
sister with such disrespect. That son of a bitch deserved
whatever he got. And if he wasn't already lying dead
in a ditch somewhere as a result of his own nefarious
dealings, then Abby sure as hell would make sure he'd
pay under the law. She didn't give a shit what Patrick
Hamilton had to say about it.

Chapter 17

KYLE TOSSED HIS PHONE ONTO THE SEAT NEXT TO him, frustrated that he still hadn't heard back from Peterman. The way the guy had talked, he was going to be questioning Rhodes right away. Hell, maybe Peterman wasn't as over everything that had gone down between them as he'd let on. Maybe he was still pissed at Kyle and going to go around him on the investigation to try to bring down Tartarus on his own.

He wouldn't have blamed him. Kyle knew he didn't deserve any help from Peterman. Still, he'd hoped the guy would come through.

Of course, thanks to Hamilton's unwillingness to provide the data to Abby again, it wasn't like Kyle could give Peterman or anyone else anything more to go on. Just his word. And he'd made sure that didn't mean shit.

God, he was a fuckup.

No wonder Mac wasn't ready to make amends after just one conversation. His father had clearly mistrusted Kyle's motives in coming to him and trying to work together. After so many years of being at each other's throats, Kyle didn't know if he'd ever be able to have a relationship with his father. But for his brothers' sakes and for Abby's, he'd keep trying.

Sighing, he snatched his phone up and called Tom. He grinned when he heard his brother's slow, easygoing drawl. "Hey, loser. How's it going?"

Tom's deep chuckle made Kyle's grin widen. "What the hell do you want now?" Tom demanded, although Kyle could tell he was smiling. "Damn, you're a needy little bastard."

"Bite me," Kyle shot back. "You got anything on Maxwell for me yet?"

"Yep. Gimme a sec."

"By the way, add to your to-do list bringing in Preston Whitmore and his dad for questioning. Hamilton stonewalled us. He's determined to handle things himself to keep it quiet."

"Dad's going to have my ass if he finds out I'm helping you," Tom said, but Kyle could hear the clacking of a keyboard in the background. "But I'll see what I can do about the Whitmores while I'm in the office today."

"Don't you ever go home, man?" Kyle asked while he waited for his brother to finish typing.

Tom grunted. "Not much point these days."

Kyle wasn't quite sure what to say. He knew what the last three years had been like without Abby, how long and lonely the nights had been when he lay awake in his bed wishing she was in his arms. He couldn't imagine what his brother had been going through after losing his wife in such a violent way. And Kyle suddenly felt like a total asshole for not checking in more often to find out.

"Tommy, don't you think it might be time to—"

"Department's not gonna run itself," Tom interrupted. "Dad's retiring in a couple of years. Someone's going to need to fill the seat."

All righty then. Message received. Clearly, his brother's personal life was off-limits. *Copy that.*

"Gabe wants it," Kyle told him, studiously avoiding the topic of his brother's dead wife. "Wouldn't hurt him to take on a little more responsibility."

Tom laughed heartily at that. "So when did you suddenly become an expert on responsibility? Didn't you just get fired from your assignment in New Orleans?"

"I wasn't fired," Kyle grumbled, the comment stinging more than he wanted to admit. "I was reassigned."

"Okay, okay," Tom replied. "*Reassigned* then. Have it your way. So you want to hear what I found out on Maxwell?"

"Lay it on me."

"Abby was right—Maxwell wasn't where he was supposed to be. But he wasn't where she thought he was either." There was more clacking. "For the first part of his business trip, he was in Chicago."

Kyle frowned. "Chicago? He lied to his own business partner about where he was going? Why?"

"Got me," Tom said. "But that's where he was. From what Abby told us about her sister's travels, it looks like he left Chicago two days before his wife did. He drove down to Indy in a rental. We have footage of him going through the tollbooths. Definitely him."

Kyle shook his head, trying to figure out why Maxwell would've changed things up on the sly. Had he known that someone was after him? Was he trying to elude the fate that appeared to have caught up to him—if the picture of the dead man was, in fact, him?

"So we should look for him down in Indy," Kyle mused.

"Guess again."

Kyle's brows shot up. "He's not in Indy?"

"Nope," Tom said. "The flight plan his pilot filed

shows he left Indy bound for Miami. And guess where the plane went after that."

"Hell if I know," Kyle told him, but the moment he said it, a thought occurred to him. "Wait, you're not telling me…"

"New Orleans."

Kyle cursed under his breath. "He was in New Orleans at the same time Emma was kidnapped."

"Well, he was supposed to be. That's where his plane went, but there's no evidence he was on it, so it's hard to say if he was in New Orleans or not. But it's definitely looking that way."

Kyle's eyes narrowed as he thought over the implications. If Maxwell had pissed off the wrong person on his trip to New Orleans, it made sense that the photo Abby had received would've come from there.

He *really* needed to get in touch with Peterman.

"Shit," Kyle cursed on a harsh sigh. "I was hoping the dead man in the photo was someone else. But it's looking less likely."

"Sorry, man."

Kyle stared at the back of the Navigator driving ahead of him, hating that he was going to have to break the news to Emma that her husband was most likely dead. And if he'd been killed by the bastards Kyle had become acquainted with while on the human-trafficking case he'd worked in the Big Easy, odds were good they'd never find Maxwell's body. It had only been by chance that he and Peterman had found the one they had.

It was the decomposing corpse of a fifteen-year-old girl who'd been savagely raped and beaten, her head bashed in until it was impossible to see the beautiful girl she'd once been. They'd only been able to identify her using dental records from the few teeth that hadn't been knocked out. Kyle tried to convince himself that she'd only been brutalized by *one* sick son of a bitch. The other, more horrifying possibility made his blood boil with rage.

The image of that poor girl had haunted him every day since then, no matter how hard he tried to forget it. He shook his head, attempting to banish it nonetheless.

"Kyle? You okay?"

Kyle started, having forgotten Tom was still on the line. "Yeah. Yeah, I'm good. Thanks for your help, Tommy."

He'd just disconnected the call with his brother when his phone rang. He glanced at the number before answering. "What do you have?"

There was a slight pause before Peterman sighed. "Not a lot."

Kyle's grip tightened on the phone. "Rhodes wouldn't talk?"

"More like *couldn't*," Peterman replied, his tone telling Kyle he was about to get some seriously shitty news. "He ghosted on us. Got out this morning and has completely vanished—hasn't even shown up at his apartment or any other usual haunts."

Kyle held the phone away from his ear and clamped his jaws tight to keep from yelling in frustration. As it was, a string of furious curses still managed to slip out.

"Dawson? Dawson, you there?"

Kyle brought the phone back to his ear but still had to take a moment to compose himself before asking, "Who was in to see him last?"

"His attorney," Peterman told him. "They brought that

slimy little shit in for questioning, but the guy is playing stupid, says he has no idea where Rhodes could be."

Kyle shook his head. "I don't know… Something doesn't feel right, Peterman. That attorney has been way too involved with Rhodes all along. He knows something."

Peterman snorted. "You don't gotta tell me that. I can smell bullshit a mile off. Why do you think you and I got along so well?"

Kyle's mouth hitched up in one corner in spite of the bad news, glad for his former partner's attempt at a little levity. "Yeah, well, don't go gettin' all sentimental on me."

Peterman grunted. "No chance of that, pal. Now what the hell do we do from here if Rhodes doesn't turn up? Without him we're fucked. Our whole case hinged on his testimony."

Kyle wished like hell he knew what to do, but unless he could figure out the crap with Abby's case and some-how connect it to the case he'd had to walk away from in New Orleans, there wasn't shit he could do.

"If I come up with anything," he finally said to Peterman on a frustrated sigh, "you'll be the first to know."

⁓

The sky was ablaze with orange and crimson by the time Abby turned off the main road and onto the winding gravel path that led to her family's cabin. She couldn't suppress a shudder as the shadows deepened, glad that they'd made good time and weren't arriving after dark. The cabin had been their refuge as children when their mother needed to get away from the prying eyes and flapping gums of the small-town biddies who couldn't seem to mind their own business where the Morrows were concerned.

Although Abby associated the cabin with peace and tranquility, the woods were a different story. She'd also hated the fact that they were miles from other neighbors, isolated from the rest of the world and surrounded by trees on pretty much every side. Even now, she felt that uneasiness creeping in on her, prickling the skin at the back of her neck and slithering down her spine.

"Do you think we'll be safe here?"

Abby nearly jumped out of her skin at the sound of her sister's voice. "Jesus!"

"Sorry." Emma giggled. "I forgot how jumpy you get at the cabin."

Abby gulped down several deep breaths before responding. "I just hate how dark it gets, I guess." She forced a tremulous smile. "But, yes, you'll be safe here. Plus, I'm sticking around with you to make sure. It's just for a few days until you feel safe going back to the house."

Emma sighed. "I don't know that I'll ever feel safe again."

Abby glanced into the rearview mirror, glad to see Tyler had conked out, his mouth hanging agape just enough that a little bit of drool had accumulated at the corner. She grinned, then wondered if he'd ever sleep that soundly again if they determined the body in the photo was his father.

Fortunately, the cabin came into view at that moment, rescuing her from having to respond to her sister's concern. She knew she should've said the right thing, should've assured Emma that she'd get over her ordeal, that in no time at all she'd be able to move on, and that her sense of security would return soon.

But the truth was, Abby had no idea if any of that would happen. She couldn't be sure that Emma would ever have a day where she wasn't constantly looking over her shoulder. Or that she'd be able to not wake up in a cold sweat. She just prayed Emma was made of stronger stuff than their mother.

Abby parked in front of the cabin, the stop jolting Tyler from his slumber. "We're here!" he shouted. He opened the car door and hopped out before she'd even shut off the engine, racing up the broad wooden steps that led to the wrap-around porch.

"You coming, sweetie?" Emma asked as she got out of the car.

Abby nodded absently. "Yeah, yeah. You go on in. I'll be there in a bit."

She sat in the car for a moment longer, surveying the two-story log cabin in front of her. To call the structure a cabin was a bit of a misnomer, though. For most people, "cabin" would bring to mind a modest little log house. But not the Morrows. Oh no. Such a humble home would've been an embarrassment. This one was two stories of sprawling luxury—complete with sunken living room, formal dining room, game room, sauna, and guest rooms galore—that just happened to be made of logs. It was a physical representation of the extravagant lies that had been part of her family's elaborate farce. Ironically, the vacation home was the only thing of value her mother had managed to hang on to when the glamorous life they'd led was revealed to be nothing but smoke and mirrors.

"Abby?"

Abby turned her attention away from the house and

toward her window where Kyle stood, his brows furrowed in concern.

"You okay?" he asked.

She nodded and opened the door, planning to help Emma unload the back of the SUV. But before Abby could take a step, Kyle pulled her into his arms and pressed a kiss to her hair. "You sure you want to stay here?" he murmured. "I can still get Tom to send someone else."

She shook her head. "Thanks, but I'm staying." She turned her face up to his and forced a smile. "I'm too old to be afraid of the boogeyman hiding in the woods."

He glanced around, surveying the woods that surrounded them, thick with full spring foliage. He was clearly on edge as well. Even though the sun was still high in the sky, the dark shadows the trees cast robbed them of much of the sunlight. "Not the boogeyman I'm worried about."

Abby made sure to keep her voice low when she said, "Do you think the kidnapper will try again?"

Kyle shook his head, but his frown deepened. "Nah, he got what he wanted."

"But you think someone else might try something," she replied.

He took her face in his hands and smiled, but it seemed forced to her. "I'm sure it's fine. You wanted to make sure Emma and Tyler had someone here watching over them after everything that's happened. Well, I feel the same way about you. I don't like the thought of you out here in the middle of nowhere without me."

She pressed closer to him. "No one said you have to go. Stay here. With me."

He groaned slightly, his sapphire eyes darkening with desire. "I'd love to. Trust me. But I think I might be taking a trip down to New Orleans."

She lifted her brows. "Why? I thought you'd moved everything up here already."

"Unfortunately, it has nothing to do with the move," he explained. "The key witness in a case I was working has gone AWOL. My former partner is searching for him and has talked to the witness's attorney, but the attorney says he has no idea what happened to the guy."

"And you have your doubts," Abby finished for him.

He nodded. "It's not adding up. And there's more. I got a call from Tom on the drive here. He discovered that Curtis might've been in New Orleans around the time Emma was kidnapped. I'm going to check it out while I'm down there to see what I can find out about the picture you received."

Abby gave a terse nod. "I'm going with you."

Kyle shook his head. "No way."

She sent a glance over her shoulder toward the cabin, making sure her sister and nephew were still inside and out of earshot. "He's my sister's husband. She might not love him anymore, but he's the father of her child. I owe it to her to bring his body home."

Kyle sighed. "You're assuming that the body's still somewhere to be found, Abby. These people aren't amateurs."

"Still," she argued, "I want to be there. With you."

His expression softened, and he leaned down to press a lingering kiss to her lips. "I'll be here tonight," he reminded her, his lips brushing against hers as he spoke. "And I'd suggest we claim a bedroom on the opposite end of the house from your family."

Abby shuddered with anticipation, her heart pounding as his lips claimed hers in a deep kiss. Her arms drifted up around his neck, her fingers spearing into his hair. "I want you right now," she panted when the kiss ended. "My *God*, I want you."

He chuckled, the sound deep and sultry. "Want to sneak away to the woods?"

She giggled. "God, yes!" But then she sighed and forced herself to take a step back and put a little distance between them. "But we should probably get the groceries inside before dark. Give me a hand?"

She started to turn away, but he grasped her hand and jerked her back to him with a laugh. The next thing she knew, he was pressing her back against the side of the SUV and slipping his hand inside her waistband.

She gasped when his fingertip made contact with the nub of her sex, but the gasp died on a moan. "That's not what I meant by 'give me a hand,'" she said, sighing. But then coming to her senses, she cast a frantic glance behind her toward the cabin. "Kyle, what if they see?"

He slid his hand down a little further, slipping a finger inside her. Her hands reflexively came up to grip his biceps, squeezing as he caressed her. "They can't," he assured her, his own voice breathless. "The car's hiding us."

Abby let her head fall back a little, wanting desperately to give in to the pleasure he elicited with every slow, sensual thrust of his finger. But her fear of being seen made her come to her senses and grasp his wrist. "Not here."

He withdrew his hand, then bent and kissed the side of her throat, nipping at the juncture between her neck and shoulder. "Where?"

Abby thought frantically. *Where, where, where...*
"The boathouse."

"Lead the way," he said with a sweep of his arm.

Abby gave him an arch look. "Groceries first," she insisted. "Then I'll give you the grand tour of the property."

After unloading the groceries in record time, Abby let Emma know she was taking Kyle on a tour of the property and might be gone for a little while. The look Emma gave her told Abby her sister knew there was more to the little walk than just a check of the perimeter, which she confirmed by making Tyler stay at the cabin.

Abby had to force herself to stroll hand in hand with Kyle toward the path that led away from the house and down to the boathouse near the private lake a couple dozen yards away. Feeling like a guilty teenager whose elder sister might be watching disapprovingly from the window, Abby giggled.

"My God," she said, laughing. "What's wrong with us? Are we really sneaking off to make out? We're adults, for crying out loud."

Kyle draped his arm around her shoulders, pulling her in close, and pressed a kiss to her temple. "Sorry. I've always had a hard time keeping my hands to myself where you're concerned."

She sent a flirty sidelong glance his way. "Hey, I didn't say I minded that. I just... I don't know. I guess I feel guilty with Emma back at the house, wondering what the hell has happened to her husband, having just come through being kidnapped and facing...God knows what next." She halted and turned toward him, grateful that his arms came around her and pulled her close. "I just feel guilty about being happy."

Kyle pressed a kiss to her forehead. "Don't ever feel guilty about that. Your sister wouldn't want you to, would she?"

Abby hardly knew. Some days she felt like she barely knew Emma anymore. Their lives had taken such different paths, and Abby had resented what she'd perceived as Emma's life of ease and luxury while she'd been left to deal with the hard stuff—like their mother's drama. She'd never stopped to think that Emma was dealing with so much drama of her own.

"I should've been there for her more," Abby confessed. "I didn't make an effort to understand what she was going through with Curtis. I just thought she was being flighty and selfish all these years and ignoring Tyler. I think she'd just shut down emotionally. I should've recognized that. I should've helped her through it instead of just getting pissed. I should've—"

Kyle cut her off with a brief kiss. When she blinked up at him, he grinned. "Now that I have your attention, mind if I weigh in on this?"

She shrugged. "Guess not."

"I don't think there's any point in regretting what you *didn't* do," he told her. "There's nothing that you can do about that. But you can help your sister *now*. You can be there for her *now*. You're a good woman, Abby. You have one of the most generous, loving hearts of anyone I've ever known."

She warmed at the compliment and could feel her cheeks flushing. But she couldn't help wondering if he'd feel the same when she finally answered his question about why she'd pushed him away. "Kyle," she began, "there's something I need to tell you."

He sighed. "There's something I need to tell you too."

She studied his expression, not liking the sudden frown that creased his brow. Her stomach sank. "You want to go first?"

He took her hand and started down the path again. "I'd rather not talk about it at all, honestly."

She squeezed his hand. "If you're not ready to talk about whatever it is, Kyle, that's okay. It can wait. I'm not going anywhere."

He sent a grateful smile her way. "You know, you say something like that and it just makes me want to kiss you again. And it really doesn't help me keep my hands off you."

She laughed. "Well then, I guess it's a good thing we're almost to the boathouse."

Chapter 18

FIELDING'S PHONE BUZZED, ALERTING HIM THAT A call was coming in. He didn't bother trying to suppress his smug grin when he saw it was from his former employer. He glanced around the crowded truck stop where he'd decided to grab some dinner on his way to his next job. Assured that no one was taking any notice of him, he took a sip of his water and swallowed the chicken potpie in his mouth before picking up the phone.

"You son of a bitch," Mr. Smith hissed without preamble. "What the hell do you think you're doing sending me a picture of a goddamn corpse? Who the fuck do you think you are?"

"I think I'm the guy who has you by the balls," Fielding said, smirking.

"I hired you for a very specific job," Smith snapped. "I didn't tell you to take out another of my *employees*."

Fielding stabbed a huge chunk of chicken with his fork. "Consider this one a freebie."

"You listen to me, you motherfu—"

"I think you're probably forgetting a few things," Fielding interrupted around a mouthful of chicken. "The first one being that you don't call the shots here, you self-righteous prick. I could put a bullet between your eyes while you're taking your morning shit, and you'd never know what hit you. So don't push me."

There was a slight pause before Mr. Smith said in a

slightly less confrontational tone, "I've paid your fee. Your association with Deputy Morrow is at an end."

"Not when you send assassins to do your dirty work like the spineless coward that you are," Fielding told him, leisurely taking another bite of his potpie. As far as truck-stop cuisine went, it was really quite good. "It's not very sporting of you."

"*Sporting?*" Smith sputtered. "What the fuck do you care?"

"It's a waste," Fielding said with a shrug. "A waste of a lovely woman, of a great deal of talent. I did my homework on her before I took this job. You're an asshole for wanting to take her out."

"She knows things," Smith pointed out, clearly speaking through clenched teeth. "I can't have her spilling her guts about what she knows."

Fielding almost laughed. This guy was such a moron. Mr. Smith might've had people taken out in the past, but he obviously didn't know shit about how to keep information from leaking. If the idiot had wanted to ensure the data didn't get out, he should've paid Fielding another two million to take Abby out, not just steal the data. It would've been more efficient, and Mr. Smith wouldn't have had to contract with the inept idiot Fielding had eliminated.

"You really think she hasn't already told people what she knows?" Fielding asked, not caring that he sounded like a condescending dick. "She's a cop. She probably has both the locals *and* the feds on your ass as we speak."

There was another pause and this time he could hear the trepidation in Mr. Smith's voice. "But she has no proof."

Jesus. Do I seriously have to explain everything to this dickwad?

"Not at the moment, but do you really think you've covered your tracks completely? *Really*?" When the guy didn't respond, Fielding added, "The kind of shit you're doing leaves a trail. If it's not Deputy Morrow—or her boyfriend—who brings you down, it'll be someone else."

"Boyfriend?" Smith echoed, totally missing the point. "What boyfriend?"

"I'm sure you'll meet him soon enough," Fielding taunted.

"I want them taken out, Fielding," Smith barked. "All of them—Emma Maxwell, Abigail Morrow, *and* whoever she's fucking. And if there's anyone else who knows anything, kill them too."

"What about the kid?" Fielding asked. "He's glued to his mom's hip right now."

"Whatever's necessary."

Fielding had thrown out the kid for consideration hoping the cold-hearted bastard would realize what he was asking, but apparently the guy wasn't above killing a child. Yeah, Fielding had read Deputy Morrow's reports on the flash drive, having run the encryption key she'd sent him. He'd gotten curious… What could he say? Considering what Mr. Smith was up to, the kind of heinous shit he was into, Fielding shouldn't have been surprised by what he was asking now. His eyes narrowed as if the son of a bitch was sitting across from him. "That kind of a job isn't cheap."

"Name your price."

Fielding did what he did for money. It was that simple. He didn't give a shit about any of the reasons he was hired by spineless asshats who were too afraid of getting their own hands bloody. But there were days when he would rather take one of *them* out instead and thin the herd by ridding the world of a worthless piece of shit. This was one of those days.

"Fifteen million," he said, throwing out a number he didn't figure Mr. Smith would be willing to pay. He'd balked at Fielding's million-dollar fee for kidnapping Emma Maxwell and extorting data from her sister.

"Done." There was no hesitation, no second-guessing. "I want it taken care of without delay."

"I have another job," Fielding replied, shocked that the guy was willing to pay what he'd asked. "I'm headed there now."

"I don't give a shit!" Smith spat. "I'm paying you fifteen million dollars. You can cancel the other job."

Fielding put another bite of his dinner in his mouth, considering the offer before him, but the food suddenly tasted like ashes. He pushed his plate back, no longer interested in eating. Fifteen million was nothing to sneeze at. He could live off that for quite a while, not have to take another job for years.

"And if I say no?" Fielding prompted.

"Then someone else will benefit from the substantial amount of money on the table."

Shit.

Fielding wasn't crazy about either of the options before him. He could take the job—and the money—but he'd have to murder several innocent people, including a freaking *kid* who had nothing to do with any of this. Or he could walk away and allow someone else to take the cash, and Deputy Morrow and her family would be just as dead.

But that wasn't his only option. There was another one…

"Fine," Fielding said. "But I want the money up front."

Mr. Smith laughed. "Are you insane? Why in the hell would I agree to that? I'm no idiot."

Fielding grunted. "Yeah, well, neither am I. You balked when I asked for the cash for the first job. And you mean to tell me that fifteen million is doable?"

"I'm motivated."

"Motivation doesn't have a cash value," Fielding reminded him. "You give me the money up front or I walk. And I give Deputy Morrow a call to let her know what you're up to."

There was a mumbled string of curses on the other end. Fielding waited patiently, absently drumming his fingertips on the orange Formica tabletop as his employer considered the proposal.

Finally, he heard a heavy sigh. "Fine. I'll pay you up front. But I want them dead within forty-eight hours. Is that clear? I want them all dead. Not one person who knows about this is to be left living. Do you understand?"

Fielding would've loved to reach through the phone and wring the guy's goddamn neck. "Yeah. I'll text you the account information where you can deposit the funds."

"But…I'm not making a drop like before?"

"Not for an amount this high," Fielding explained. "This is the kind of sum that makes guys like you do something stupid—like double-cross me. Or try to kill me at the drop-off."

Fielding could hear the guy gulp on the other end and knew he'd guessed pretty accurately.

"I want the money deposited tomorrow or the deal's off."

He hung up before Mr. Smith could respond and immediately texted him the information for one of his foreign bank accounts that was registered under a dummy corporation and layers and layers of fake identities.

With that taken care of, Fielding brought up the photo of the dead assassin that he'd sent to his employer and attached it to another text message.

He hit Send and dropped the phone into the pocket of his jacket. Then he dropped a hundred-dollar bill on the table to cover his dinner, along with a hefty tip for the bleached-blond waitress who reeked of cigarette smoke. It was a risk—she might actually remember him for a tip like that. But it was one he was willing to take. Soon it wouldn't matter. He'd be taking an extended vacation in the Caymans by the end of the week.

Chapter 19

KYLE STARED AT THE FIRE BLAZING IN THE CABIN'S massive stone fireplace, watching in fascination as the flames moved in a sensual dance. His eyelids were getting heavy, the long drive to the cabin and the quiet serenity of the place making him relax to the point that his entire body felt like it weighed about twice as much.

"Are you bored too?"

His head snapped toward the sound of Tyler's voice. "We've only been here for a few hours," Kyle said with a grin. "You can't tell me you're bored already."

Tyler rolled his eyes and flopped down on the sofa next to him. "There's no cable or wireless. What am I supposed to do while I'm here?"

"You could try reading," Kyle suggested. "That's what my brothers and I always did when we went camping with my parents."

Kyle couldn't help the sad smile that came to his lips when he thought about those trips with his parents. Mac always turned them into some kind of survivalist-training boot camp, but his mom had made sure that they had fun too. She'd have s'mores and homemade lemonade ready when they got back from the daily mandatory three-mile hike. And when it was time for them to settle in for the night after telling ghost stories around the fire and they were all too scared to go right to sleep, she'd make sure each of them had their own flashlight so that they could read the latest *Spider-Man* or *X-Men* comic books for a while.

"I can't read," Tyler complained, interrupting Kyle's thoughts. "I forgot my e-reader."

Kyle laughed. "You mean to tell me you don't have a single book around this place?"

Tyler shrugged. "Maybe in the library."

"That's probably a good place to look," Kyle said, ruffling the boy's hair. "Maybe you'll even find some Robert Louis Stevenson. *Treasure Island* was my favorite when I was your age."

Tyler sighed. "I guess…" He paused for a moment, looking up at Kyle through long lashes. "Mom said she's going to bed early. Is she going to be okay?"

Kyle nodded. "Yeah, I'm sure she will be. She's just tired."

Tyler nodded. "Okay. Well, I'll find a book and read, I guess, but I'm not going to sleep early since I don't have to go to school tomorrow. Aunt Abby said she'd call and let them know."

"Then I'm sure she will," Kyle said with a terse nod.

He watched Tyler sulk away, his disappointment at the cabin's lack of technology clearly putting a damper on his vacation from school. Kyle was still smiling when Abby came into the room pulling on a bright blue cardigan that made her eyes an even more electric shade of blue.

"Going somewhere?" he asked, hoping like hell she'd say no. All he wanted to do was drag her into his arms and pick up where they'd left off down in the boathouse. They'd continued their make-out session there, but it'd only whetted his appetite for more. Hearing her quiet gasps as she fought to keep from crying out drove him wild. If the boats hadn't been in sore need of a good scrub-down, their sojourn there would've ended much differently...

"Emma's asleep," she told him. "And I just passed Tyler in the hallway. He said he was going to bed to read for a while. I thought I might go outside and sit on the porch. Care to join me?"

Not really the answer he'd been hoping for, but he had to admit that the thought of sitting with her under the stars was just as alluring. "Wouldn't miss it."

He was careful to make sure the screen door didn't slam shut when they went out onto the front porch, not wanting to draw Emma or Tyler from their beds to see what all the racket was. Plus, he'd had to share Abby with them for the whole evening. He wanted her to himself for a little while before he had to leave the next morning.

"I tried to call to book a flight to New Orleans," he told her as they curled up together on the porch swing. "But I wasn't able to get a signal out here."

"Cell phone service can be pretty spotty out this way," she told him, draping her leg over his thigh and resting her head against his chest. "It gets better a few miles down the road. If you don't want to wait until morning, we can drive down that way."

He shook his head and pulled her closer. "It'll keep. I'm where I want to be right now. I already hate that I have to leave you for a few days."

"That was your choice," she reminded him, "not mine. I still think I should be going with you."

"You'd just spend the entire time worried about Emma and Tyler because you weren't here," he pointed out. When she lifted her head to argue, he gave her a pointed look. "Am I wrong?"

"No," she begrudgingly admitted. "You're not. You know me far too well. I'd be a nervous wreck. I know this is the best place we could've taken them. No one really knows about this place but family." She laughed. "You saw the road to get here. No one passing by would even know it's there! So I guess I should be telling *you* not to worry either."

Kyle's arm tightened around her. "That's definitely a comfort. But it's more that I just don't want to be away from you for that long."

She lifted her eyes to him and offered him a broad smile. "I'm glad you're here, Kyle. I've missed you."

"I've missed you too," he murmured, pressing a kiss to her hair. "*God*, I've missed you. There were so many times I almost called, but I wasn't sure you'd want to hear from me. I just wanted to hear your voice, talk to you about my day—especially during my last couple of months in New Orleans."

She reached up and cupped his cheek and brought his face down to hers for a lingering kiss. When it ended she said, "You can tell me about it now. I'm listening."

He took a deep breath and let it out on a long sigh, steeling himself to dredge up the memories that he'd been trying to suppress for months now. "One of the cases I'd been working on in New Orleans had to do with a human-trafficking operation."

"Are you serious?" She was visibly taken aback, pulling out of his embrace. The better to peg him with a pissy look, from what he could tell.

He nodded warily. "I know I should've mentioned it sooner—"

"Damn right you should've!" she shot back. "Why

didn't you say anything after you read my reports for Hamilton? You might've had information that was relevant to *my* case."

He sighed, his shoulders sagging. "I didn't want to make connections that weren't there just because I wanted them to be. That's not good detective work, Abby. You know that."

She studied him for a long moment before her irritation with him for holding out on her dissipated. "Tell me about your case," she prompted, although her solicitous tone sounded forced. "I'm listening."

He hesitated, fearful of what might happen once he opened the dam that had been holding back the horrific memories. But then her expression softened and she took his hand and laced her fingers with his. She turned so she was facing him, giving him her undivided attention.

When he saw the love in her eyes, felt the warmth of her palm against his, he nodded, more to himself to confirm it was time to tell her the truth than for any other reason. "I inherited the case," he began. "It was one that the New Orleans office had been working on for a few years. The guy who'd been assigned before me had been a good agent, but the stress of it finally got to him. He requested a transfer to Seattle."

"Is that what happened to you, Kyle?" Abby pressed gently. "Is that why you came back to Indiana? Did you wash out?"

He had to laugh out loud at that one. "No, I really did get transferred. And a thirty-day suspension. This week off isn't exactly a vacation. It's the final week of my mandated leave."

Abby's eyes went wide. "What happened?"

"I was obsessed with the case in New Orleans, Abby," he explained. "I was willing to do whatever it took to bring down those sons of bitches—even if that meant being accused of using excessive force to bring in a key witness who was trying to skip town. The guy filed a complaint against me. And considering I was already pretty much at the top of my boss's shit list, he didn't exactly need much of a reason to send me packing."

"But you did great at the academy," Abby said, defending him. "And they loved you in Miami. Why did this jackass in New Orleans have it in for you?"

He vaguely wondered how she knew so much, but was gratified by her defense of him nonetheless. "Let's just say my family legacy preceded me."

She groaned. "*Idiots*. You're more than your family history, Kyle. And they're morons for not seeing what an incredible man you are."

He brought her hand up to his lips and pressed a kiss to her palm. "This is why I love you."

She smiled and leaned forward to brush a kiss against his mouth that ended far too soon for his liking.

When she pulled back again, he continued, "Anyway, so this case fell into my lap when I started and quickly became my focus at the expense of everything else. And it got worse when we found *her*."

Abby shook her head. "Who?"

"Her name was Rosalie Sparks," he replied. "She'd been a beautiful fifteen-year-old with a promising future. Until she went missing. She'd met some guy online and convinced herself she was in love with him, that he was her soul mate. He told her he was a sixteen-year-old boy who had a shitty home life and played on her sympathies. Their exchanges started out pretty harmless, but they began having some really explicit conversations in their chats. Eventually, this guy convinced her to send him pornographic photos of herself. Not long after that, he talked her into meeting him."

Abby cursed softly and tenderly caressed his arm, instinctively knowing that the story wasn't going to end well.

Kyle scowled, the thought of that sick asshole preying on Rosalie making him wish he could castrate the bastard and shove his balls down his throat. He heaved a sharp exhale. "Some guy walking his dog uncovered Rosalie's remains about a year later."

"Oh my God…" Abby closed her eyes for a moment. "Her poor family."

He pulled a hand down his face, remembering the day he'd had to deliver the death notification to Rosalie's parents. Her mother had handled it a little better, having already resigned herself to the fact that her daughter would never return. But the father had held out hope. Kyle could still hear the man's heart-wrenching sobs.

"Rosalie had been beaten and raped," Kyle went on. "Her head was bashed in."

Abby gasped. "Good God."

"It was one of the most horrific crime scenes I've ever seen," Kyle told her. "At first we thought it was another case of a young woman being lured to her death by a lone sexual predator. But then the medical examiner found a mark on the inside of Rosalie's right thigh, a brand that we'd found on several other men and women who'd been arrested in a prostitution ring operating as an illegal massage parlor."

"Was Rosalie working there too?" Abby asked, her brows coming together in a frown.

"That was the big question," Kyle told her. "We questioned the prostitutes we'd arrested and began to piece together how their operation worked. Not surprisingly, it was run by a woman who was bringing girls and young women into the U.S. with promises of work, marriage, a better life, but then forced them into prostitution or domestic labor."

"Unfortunately, that kind of thing is growing more common," Abby told him. "But those sorts of operations are small scale compared to what Tartarus is involved in."

"True," Kyle admitted, "but soon we were able to tie the massage-parlor operation back to another investigation that my predecessor had begun. He'd busted a group for human trafficking after state troopers pulled over a box truck with dozens of dead illegals in the back. Everyone thought the group was just a bunch of freelancers trying to exploit people desperate to get into the country. But we kept making more connections, finding more of these seemingly small freelance operations, and discovered they had a common thread—a kind of parent company that they all reported to."

"And you think that parent company might be Tartarus?" Abby asked. "I mean, Curtis isn't the only asshole out there doing this kind of thing."

Kyle raked a hand through his hair. "I know… It's just… It's a gut feeling, Abby. I can't explain it. There were little things that kept cropping up in your reports, similarities that jumped out at me."

"Okay," she said, her voice taking on that particular tone that told him her mind was racing as she mentally sifted through all the information. "What about Rosalie? So far, everything you've mentioned has dealt with groups preying on people literally dying to get into the U.S. But Rosalie doesn't fit that description."

Kyle shook his head. "No, she didn't. That's why the brand was so confusing. Luckily, we caught a break when a male prostitute the New Orleans cops brought in started singing like a canary to try to avoid jail time. The stuff he was giving up prompted them to call us in."

Abby's spine stiffened as she waited for what Kyle was about to tell her. She was so beautiful in the moonlight, her eyes wide and alert, her brilliant mind ready to absorb his every word. He couldn't help reaching up and briefly caressing her cheek with the back of his fingers. He needed the contact, needed to feel the silky smoothness of her skin before he shared the rest of the story.

When his hand dropped away, Abby took it in both of hers, not saying a word.

Kyle took a deep breath and let it out on a long exhale, wishing the process could cleanse his soul of the heaviness that weighed on it. "This guy—Harlan Rhodes—told us about the way his bosses recruited new people, sometimes for use here domestically, but more often to satisfy the appetites of American businessmen and others traveling abroad."

"Sexual tourism," Abby spat, her tone betraying the level of her disgust.

"Exactly. Rhodes said that he was one of the recruiters, often interacting with kids living on the street, offering them a way out of their current life. He said some of the people they recruited ended up being 'kept' by clients that took a liking to them, making them exclusive 'property.' But they were all branded, marked like cattle, as a reminder to the client that they were just loaners and that the clients had better not forget that."

"And you believe Rosalie was being kept by someone?"

Kyle nodded. "Yeah. We showed Rhodes a photo of Rosalie, and he confirmed he'd seen her coming through the network. But she was different, he said. He claimed most of the recruits from the U.S. are *willing* participants in what's going on, that they know what they're signing up for. I doubt that's true, but I guess in Rhodes's case, perception was reality. Anyway, he said a lot of the underage victims had been recruited online by men pretending to be teenage boys."

"Jesus," Abby breathed. "That adds a whole new threat to the crap happening online. It's bad enough having to worry about pedophiles trolling or psychos luring their kids into a dangerous situation, but now parents also have to worry about their kids being abducted and forced into sexual tourism?"

Kyle leaned forward, bracing his arms on his knees. "After everything I've seen with this case, the idea of being a parent someday scares the shit out of me."

"So, what happened to Rosalie?" Abby asked in such a clipped tone that Kyle sat up to better study her expression.

When he couldn't get a read on what had caused the abrupt change in her demeanor, he continued. "I guess Rosalie fought against her handlers, tried to escape. They never got around to shipping her overseas. Instead she was given to a man Rhodes only knew as 'the Cowboy.' From what Rhodes could gather, the Cowboy was one of the high-up bosses. When they had the occasional new recruit who didn't behave, they were given to the Cowboy to break—hence the nickname."

"That poor girl!" Abby gasped. "I hate to think what he put her through."

"Unfortunately, we were able to get a pretty clear picture of what someone put her through—whether it was him or whoever he gave her to."

"And you think Tartarus was behind this?" Abby asked softly.

When he glanced her way and met her gaze, he could see doubt in her eyes. He couldn't blame her. It sounded ridiculous even to him. Yeah, her brother-in-law was into some really shady shit and, if by chance he was still alive, deserved to rot in prison for his own human-trafficking operation. But was he really the one behind the atrocities Kyle had discovered in New Orleans? The connections he'd been making in his head sounded even more tenuous now that he was saying them aloud.

"Hell, I don't know," he grumbled, launching to his feet and striding several paces down the porch to lean against the railing. He heard Abby's light footsteps behind him. A moment later, her arms encircled his waist and she pressed her cheek against his back.

The warmth of her tender embrace was enough to make his throat go tight. Having to talk about Rosalie Sparks, having to relive the horrors he'd witnessed and being left to imagine the unspeakable acts of violence, had his gut twisting with emotion.

As if sensing his internal turmoil, Abby pressed a kiss to his back, then pulled away enough for him to turn in her arms so that he was facing her. Without a word, she gazed up at him, her expression so full of sympathy and

226 KATE SERINE

understanding that Kyle's heart broke wide open. He closed his eyes against the sudden blur there and choked back the tears that he wasn't about to let her see, lest she think he was a total fucking pansy.

But then her palm was resting on his cheek, her thumb caressing his skin, offering him the silent love and support he'd sorely needed for months. And then she was slipping her arms around his neck and drawing him closer, pulling him to her. He buried his face in the curve of her neck, holding on to her as if his life and his sanity depended on it. And, hell, maybe they did.

He didn't know how long they stood this way before he finally released her and took a step back, putting a little distance between them, suddenly embarrassed for showing how much the case had gotten to him.

"Sorry," he murmured.

Her brows came together. "For what? For being compassionate and caring? For giving a damn about the victims who count on us to find justice for them? Don't ever apologize for that, Kyle. It makes you who you are. And it's just another reason I fell in love with you."

She took his hand then and tugged him toward the house. He followed without question, his pulse quickening with each step. By the time they reached the end of the upstairs hallway that was farthest from where Emma and Tyler slept, the blood was pounding in his ears and his groin.

He didn't even wait until they crossed the threshold to drag her into his arms and press his lips to hers in a harsh kiss. He wasn't being gentle, he knew. But Abby didn't seem to mind. Her kiss was just as hungry and savage in return, her tongue tangling with his in that maddeningly sensual way she had that drove him wild.

They stumbled into the bedroom and Kyle managed to shut the door behind them without slamming it in his haste to get her inside. Then he was pulling her shirt over her head and unhooking her bra with a quick flick of his fingertips. The next instant, he was bending her back, taking one of her nipples into his mouth. He kneaded one breast as he laved and teased the other with his tongue and teeth, making her moan softly.

But he didn't resist when she pulled his head up and claimed his mouth, carefully pulling him back with her toward the bed and fumbling with his fly as they went. When she slipped her hand down between them, he shuddered. And when she began to caress him, smoothing her palm up and down his shaft, he groaned.

"Jesus, Abby," he ground out. "You keep doing that, and I'm going to throw you down on that bed and fuck the hell out you."

She giggled, a deep, throaty sound that made his dick twitch. "Whatever do you mean?" she rasped, continuing to stroke him. "Do you mean…like *this*?"

Chapter 20

THE SOUND KYLE MADE IN RESPONSE TO HER taunting rumbled deep in his chest like a growl. So Abby wasn't entirely surprised when he tackled her onto the bed and claimed her mouth in a kiss so animalistic she felt like something primal had been unleashed. Nor was she surprised when he roughly stripped her of her jeans and panties, while also managing to shed his own and grab a condom before plunging deep into her with such a savage thrust that she gasped, curling into him.

Then he was thrusting with that same savagery, stroke after stroke, burying himself so deep that all Abby could do was rock with him, gasping at the intensity of the pleasure washing over her. She shattered within moments, biting back the cry that no doubt would've wakened her sister and nephew down the hall.

"Oh my God," she panted, her thoughts reeling. "Oh God, yes."

But at her words his strokes became slower, more sensual, which brought on a different level of pleasure, one that went beyond the physical. She moved with him, arching into him, accepting all that he gave, her hands drifting down his arms and over his shoulders, her fingers hungry for every inch of him.

Abby gazed up at him. His eyes were closed, his long, dark lashes brushing against his cheekbones. His full lips were slightly open, his pleasure playing across his features. As if sensing her gaze, he opened his eyes and the intensity of the desire she saw there made her heart swell.

She reached up with both hands to grasp the back of his neck and pull him down to her. His lips brushed lightly over hers in just the whisper of a kiss—not nearly enough to satisfy her. But before she could urge him to kiss her again, he shifted slightly, rolling to his side, bringing her with him, and draping her leg over his waist.

Now that they were stretched out next to each another, he pulled her in against him, languidly ravishing her mouth as they made love unhurriedly.

"I could do this all night," he murmured against her lips.

She chuckled, liking the sound of that plan. But even as a grin curved her lips, another release rushed up on her, making her shiver as heat and light exploded within her body. But it seemed Kyle wasn't finished with her yet.

He rolled onto his back, bringing her with him so that she was straddling him. Abby rolled her hips in concert with his, letting her head fall back on her shoulders. He ran his hands lightly up and down her ribs, finally tangling in the length of her hair. As his own release grew imminent, he grasped her hair in his fists, their unhurried movement now becoming more purposeful, more precise, until he suddenly grasped her hips and plunged in with a few deep strokes before he came with a long groan.

Abby was grinning when he sat up and eased her onto her back before he withdrew. She was *still* grinning when he returned to the bed and slipped under the sheets, pulling her into his arms.

She heaved a long sigh and lazily caressed his chest,

wishing he was staying there with them, but as reality began to settle upon them, the truth that he was leaving in the morning stubbornly intruded upon the more pleasant thoughts that were beginning to form.

"Will you be okay?" she whispered.

His fingertips trailed up and down her arm. "About the case?"

"That and going back to New Orleans," she replied. "I don't like the idea of you going alone. I should be with you. You don't know what these people might be capable of if they're cornered, Kyle."

He pressed a kiss to her hair. "I appreciate your concern, sweetheart, but I'm only going down there to try to find Rhodes and ask him some questions. I'm not planning to rush in half-cocked, demanding answers. Rhodes was already pissed at me. If I go in there all badass, he's going to clam up again."

"And what if his bosses come looking for you?" Abby demanded, her heart beginning to race as she considered the danger he might be walking into. "What then?"

"Then I'll deal with it," he assured her. "It'll be fine. Trust me."

She lifted her head from his chest so that she could hold his gaze and get a read on whether he was as unconcerned as he seemed or if it was all an act for her benefit. When he gave her that cockeyed, arrogant grin of his, she sighed. "I do trust you. But that doesn't mean I'm going to worry any less."

He cupped her cheek. "I'll be home before you know it."

"And then what?" she asked before she could bite back the words. Before her questions could open up an entirely different conversation, she quickly amended,

"How are Emma and Tyler supposed to just go back to their normal routine?"

Kyle's brows came together as he considered the question. "I'm hoping that when I return, I'll be able to answer some of Emma's questions, the biggest one right now being what happened to your brother-in-law."

Abby closed her eyes at the thought of the horrible fate that might've befallen Curtis and how the truth of his criminal activities and the manner in which he'd paid for those actions would hurt her family. She edged closer to Kyle, seeking the comfort only the warmth of his arms seemed able to provide.

"I don't know what to tell them," she murmured. "I don't know how to break it to Ty that his father is a heartless, greedy son of a bitch who used people in heinous ways."

"Then don't," Kyle replied. "Let his mother figure out the best way to handle that news. It should come from her."

Abby shook her head a little. "Emma's never been able to handle conflict or confrontation. That always fell to me. Even when she and Curtis were fighting and he'd storm off in a rage to some corner of the world to sulk, I'd have to be the one to call him and try to smooth things over between them. I wish I'd never bothered."

Kyle lifted her chin with his knuckle so that she was looking up into his penetrating gaze. "You can't save everyone from pain in this one, Abby." When she tried to look away, his hand shifted so that he was lightly but firmly grasping her chin. "I know you, sweetheart. I know you would shield them all from harm if you could. You've been doing it your entire life. But all you can do is be there for them while they're hurting and pull them through to the other side."

She reached up and caressed his strong jaw, knowing his advice was offered from experience. She hadn't known him when he'd lost his mother to cancer, but she'd heard him talk about her often enough to feel like she knew how deeply Theresa Dawson had loved her boys and how much they'd adored her. Abby could only hope her own children might feel that kind of unconditional love for her someday.

He pressed a kiss to her forehead. "You are the strongest woman I know, Abby. But if you need *me*, I'm here."

Abby closed her eyes and nestled into him again, wishing she was half as strong as he believed her to be, wishing she'd been strong enough three years before to tell him the truth and not let him leave town without knowing how much she loved him.

"Kyle," she whispered, "there's something I have to tell you."

―᭤᭤―

Kyle stiffened at the tone in her voice. It was the same tone he used when delivering death notifications to the family of victims. Whatever Abby was about to tell him, it wasn't good.

When she sat up and turned her back to him to let her legs hang over the side of the bed, his stomach twisted with apprehension. But he'd just told her he'd be there for her, so he sure as hell wasn't about to go chickenshit on her now when she was clearly reaching out to take him up on his offer.

He sat up and scooted closer, wrapping an arm around her waist and pressing a kiss against the back of her shoulder. "I'm here, sweetheart. You can tell me anything."

She took a deep breath and let it out slowly, her shoulders dipping in dejection on the exhale. "I fell in love with you the first time I saw you," she told him. "The moment our eyes met, when you shook my hand… the effect was staggering. I'd never responded to anyone that way."

He chuckled, using it to cover his sudden relief. "Sorry?" When she didn't share in his amusement, he pressed another kiss to her skin and then rested his chin on her shoulder. "If it helps, I felt the same way about you. It killed me that we were going to be working together, that I'd have to see you every day and not be able to touch you."

She briefly pressed her head against his but then pulled away a little, subtly distancing herself from him. "When you announced you were leaving, I just… Well, I knew we couldn't have a future, but I wanted to be in your arms just once. That day at the lake was unbelievable. Unfortunately, I realized it wasn't going to be as easy to let you go as I'd thought."

"It wasn't easy for me to leave either," he assured her, meaning it. Knowing he'd have to tell her good-bye had hung over him like a dark cloud the entire summer, coloring every moment of happiness they'd shared. "I'd hoped that we could continue things long distance after I left. I wanted to make it work, Abby. If I hadn't, I wouldn't have told you how much I loved you."

She nodded but didn't speak for a moment. And when she did finally go on, her voice was tight as if choked by emotion. "I had hoped so too. But then"—she took a deep shuddering breath—"two days before you left, I went to the doctor because I'd missed my period."

Kyle's stomach dropped at warp speed, and he drew away from her, having a pretty damned good idea what he was about to hear next but not believing it at the same time. Abby wouldn't have kept something like that from him. Not Abby. Not the woman he wanted to spend the rest of his life with. He ran a hand down his face, waiting for her to speak, needing to hear it from her.

She cleared her throat. "The doctor confirmed I was pregnant."

Sorrow and rage hit Kyle like a ton of bricks. Suddenly Joe's apology in the bar made sense. And that just added to Kyle's fury. *He* hadn't known that Abby was pregnant, and yet somehow his *brother* had?

"Abby..." he croaked. He had to work to keep his voice even when he continued. "Did Joe and Sadie know about this?"

"Sadie did," she admitted. "She's my best friend. I had to confide in someone. But I didn't say a word to Joe. I swear it."

Kyle's jaw began to ache, and he forced himself to quit grinding his back teeth in order to say, "Since I don't currently have a toddler running around calling me 'Dad,' I assume you got an abortion."

She spun around on a gasp, her eyes wide, horrified. "What? No! You think I wouldn't want to have our child? It was a precious—albeit unexpected—gift."

He frowned at her, perplexed and impatient to know the rest. "So what happened then?" he demanded, his voice overly loud. "Did you have the baby?"

She shushed him with a glance toward the door. "Lower your voice!"

"Do we have a kid somewhere that I didn't even know about?" he hissed.

She lunged to her feet, pacing naked in the confines of the room. As hurt and upset as he was, Kyle couldn't help but appreciate the way the moonlight coming in through the window played upon her fair skin and pale hair, giving her an almost ethereal glow.

"No."

The single word brought him out of his reverie and his gaze snapped to her face, which was twisted with sorrow. "You miscarried," he guessed.

She nodded. "A few weeks later."

He wanted to go to her, to wrap her in his arms and soothe away her sorrow. But his hurt at being kept in the dark made him stay where he was. "Why didn't you tell me any of this before now?"

Abby wrapped her arms around herself and ran her hands up and down her arms, clearly needing the comfort he was being an ass about withholding. "You were leaving," she said as if that explained everything. "You had plans, a future. I didn't want to ruin that for you."

He felt the heat in his cheeks as a new wave of anger washed over him. "You thought that I'd choose a job over you and my *child*?" As soon as he said it, he realized this was the same thing he'd accused his father of all these years. Was it so hard to imagine that Abby might think he'd be the same kind of father? He threw back the covers and started gathering his clothes. "Don't you know me better than that?"

She came to him and grabbed his bicep. "Yes," she

said, her eyes pleading with him to understand as they
met and held his furious gaze. "I do. That's why I didn't
tell you."

He shook his head. "What the hell are you talking
about?"

"I knew you'd stay." Her grip on his arm tightened
slightly. "I didn't want you to give up everything you'd
dreamed of because of me. I didn't want our relationship to have that hanging over us. I would've always
wondered—you would've always wondered—if we
were only together because we felt like we *had* to be. I
saw what that did to my parents. I didn't want that for
us. For *you*."

Kyle stared at her for a moment in disbelief. He
understood what she was saying, understood where she
was coming from and why she hadn't told him. But it
didn't take away the sting of not knowing. The fact that
she'd doubted the depth of his love for her, that she'd
made a decision that had been *his* to make, hurt him
more than he cared to admit. He jerked his arm out of
her grasp and pulled on his pants.

She reached out to him, but her touch fell short.
"Kyle, please try to understand…"

He strode toward the door. "I understand, Abby," he
snapped as he grasped the doorknob. "I just need some
time by myself right now."

Kyle closed the door softly behind him in spite of
his urge to slam it and strode down the hall on bare feet
so as not to wake Emma or Tyler. He'd planned to just
duck into one of the other rooms and crash for the night
until he could leave at first light, but he somehow knew
he wouldn't be able to sleep even if he tried.

Adrenaline was pumping hard through his system and his thoughts were racing as he replayed that day three years ago when Abby had lied to him and told him that she didn't love him. He should've seen that she wasn't being honest. He should've known that something was off. But as he pulled his shirt over his head and jogged down the steps to the first level of the cabin, he began to wonder. *Had* he sensed that something was off? Had he *wanted* her to push him away?

As much as he wanted to deny it, he couldn't help but wonder. The strength of his feelings for Abby had scared the shit out of him. He couldn't hide how he felt about her, couldn't bear the thought of leaving her. Had he secretly been relieved when she said she didn't feel the same way?

He shook his head as he dropped onto the couch to pull on his shoes. "No," he said aloud to himself, shaking his head even more emphatically. It had torn him apart when he'd walked away that day, had torn him apart every day since.

So why the hell was he running away now?

This thought brought him up short.

Damn it.

He was running away because that's what he did when he was hurting. He ran away so that no one would see his pain, so that he wouldn't have to admit to anyone what he was really going through. He'd done the same fucking thing when his mom was dying. Instead of reaching out to his dad, he had pushed him away, not wanting the man he worshipped to see him as weak. Little had he known how much his dad was hurting too.

And now he was pushing Abby away.

He glanced toward the stairs, knowing he should go back up and talk to her, but he had a feeling that with the mood he was in right now, he'd end up saying things he'd regret later and jeopardize the future he wanted and hoped she wanted too.

It was better if he just left, put some distance between them for a couple days. He needed some time to sort through the jumble of emotions he was experiencing. He was going to have to leave in a few short hours anyway so he could get to the airport and book a flight to New Orleans.

He grabbed his keys and let himself out the cabin's front door, but he paused for a moment to stare up at the second floor of the palatial cabin, wondering if Abby was watching from the window.

He should go back in, at least tell her good-bye. He should tell her that he loved her and that he wanted to spend the rest of his life with her. But the ache in the center of his chest and the lump of anger and sorrow that was choking him kept him rooted where he was. Kyle stubbornly set his jaw and got in his car. He'd call her on the way to the airport, after he had a chance to cool down, and assure her that they'd sort it all out when he got back. He hoped to God that was true.

Abby let the curtain fall back across the window when she could no longer see Kyle's taillights and wiped the tears from her cheeks. Her body was still sensitive from their lovemaking, her lips raw and swollen from his kisses. She'd never known that kind of soul-shaking passion with anyone but Kyle.

And now he was gone.

Her fear of how he'd react to the truth she'd kept from him had come true. The look on his face when he realized why she'd pushed him away three years ago, the fury in his eyes when he briefly thought she'd given the baby up, was a look she hoped never to see again.

Of course, she might've just ensured that she'd never see any part of him again.

The heartbreaking prospect that she might never feel the warmth of his arms again chilled her down to her bones. She wrapped her arms around her torso, trying to hold in the shivers that racked her body, but they came anyway.

A single sob shook her shoulders as she turned back to the bed that was still warm from where they'd lain together. She slipped under the covers and buried her face in her pillow, which still held the masculine musky scent of his aftershave, and let the tears come.

Chapter 21

KYLE HAD BEEN SO UP IN HIS OWN HEAD THAT HE wasn't even sure where he was going until he found himself parked in Joe and Sadie's driveway. Dawn was just beginning to creep over the horizon, sending out tentative tendrils of light that sparkled on the early morning dew. For a long moment, Kyle just sat in the car, staring blankly ahead, exhaustion weighing down his arms and legs and making it impossible to even open the door and get out.

He wasn't sure how long he'd been sitting there scowling when the front door opened and Joe came out of the house in nothing but what looked like hastily donned jeans. Frowning, he rubbed his arms to generate warmth as he cautiously approached Kyle's car.

Kyle met his brother's concerned gaze through the window but made no move to roll it down until Joe tapped lightly on the glass with his knuckle. With a harsh sigh, Kyle rolled down the window, then averted his gaze, too pissed to be the first one to say a word.

"Kyle?" Joe asked, his confusion at seeing his brother evident in his tone. "You okay, man? What's going on? I thought you were going up north with Abby and her sister."

Kyle's eyes narrowed, but he continued to stare straight ahead. "Why didn't you tell me?"

"Tell you what?"

At this Kyle finally turned his head to peg his brother with a furious look. "You know what, you asshole."

Joe straightened and took a step back as Kyle moved to get out of the car. "I don't know what the hell you're talking about, Kyle."

Kyle slammed the car door and took an angry stride forward, but his older brother stood his ground, not intimidated in the least. "Yeah right," Kyle snapped. "I oughta clean your fucking clock!"

Joe's gaze hardened, and Kyle saw him spread his feet a little, taking up a fighting stance. "You could try, baby brother. Or you could get your ass inside and tell me what *the hell* is going on."

Kyle considered the options Joe had offered, his anger at them for keeping Abby's secret causing him to lean heavily toward the former when movement out of the corner of his eye caught his attention. He glanced away to see Sadie standing in the doorway, wearing a pale pink bathrobe, her hair tousled from sleep.

"Joe? What's going on?" she hissed in a loud whisper.

But Kyle was already striding angrily toward her, his finger pointed at her in accusation as he spat, "I trusted you, Sadie!"

Her eyes went wide as she sent a confused look toward Joe. But Kyle only caught a glimpse of her confusion before Joe stepped smoothly in front of him and shoved him back. "You better think about your next move very carefully," he warned. "You take one more step toward her, and I'll make good on my earlier threat. You think I'm joking, you try me."

Kyle looked over Joe's shoulder to peg Sadie with his furious gaze. "All the times we talked," he replied, forcing himself to keep his voice at a reasonable level, "all the times I listened to you crying over how much you missed Joe—and you never thought to maybe clue me in on what had happened to Abby? How could you keep that from me?"

Sadie's expression immediately went from confused to contrite. "Come inside, sweetie."

Kyle wasn't sure if she was talking to him or his brother, but his shoulders sagged when he saw the sorrow and sympathy in Sadie's eyes and took a step forward to take her up on the offer. Joe grabbed his bicep, his grip asking a silent question. Kyle gave him a curt nod. "I'm good. I'm sorry, man."

Joe shifted his grip to Kyle's shoulder as he ushered him in, his hold now more one of silent support than thinly veiled warning, reminding Kyle that his brother was there for him, that he had his back—just like he always had.

"I'm sorry, Joe," Kyle mumbled again, his voice cracking under the strain of his tumultuous emotions and bone-deep exhaustion. "I just—"

"It's all good, man," his brother told him, pulling him in for a brief sideways hug before releasing him and leading him into the kitchen where Sadie was already making coffee for the three of them. "So what the hell happened?"

"Abby told him about the baby," Sadie supplied.

Joe's eyes went wide. "You didn't know?" He muttered a string of curses under his breath, then ran a hand down his face. "I'm *such* an asshole. When I made that comment in Mulaney's…"

Kyle waved away his brother's apology as he pulled out a bar stool at the island. "I need to know why you kept this from me, Sadie. Why didn't you tell me when I left that summer for Quantico? I would've come back to be here with her through everything. Did you guys really think I would've let her carry my kid without being around for her? Or that I'd abandon her during the miscarriage?"

"Of course we knew you'd come back," Sadie assured him. "That's why Abby didn't want you to know—not right away anyway. She didn't want you to miss your opportunity. It wasn't an easy decision for her, Kyle."

Kyle put his elbows on the counter and hid his face in his hands for a long moment, trying to sort through everything. When he felt Sadie's hand on his back, he looked up to see her sitting on the bar stool next to him. "I'm sorry, Sadie," he said. "I just… It just kills me to know what she went through without me there to support her, to help her through it."

She smoothed his hair away from his brow and pressed a kiss to his forehead. "I know, sweetie. I'm sorry you just found out now. But you have to understand where Abby's coming from. She didn't want you sticking around because you felt like you had to."

Kyle quirked an eyebrow at her and gave her a mildly chastising look. "You should know us Dawson boys better than that. No one can make us do what we don't want to." He sent a meaningful nod toward his brother. "And you know that guy's been in love with you since we were kids, right?"

Sadie flushed prettily and sent a loving glance toward Joe. "Yeah. I kind of had my suspicions."

Joe chuckled and took her hand, bringing it to his lips and pressing a kiss to her knuckles.

"Then put him out of his misery and marry him, will ya?" Kyle said, pushing back from the bar.

A smile curved Sadie's lips, and she reached across the bar to pull Joe toward her for a kiss.

"I'm going to go crash in the guest room," Kyle called over his shoulder as he left the room. "You kids do what you gotta do..."

He heard Sadie squeal with laughter and had to grin, figuring his brother was probably going to whisk her back to bed for a while to take Kyle's advice. He climbed the stairs and purposely headed toward a room at the back of the house—furthest from Sadie and Joe's. As happy as he was for his brother, he didn't need to hear anything going on between the two of them.

After shutting the door behind him, Kyle did a quick search on his phone and found the number for the airline. They could get him on a flight later that afternoon. It wasn't going to be cheap, but if he could get some answers, the cost would be worth it. With that taken care of, he stretched out on the bed, eager to finally get a little sleep.

But as exhausted as he was, sleep wouldn't come. The way he'd left things with Abby weighed too heavily on him. He checked the clock. It was still early, but he knew from experience that she was an early riser. Taking the chance she might already be awake, he took a deep breath and dialed her number.

When she didn't answer, his heart sank. But when the call went to voice mail, his mouth suddenly went dry, and he wasn't sure what to say. "Hey, uh, Abby, it's me," he fumbled. "I, uh, just wanted to say I'm sorry I left like I did. I was just hurt. And pissed. And... Shit.

I don't know. Anyway, I'm leaving for New Orleans this afternoon. I'll try to call again before I go. I just… I love you."

He hung up and tapped his phone against his forehead with a groan. As apologies went, it was pretty fucking lame. He almost called her back to try to say something more eloquent, but if she was avoiding his calls on purpose, that was just going to make the situation worse.

He heaved a sigh and tossed his phone onto the bed beside him and closed his eyes. He'd wait until he'd slept a while and then call her again. Maybe then he wouldn't sound like a total moron.

He wasn't sure when he drifted off but when his phone rang, jolting him awake, he was still in a sleep fog and didn't quite realize he'd answered the phone until he heard his brother Tom's voice in his ear.

"Kyle? You there?"

Kyle scrubbed his face with his hand, trying to rid himself of the last vestiges of sleep. "Yeah. Yeah, I'm here. What's up, Tommy?"

"Where are you?"

Kyle shook his head a little, trying to remember. "Uh… Joe and Sadie's. What time is it?"

"Noon," Tom said, his tone clipped. "I've been trying to reach Abby."

This brought Kyle completely awake. "Why? What's going on?"

Tom's voice held an edge of frustration when he said, "I called Detroit PD to see about bringing in Whitmore and his father for questioning. Turns out Donovan Whitmore, Preston's father, was admitted to the ER around two a.m. after suffering a massive heart attack. Two guesses who was with him when the ambulance arrived."

Kyle cursed under his breath. "Patrick Hamilton. He broke the news to dear old dad about his son's activities, I'm guessing."

"Odds are."

"Is the old man going to pull through?" Kyle asked.

Tom sighed. "Not looking good. Apparently, he's on life support."

"What about Preston Whitmore?"

"Missing."

Kyle's blood went cold. "Missing? Missing how?"

"Hell, I don't know," Tom snapped. "Missing like everyone else goes missing, Kyle."

"Jesus, Tom, what's your problem?" Kyle retorted. "I'm just asking, man. It's kind of an important detail."

There was a heavy sigh on the other end of the line. "Sorry. I'm just in a shitty mood."

Kyle waited, ready to listen if Tom needed him to, but when his brother didn't go on, Kyle prompted, "So, what did you find out about Preston Whitmore? Was he officially reported missing by someone or just didn't show up for work?"

Tom cleared his throat a couple of times, and Kyle could almost picture his eldest brother giving himself a figurative smack upside the head to get his act together. "Whitmore was reported missing by his personal assistant when he didn't show for a meeting. And get this— that meeting? It was supposed to take place the same day Emma Maxwell went missing. Detroit PD searched his apartment. Nothing was missing from what anyone could tell. There were no signs of a struggle."

Kyle was struck mute for a moment as his mind rapidly strung together what the man's disappearance could indicate. It certainly didn't do anything to make him look less guilty, but another possibility began formulate. "Who was he supposed to meet?"

"His assistant didn't know. Whitmore had put it on his calendar himself and didn't indicate who he was meeting, just where he was going. And you ready for this? The meeting was in New Orleans."

A chill crept over Kyle's skin as the possibility he'd been considering became more concrete. "You're shitting me."

"Nope," Tom assured him. "According to his company jet's flight records, he got on the plane that morning as planned. But then there's no trace of what happened to him after he landed. He was just *gone*."

Kyle cursed under his breath. "You thinking what I'm thinking?"

"He's been offed as well?"

"Maybe," Kyle hedged, raking a hand through his hair. "Or maybe he's been offed *instead*."

"You think it's him in the photo Abby received and not Curtis Maxwell?" Tom asked.

Kyle pinched the bridge of his nose and squeezed his eyes shut, trying to recall the photo Abby had shown him. "We couldn't tell for certain that the dead man was Maxwell. He was beat all to hell. All Abby had to go on were his hair color and his clothes. What's Whitmore look like? Does he have the same hair color and build as Maxwell?"

"Got me. Hang on a minute." Kyle could hear the clacking of Tom's keyboard as he typed. "Shit."

"That's not what I was hoping to hear, Tom," Kyle drawled.

"Sorry, man," Tom said. "But they could be brothers."

Kyle's scowl deepened. "I gotta know who Whitmore and Maxwell were supposed to be meeting with in New Orleans."

"I talked to the detective looking into Whitmore's disappearance," Tom told him. "He's going to keep me in the loop as a favor to Dad."

"Dad?" Kyle echoed. "Christ, is there anyone in the Midwest who doesn't owe the Old Man a favor?"

Tom chuckled. "Nope. And lucky for us. I'll let you know if anything else turns up. You want to try to get in touch with Abby and let her know?"

Kyle ran a hand through his hair. "Yeah. I'll give Abby a call on my way to the airport."

"Airport? Where the hell are you going?"

"As luck would have it, I've already booked a flight to New Orleans to question a suspect in another case."

"That's an awful lot of too much coincidence," Tom mused. "I don't like you heading down there alone, Kyle."

"Don't worry," he assured his big brother. "My former partner is helping me out."

"I thought he hated you."

Kyle laughed. "Yeah, well, I guess my charm finally won him over."

The minute he hung up with his brother, Kyle tried Abby's number again—and again got her voice mail. He had a moment of intense panic and was ready to hop in his Mustang and race back to the cabin when he remembered what Abby had said about the cell phone service in the area.

Damn it.

He'd thought maybe she'd been screening his calls when he'd tried earlier. Now it occurred to him that she might not even know that he'd called at all. *Great.* So much for his big apology. For all she knew, he was still furious with her.

And now he had to get his ass moving so he wouldn't miss his plane. He called again on the way to the airport, praying that maybe she'd check her voice mail sometime soon. If Curtis Maxwell was still alive, that added a whole new spin to the sick and twisted drama the man was starring in…

———

Abby checked the screen of her phone again and held it above her head, turning a little in search of the elusive signal before heaving a frustrated sigh and returning her gaze to the woods that framed the little lake behind the cabin where Tyler was fishing without much luck.

"He'll call."

Abby turned away from the idyllic scene to gaze at her sister lounging in a chaise on the opposite side of the deck and offered her a grateful smile. "I should've told him sooner, Em. I don't blame him for being angry about it."

Emma shrugged as she took a sip of her coffee. "What's done is done, Abby. You just have to move forward."

Abby studied her sister for a long moment, impressed to see the newly defiant lift of her chin. Maybe she'd be okay after all… "Still, I shouldn't have let him leave like that."

"Didn't really have much of a choice from what it sounds like," Emma told her. She rose from the chaise and walked to the railing to watch her son more closely. "I'm sure he got home safely."

Abby nodded but didn't speak, glancing at her phone once more. She hadn't slept at all. She'd tossed and turned, replaying her conversation with Kyle and unable to forget the look of betrayal in his eyes. Finally, feeling trapped and claustrophobic inside the cabin, she'd given up and had come out on the deck. She'd been sitting there since dawn, listening to the birds and the other sounds of morning for several hours before her nephew and sister had joined her, bringing out a tray of brunch.

Emma hadn't even asked about why Kyle wasn't there. She'd just seemed to know. When Abby had teared up, Emma had sent Tyler down to the boathouse for the fishing gear so that they could talk.

"We really should invest in a phone line out here," Abby mumbled, glancing down at her phone again. About the only thing it was good for was telling the time. It was well past noon now, but the hours couldn't pass quickly enough to suit her. She grumbled, "I feel so cut off from everything without any cell service. What if there's an emergency?"

Emma turned to give her an amused grin. "We spent a great deal of time here as kids without any mishaps, Abby."

Abby got to her feet, suddenly antsy. "It only takes one."

"Hey," Emma said with forced enthusiasm. "Do you want to go for a boat ride? We haven't taken the boat out in ages!"

Abby laughed, picturing the rowboat that she had been surprised to find still in the boathouse when she and Kyle had gone down there for their heated make-out session the day before. "That old thing is probably half rotten! There's no way you're getting me in that boat."

"A walk then," Emma suggested. "Just the three of us."

Abby started to decline the offer, but paused when she saw the hopeful look on her sister's face. Maybe she wasn't the only one who needed to keep her mind off things.

"Alright," she relented. "But we're not going far. You know I'm not a fan of these woods."

"Tyler!" Emma called down to her son. "Come on up, buddy. We're going for a walk." She then drained her coffee and hurried toward the door to the house, her enthusiasm contagious. "I'm going to go change my shoes. Don't go anywhere."

Abby laughed. "Where am I going to go? There's nothing around here for miles."

Emma winked at her, then disappeared inside. Abby frowned as soon as her sister was gone, wondering if Emma was as okay as she appeared to be. The sudden change in her personality, the cheerfulness in spite of what she'd gone through while she was missing, were great to see. But Abby didn't quite trust it. She'd been there during every one of her mother's breakdowns, and each of them had started with a period of what appeared to be joy and contentment. But then the depression would descend with a vengeance.

She sighed, hoping she was worrying for nothing. Even so, she silently sent up a prayer that nothing would destroy this fragile happiness that Emma seemed to be enjoying.

"Ready?" Emma chirped, emerging from the house just as Tyler joined them on the deck carrying his fishing gear.

Abby forced a smile and tucked her phone in her back pocket. "You bet."

Chapter 22

As Kyle made his way to the gate for his flight, apprehension about leaving Abby at the cabin without additional backup began to make him twitchy. Luckily, they'd already begun preboarding when he found an open seat in the crowded waiting area. He dropped his overnight bag at his feet before squeezing into the narrow vinyl-covered chair to wait until they called his row. The sooner he could get to New Orleans and back to Abby, the better.

"Headed to the Big Easy?"

Kyle frowned and glanced around in confusion before he realized the man across the aisle had spoken to him. "Sorry?"

The man offered a friendly smile. Clearly he was an extrovert. Awesome.

"I was just asking if you were heading to New Orleans."

Kyle eyed the guy up and down with a quick glance, subtly sizing him up. He looked like he could be everybody's favorite neighbor—ordinary, nondescript. The guy who kept his lawn nice and trim and waved to all the cars driving by.

"Yeah," Kyle said, offering a curt smile in return.

"Business or pleasure?"

Kyle suppressed his irritation at being engaged in conversation and said, "Business."

"Me too." The guy's smile widened. "What kind of business you in?"

Speaking of business, Kyle wanted to tell the guy to piss off and mind his own. But for some reason he found himself continuing to answer the man's questions. He had to give the guy credit. He had a way of drawing out information. But Kyle was a pro at evading. "Government work," he hedged, keeping it vague.

The guy nodded. "Ah, gotcha." He looked at Kyle expectantly, clearly not willing to end their conversation there.

Kyle suppressed a sigh. "What about you? What kind of work are you in?"

"I'm an independent contractor," the guy said with a shrug. Then he gave Kyle an amused grin. "I've worked with some government guys before. Who knows? Maybe I've even done a job for one of your bosses."

Kyle's brows twitched together briefly. "I doubt it."

The guy laughed. "Hey, it's a small world. You never know."

"Are you from New Orleans?" Kyle asked, trying to change the subject.

"Nah," the guy replied. "Just passing through. How 'bout you?"

Kyle shook his head. "Same."

A woman's voice suddenly filled the area, the words garbled and crackling, but Kyle could understand enough to know that his row was being called to board. He got to his feet, glad to be moving again.

"That you?" the guy asked, gesturing with his thumb toward the ceiling as if the gate attendant was some divine voice calling the passengers to their final destination and not the harried-looking woman behind the podium with the edge of her uniform blouse coming untucked.

"Yeah," Kyle said, shouldering his carry-on. "It was good talking to you. Have a good trip."

The guy extended his hand. "You, too…?"

It took a moment for Kyle to realize the man was waiting for Kyle's name. For a second he thought about giving a fake name, but why bother? It wasn't like he and the guy were likely to cross paths again. "Kyle," he supplied. "Kyle Dawson."

The guy shook Kyle's hand with a hearty grip. "Kyle? Good to meet you. Take care now."

Kyle gave him a curt smile and headed toward the growing line of passengers at the gateway. But he'd only gone a few steps before he paused to turn back to get another look at the guy. "You seem familiar for some reason. Have we met before?"

The man laughed a little. "I get that all the time. I guess I just have one of those faces. I look like everybody. And nobody."

Kyle nodded slowly. "Guess so. Well, see you around… Sorry. Didn't catch your name."

"Fielding." The guy's smile widened. "Greg Fielding."

Kyle raised a hand in farewell. "See you around, Fielding."

Fielding gave him a nod. "Yep. You bet."

As soon as Kyle had boarded and stowed his carry-on, he took out his phone and called his brother.

"Aren't you supposed to be on a plane?" Tom quipped by way of answering the phone.

"I am," Kyle said in a rush. "And I only have a few minutes before they make us turn off our phones. I need you to do me a favor."

"This is becoming a habit, baby brother."

"I'll owe you one."

"One?"

"Okay, a shit-ton. Could you just do this for me?"

"Alright. What?"

"I need you to see what you can find on a guy named Greg Fielding. He's an independent contractor who's done some government work. I don't know anything else about him."

"Seriously? This is what you're giving me to work with? That's not exactly an unusual name."

"Fine," Kyle snapped, holding up his index finger to indicate to the flight attendant that he needed just a minute longer. "Give it to Gabe. He loves this kind of down-the-rabbit-hole shit."

"Is this related to the case?" Tom asked.

"No, just a hunch," Kyle admitted. "I met this guy in the airport a minute ago and there's something off about him."

Tom laughed. "Jesus, Kyle. Are you kidding me? If I ran a check on every guy I came across that seemed a little off…"

"Humor me, will ya?" Kyle said. "I'm going to be on a plane with this guy for the next two hours."

"I won't have anything before you take off," Tom reminded him. "Won't do you much good if I find anything on him."

"Trust me, I'm aware of that."

"Sir," the flight attendant was down in his face now, trying very hard to be pointed but polite. "We're preparing for departure. I need you to stow your phone until the pilot gives the okay."

Kyle gave her his most charming smile and nodded

and said into his phone in a rush, "Just text me what you find, Tom."

———∼∼∼———

Fielding settled into his seat a few rows back from Kyle Dawson, trying not to frown as he mulled over his meeting with the FBI agent who was screwing Abby Morrow. What in the hell was the agent doing on a flight to New Orleans when Deputy Morrow was clearly still in danger? Didn't they get his fucking text?

Figured.

That's what he got for trying to be a nice guy and even the odds a little.

Still...

As much as it irritated him that his attempt to warn Abby Morrow had gone unheeded, the thought of those pricks hurting her made his stomach lurch. Maybe he'd send another text, make sure Deputy Morrow got the idea. He certainly had a few that could get the point across. Or maybe he'd just let things run their course. It's not like he had any skin in the game. And unless something showed up in the papers, he'd never know about it anyway. Not where he was going to be luxuriating for the foreseeable future.

Anyway, it didn't matter. He'd already confirmed that fifteen million from his employer had been wired to his account, as instructed. Boy, that bastard was going to be pissed when he realized Fielding had taken the money and skipped out on him without offing the deputy and her family. But clearly his employer was desperate. And desperation often overrode sense and reason.

He almost hated to leave and miss all the fun when his

employer realized he'd been double-crossed. He almost felt sorry for the moron. Which is why Fielding had agreed to take this last job when Mr. Smith had called that morning. Apparently, there'd been a development and there was another million in it for Fielding if he'd take care of a little problem down in New Orleans first.

It was a shame that his final job before an extended vacation wasn't even remotely interesting. Disposing of a body, of all things. Shit work. To have to end his career where he'd begun was like getting busted down from general to private.

But apparently these jackasses couldn't be bothered to even do that much on their own and were willing to pay out the ass to keep their hands clean. And a million dollars could buy a fuck-load of humility. So here he was on a plane to New Orleans.

Whatever amateur they'd hired to off the guy in New Orleans was going to leave the stiff in some abandoned warehouse for Fielding to get rid of it. He was thinking acid was probably the way to go. Then again, the bayous offered a nice alternative with the population of gators that were always looking for a free lunch.

Fielding settled back in his seat and crossed his arms over his chest. As the plane taxied down the runway, he closed his eyes and began counting back from one hundred, determined to get some shut-eye before he arrived in New Orleans. It was going to be a long night, and he needed to have his wits about him.

Before heading to the abandoned building, he was planning to tag along with Agent Dawson and find out what he was up to in the Big Easy. He actually kinda liked the guy.

Aside from the little display outside Deputy Morrow's house the other night in the storm, which Fielding couldn't help but admire, Dawson seemed like a decent investigator. The way Dawson had been studying him from the moment they made eye contact, he could tell the agent instinctively sensed something off about him.

He'd come across quite a bit of information about the famous Dawson family when he'd read up on Abby Morrow, but he hadn't had the opportunity to see one of them in action on the job. Until today. Now he understood why their names got bandied around by law enforcement and criminals alike with a mixture of rage, jealousy, and awe. Hell, if Fielding hadn't been used to constantly watching for tells that someone had made him, he never would've noticed that the guy was assessing him, judging him while they'd chatted. Dawson was just that good.

It'd be a damned shame if their jobs happened to intersect…

⟶⟵

Kyle slung his carry-on over his shoulder and took out his phone, turning it on to see if he had any text messages from his brother—or Abby. But he still hadn't heard from either of them. Impatient, he tried calling Abby again but only got her voice mail. He didn't even bother leaving a message this time.

Then he tried Tom. Surprisingly, he didn't get an answer there either. *What the hell?* Tom *always* answered his phone. He hung up and was getting ready to try again when Gabe's number came across the screen.

Frowning, Kyle answered. "Hey, Gabe. What's up?"

"Tom asked me to look into that guy you were asking about," he said.

Kyle started walking down the crowded corridor, heading for baggage claim to grab the duffel bag in which he'd checked his gun. "Yeah? And?"

"Well, there are about a hundred guys with that name," Gabe informed him, "but none of them are contractors of any kind, not that I could find."

"Maybe the guy was lying to me about what he did," Kyle suggested.

"Got me," Gabe replied. "I just know I couldn't find shit on anyone meeting your criteria. You got a physical description of the guy?"

Kyle slowed his stride. Hell, he wasn't sure how to even give a description of the man. "Uh…mid-forties, maybe? Brown hair. Brown eyes. He just looked…ordinary. No distinguishing characteristics of any kind."

"Well, thank you, Agent Dawson," Gabe drawled. "That description is immensely helpful. You just described about eighty percent of the population, numbnuts."

Kyle's mouth hitched up at one corner, glad his brother was teasing him again. That was definitely a good sign. "Sorry, man. That's all I've got. What can I say? The guy doesn't stand out in any way."

"I don't know what to say then," Gabe replied. "The guy's a ghost, Kyle. There's nothing on him anywhere."

Kyle came to a halt, causing the person behind him to slam into him. He threw a glance over his shoulder as the man sent an irritated epithet his way. He mumbled an apology and returned his attention to the conversation with his brother.

"Thanks, Gabe," he murmured, his brows furrowed. "I appreciate you taking a look."

He hung up his phone and stood there, lost in thought for a moment before he finally continued on his way to baggage claim. By then, the area was a flurry of activity with passengers milling around the carousel.

Kyle saw his duffel bag come around and snatched it up. When he turned, he found himself face-to-face with Fielding.

He gave him a curt nod in greeting and started to go around, but he'd only gone a few steps when he heard Fielding call out, "Be seeing you around, Agent Dawson. Take care of that pretty little deputy of yours."

Kyle whirled around in an instant, his heart pounding. "What the fuck—?"

But Fielding was gone.

Kyle frantically searched the crowd, but Fielding had vanished.

Like a ghost.

Kyle let out a string of furious curses, earning a horrified look from more than one passerby. He raked a frantic hand through his hair.

*God*damn *it!*

He didn't like it. He didn't like it at all. As he swiftly strode toward the airport exit to catch a cab, he called Abby again.

"Abby, baby, please call me when you get this," he said in a rush. "I need to talk to you right away. Please call me, sweetheart."

The next call he made was to Peterman. "I'm here."

Chapter 23

ABBY BOUNCED HER KNEE RHYTHMICALLY AS SHE nibbled on the salad Emma had prepared for dinner, her nerves not any better after their walk earlier. Or their game of pool. Or the movie they watched. She still couldn't get to her phone and felt completely cut off from the world. And from Kyle.

She desperately wanted to talk to him, to try to explain again why she hadn't told him three years ago, hoping that maybe by explaining her reasons again he would understand. But her damned signal was completely nonexistent where they were.

"I'm going to town," she announced abruptly, shoving her chair back from the table.

Emma and Tyler both stared at her for a moment before Emma gestured with her fork toward Abby's salad. "You haven't finished eating."

Abby backed away from the table, eager to get going now that she'd decided to leave. "I know. It's delicious. Really it is. I'll eat the rest when I get back. I won't be gone long." She glanced to Tyler and grinned. "How about I get some ice cream while I'm there?"

"Sweet!" he cheered. "I like mint chocolate chip."

"You got it, buddy." But as she said it, Abby felt a twinge of guilt at having to leave them alone for even the hour she might be gone. "You know what? Why don't you both come with me? We can go to the ice cream shop instead."

"Can we, Mom?" Tyler asked.

Emma studied Abby for a moment, then patted Tyler's arm. "Why don't you stay here with me? I want you to show me the new game you got for your birthday. I think I'd like to learn to play." When Abby opened her mouth to protest, Emma added, "Besides, I'm thinking Aunt Abby has a call she'd like to make while she's in town."

Abby gave her sister a grateful smile. "Okay, then. I'll grab some ice cream and be back in a jiffy." She hurried back to the table and dropped a kiss to the top of Tyler's head, then gave her sister a quick hug. "I'll be gone maybe an hour at most."

Emma shooed her away. "Go. We'll be fine."

Abby blew them a kiss before hurrying toward the door and snatching up her purse on the way out.

She was only a few miles down the road before she took her phone out to check for a signal.

"Damn it!" she hissed. "*Still* nothing."

She tossed the phone onto the seat beside her and turned her attention back to the road. She'd just have to wait a few more minutes until she was actually in town. That last couple of miles felt like forever. When she finally pulled into the parking lot of the tiny grocery store tucked in between a bait-and-tackle shop and a take-and-bake pizza place, she snatched up the phone and heaved a sigh of relief when she saw she finally had a signal.

She also saw how many missed calls and texts she had. Many of them from Kyle.

"Jesus," she whispered. "What the hell?"

She took a deep breath and let it out slowly before playing the first one from Kyle. When she heard his apology, the heartfelt emotion in his voice, her eyes filled with tears. She closed her eyes and let her head fall back against the headrest of her seat, letting relief wash over her.

Then she gave herself a mental shake, her spirits lifted now that she'd heard his voice and knew in her heart that they'd be okay. They'd talk it out when he got back from New Orleans. It'd all be fine.

With a renewed sense of hope, she got out of the SUV and went into the grocery store, playing the rest of her messages as she gathered a few items into the cart. But her raised spirits came crashing down again as she listened to the rest of her voice-mail messages, one urgent message after another from Tom and Kyle.

As she pulled a carton of mint chocolate-chip ice cream from the freezer, she dialed Kyle, eager to hear his voice. He answered on the first ring.

"Abby!" he said on a relieved sigh. "Thank Christ! I've been worried out of my goddamned mind."

"I'm okay," she assured him, her brows coming together at the concern in his voice. "I didn't have a signal. I had to come into town to check my voice mail. I had several from Tom telling me to call right away. What the hell's going on?"

Kyle quickly filled her in on the Whitmores and his suspicion that her brother-in-law might not be the man in the photo after all.

She shook her head, trying to sort through it all. "Curtis might actually be alive? Why wouldn't he contact Emma or Tyler if that's the case? Is it possible he's being held somewhere? That maybe whoever's behind this hasn't harmed him yet?"

"I'm going to check into it while I'm here in New Orleans," he told her, but she caught a note of caution in his voice. He was trying to keep her from getting her hopes up. "I'm on my way now to meet with Peterman and see if we can get access to question Rhodes."

"Just be careful, Kyle," she pleaded.

"Don't worry," he assured her. "I'll be fine. I'm just here to ask a few questions."

There was a long, awkward pause before Abby finally took a deep breath and said, "I'm sorry. About earlier. About how I told you everything. I should've told you sooner... I should've—"

He interrupted her with a heavy sigh. She knew what that sigh meant. She could picture him running a hand through his dark hair, his eyes squeezed shut in a pained frown of frustration. She'd seen it the day she'd broken things off with him, had seen it the night before when she'd told him the truth.

"We'll sort it out, Abby," he finally said, his voice gentler than she was expecting. "I just need a little time. I promise, when I get back to— Shit. I gotta go."

"Kyle, is everything okay?" Abby asked in a rush, but he'd already hung up. She tried calling him back, her heart pounding with dread, but the call went to voice mail. Her knees suddenly feeling weak, she hurried to the counter to pay for her groceries, barely registering the cheery comments the cashier made to her.

Abby forced a smile, nodding absently as her thoughts whirled. She waved a good-bye and grabbed her bag, hurrying out to her car and dropping the bag in the passenger seat before getting behind the wheel. Then she remembered all the missed texts she hadn't bothered reading in her eagerness to talk to Kyle.

There were a few from Tom and Kyle, both insisting that she call them right away. Then she saw two from a blocked number. Her breath caught in her chest and her fingers trembled as she went to the first one.

My gift to you.

The man in the photo was clearly dead, his neck broken if the angle of his head was any indication. He was dressed in black, and a black knit cap lay on the ground beside him in what looked like some kind of ravine.

But who was he? She didn't recognize him, had no idea why the sender would consider the dead man a gift.

She went to the next text message. This one didn't contain a photo, just a message: A "thank you" would be nice. If not for my intervention, you and your boyfriend would be dead. P.S. Please give my regards to your lovely sister.

She frowned, wondering what the hell he was talking about. The dead man in the photo had been killed while trying to kill her and Kyle? That was hard as hell to believe. Why would the bastard who'd abducted her sister try to save her life from some unknown assailant? And how had he known someone was going to try to kill them?

Or was this all just a ruse? For all she knew, the man in the photo could've been anyone, could've been a fake. *Fake.*

She scrolled back through her messages until she

found the one that had been sent from New Orleans. She brought it up, looking it over with fresh eyes. The man in the photo was definitely the same build as Curtis and appeared to have the same hair color. And even behind the bruises and blood he *looked* like her brother-in-law. But as she looked closer now without emotion and fear clouding her judgment, she could see the slight differences... A cleverly constructed fake.

But why?

Or, more importantly, *by whom*?

"I thought I was meeting you at headquarters," Kyle said, trying to shove his carry-on into the trunk of Peterman's Lincoln. For a guy who was so uptight, the trunk of his personal vehicle was a serious frigging mess. It was almost completely full of shit. "Why the change of plans?"

Kyle's eyes swept over everything, trying to figure out if he'd be able to fit his other bag in among the clutter. It looked like the guy had emptied out his frigging garage. There were tools, drop cloths, a spare tire, and a gas can that Kyle hoped was empty. Who the hell drove around with a gas can in their trunk in the Louisiana heat, for chrissake?

Peterman shoved aside some blankets and a tire iron to make room for Kyle's duffel bag. "Thought it'd save us some time if I just met you at the airport instead of you having to try to deal with a cab and all that."

Peterman grabbed the edge of the trunk lid and started to slam it shut but Kyle caught it. "Hang on. Gotta grab something out of my bag." He quickly unzipped his duffel bag and slipped his hand between a couple of shirts to pull out the gun case where he'd secured his sidearm before shoving it into his checked bag. He quickly entered the combination on the lock and took out his unloaded weapon. "Can't forget this."

Peterman chuckled. "You think we're going to be ambushed on the way to meet with Rhodes?"

Kyle offered him a cockeyed smile, glad his former partner didn't seem to harbor any lingering animosity toward him. Too bad they hadn't been able to get along when they had been partners. He grabbed the clip he'd brought—a "reasonable" amount of ammunition by TSA standards—and loaded the gun before tucking it into the holster at the small of his back and slamming the trunk. "Can't be too careful. How'd you finally find Rhodes?"

"Didn't. He contacted me," Peterman explained as he got behind the wheel. He started up the Lincoln and pulled away from the curb, merging into the airport traffic. "Well, his attorney did anyway. Said he had persuaded Rhodes to talk to us."

Kyle's brows lifted. "That's an interesting turn of events. What do you think made the attorney suddenly want to work with us on bringing him in?"

Peterman shrugged. "Got me. But he didn't want to bring him into headquarters. Worried about being recorded and incriminating himself. So we've arranged an alternate location."

Kyle's brows came together in a frown. "How'd you manage that?"

"It's called *networking*, Dawson," Peterman said with a grin. "You might try it sometime instead of pissing off everyone you work with. You'd go farther."

"Thanks for the tips on how to make friends and influence others," Kyle drawled. "Glad to see those self-help books are working out for ya."

Peterman laughed aloud at this, making Kyle grin. Yeah, it was definitely too bad they hadn't gotten along before. Of course, Peterman was right. The fault was mostly Kyle's, and it was a mistake he was determined not to make again in his new assignment back home. He was done with the rebellious bullshit. It was time to grow the fuck up and get over his daddy issues. If not for his own good, then for the sake of his relationship with Abby.

And as soon as he got back home, he was going to spill his guts, lay it all out there, and ask her to spend the rest of her life with him.

"You married, Peterman?" Kyle asked out of the blue, genuinely curious to know more about the guy since he'd never really bothered before.

Peterman grunted. "Used to be. The bitch took everything I had and then some. You should see the alimony check I have to write every month. You'd think I was a fucking millionaire."

"Sorry, man," Kyle said sincerely.

Peterman shrugged. "Good riddance, you know? The only thing she let me keep was my baby girl."

Kyle's brows twitched together at the slight hitch in Peterman's voice at the mention of his daughter. A daughter he didn't even know Peterman had. He probably should have. And now, come to think of it, he seemed to recall him mentioning something... "How old is your daughter?"

Peterman's jaw tightened, then he coughed, clearing his throat before answering, "Sixteen."

Kyle nodded, somewhere in the back of his mind wondering if his and Abby's baby had been a boy or a girl. Not quite knowing what else to ask about the daughter that Peterman seemed reluctant to talk about, Kyle switched back to what seemed like safer ground. "This is a nice car. Is it new?"

Peterman cast a glance his way, then shrugged. "I got it a few months ago. You really *weren't* paying attention at all while we were partners, were you?"

Kyle shifted uncomfortably. "Sorry. I was dealing with some shit, man. It had nothing to do with you."

Peterman glanced away from the road to give Kyle a probing look as if he wasn't quite sure how to process what Kyle was saying. "Didn't think it did."

Kyle cleared his throat and glanced around the car, taking it in. The thing was loaded with all the bells and whistles. Clearly, seniority at the Bureau had its perks. Peterman had to be pulling down a fat salary to afford such a nice ride, especially with the alimony check he said he was sending to his ex.

Kyle thought about his tiny apartment, still unpacked. Maybe it was time he looked at buying a house, settling down… He chuckled to himself, wondering when the hell he'd become all domestic and shit. Some rebel he was. He had a feeling that his days of pizza and Chinese takeout every night were coming to an end.

"What's so funny?" Peterman asked, breaking into Kyle's thoughts.

"Just thinking about my…" Kyle paused. "Hell, I don't even know what to call her. Girlfriend, I guess? She's the one who I've been working the case with in Indiana."

Peterman chuckled. "Yeah, well, sounds like that's

not all you're working. She's one nice piece of ass, Dawson. I'll give you that."

Kyle straightened at the comment, turning to study Peterman's profile. "How do you know anything about her?"

Peterman sent a nonchalant look his way. "What? You didn't think I'd check into the woman you said you were working this case with when you called me?"

Kyle studied him for a moment longer, searching for any signs of a hidden agenda, but Peterman seemed on the level. "Sure. Just use some respect, man. You talk like that about her again, and I'll drop you."

Peterman lifted his hands from the steering wheel briefly in a mea culpa gesture. "No disrespect meant."

"So where the hell are we meeting with Rhodes anyway?" Kyle asked, changing the subject.

"Just outside of the city," Peterman told him. "We'll be there soon."

Fielding was careful to stay back from the silver Lincoln, not wanting either of the men to pick up on the fact that they had a tail. He'd paid handsomely to have a car delivered to him at the airport terminal, but it'd been worth it. If he'd had to hail a cab or get a rental car, he would've missed Agent Dawson getting into a car with someone who looked like an FBI agent. A colleague in law enforcement, Fielding guessed. They certainly hadn't greeted one another as friends.

So where the hell were they going?

If Dawson's companion was a fellow agent, why weren't they going to FBI headquarters, which was in the opposite direction by several miles now? Fortunately, Fielding had a couple hours before it was time to do his job, so he had time to follow for a while and satisfy his curiosity about their final destination.

"What are you up to, Agent Dawson?" he mumbled to himself, narrowing his eyes against the sun.

Suddenly, Fielding's phone alerted him to a new text message. With a groan, he snatched up his phone and glanced at the message. His eyes went wide when he saw who the message was from. But his lips curved into a satisfied smile when he saw what the message actually said.

Thank you.

It seemed the pretty little deputy had finally received his text messages. He'd been beginning to wonder if he'd been wrong to do her such a considerable favor. It turned out she'd been worthy of his benevolence after all.

It was too bad he hadn't been sent to abduct Abby Morrow. He had a feeling she wouldn't have been nearly so timid or frightened while under his care. Her sister had been a compliant little mouse. And while that certainly made his job easier, it had taken all the sport out of it.

But Abby had made up for it by following all his rules during their little game.

It was really too bad that their association had to end. He would've liked to continue to test the full limit of her investigative abilities by really putting her to the test in a *true* battle of the wits. Now *that* would've been a game worthy of her talents—and his.

And then perhaps he could've been the one making

out with her in the thunderstorm, stripping her of her
clothes in her entryway, fucking her against the wall…

He shifted a little in his seat as he remembered the
scene he'd glimpsed through her window.

Fielding shook off the fantasy and focused his attention back on the road and the Lincoln several cars ahead.
The driver was taking an exit.

Fielding frowned and did a double take when he saw
the highway sign indicating where they were headed.
The driver's destination seemed to be in the same direction as where Fielding would be heading for his own
job. That would certainly make it easier to keep his
appointment. What a fortunate coincidence.

Except that Fielding didn't believe in coincidences.

Chapter 24

"You dragged my ass all the way out to some *warehouse*?"

Peterman gestured vaguely with his arm toward the few boxes and crates that remained in the abandoned building. "Rhodes's attorney thought this might be the best place to talk with him off the record," he said. "You can ask him what you want here without anyone listening in."

Kyle glanced around the vast expanse of the warehouse, illuminated only by the single fluorescent light hanging from the ceiling near where Peterman stood. The rest of the light fixtures that Kyle could discern in the waning evening light appeared to have been broken or disabled long ago. In the darkness, he heard the scurry of one of the local wildlife that'd apparently taken up residence in the building since its human occupants had vacated.

He didn't like this. Not one fucking bit.

"So where's Rhodes?" Kyle asked, working to keep his voice level. "Shouldn't he be here?"

Peterman shifted uneasily on his feet, beginning to look a little nervous. "I'm sure he'll be here any minute. Just be patient."

The hair on the back of Kyle's neck prickled in warning. When a soft shuffle in the shadows drew Peterman's attention away, Kyle snatched his gun from the back of his waistband and had it trained on Peterman when the man turned back around.

"What the fuck, Dawson?" Peterman cried, instantly raising his hands.

"Who are you working for?" Kyle demanded. "Maxwell? Whitmore? Hamilton? *Who?*"

Peterman shook his head frantically. "I don't know what the fuck you're talking about! I'm not working for anybody."

"Bullshit!" Kyle barked, taking a few cautious steps forward. "Take out your weapon and put in on the ground where I can see it. Your backup too." Peterman gave him a quizzical look. "Yeah, I paid a little more attention than you think, Peterman." He gestured with the muzzle of his gun. "Let's go."

Peterman reached around to the small of his back and slowly withdrew his weapon, letting it hang from his index finger as he held it up where Kyle could see it. Then, without taking his eyes off Kyle, he squatted and set it on the concrete floor. While he was kneeling, he lifted the leg of his pants and undid the Velcro strap that secured his backup weapon against his calf.

"How much are they paying you for information?" Kyle hissed. "How much did it take for you to sell out?"

"You gotta believe me," Peterman said, as he slowly rose to his feet, hands still raised. "I'm not involved in this, Dawson."

"It all makes sense now, Peterman," Kyle retorted. "Someone tipped off Rhodes that we were coming to bring him in. That's why he ran. And you tried to stop me when I went after him."

"I wasn't trying to stop you!" Peterman shouted. "I was trying to keep you from getting your stupid ass killed! You were my partner, Dawson. That's what partners *do*."

"Then who tipped him off that we were coming?" Kyle demanded, beginning to doubt his own suspicions. "Huh?"

"I have no fucking clue! Damn it, Dawson!" Peterman growled. "I'm not a dirty agent! This case is just as important to me as it is to you. I was there when we found Rosalie Sparks, remember? That has haunted me just as much as it's haunted you. Why the fuck do you think I'm helping you now? I want those assholes caught just as much as you do!"

"So where's Rhodes then?" Kyle spat. "Why drag me out to a deserted warehouse? Who the hell paid you off to get me here, Peterman?"

Peterman's face twisted with emotion, then his shoulders sagged. "I'm not working for them, Dawson. I swear to God. It's not like that."

Kyle's grip on the gun tightened. "Enlighten me."

"They—" He glanced away for a moment, composing himself. "They've got my daughter. They've got my baby girl, Miranda. She's only *sixteen*. They said if I didn't bring you out here, she'd get passed around from man to man and then they'd gut her and drop her on my doorstep."

Kyle lowered his weapon on a horrified curse. "Jesus Christ."

"I don't know where the hell Rhodes is," Peterman repeated. "I swear it. His attorney called me to set it up—"

The sharp crack of the shot abruptly cut off Peterman's words as the bullet struck him in the chest. Kyle whirled around to face the assailant and nearly fired a round just as the man emerged from the shadows, but thank God he'd caught sight of the terrified, sobbing girl being used as a human shield before he'd fired.

Kyle's eyes went wide when he saw who was peeking out around her, keeping her in front of him like the coward he was. One hand grasped the girl's arm while the other held a gun to her side. She was gagged and her hands were bound, her entire body trembling. When she saw her father lying on the ground, a terrible little wail escaped her. Fury raged in Kyle's blood.

"Miranda, honey," Kyle called out. "Miranda, look at me. Don't look over there. You just look at me, okay?" He then turned his furious gaze on her captor. "You son of a bitch."

Rhodes grinned, his lips curving into a mockery of a smile. "Agent Dawson, so good to see you again. And you too, Agent Peterman—" He sent a pitying look toward Peterman's body, then offered Kyle a pout. "Well, I guess he won't be joining in our conversation after all."

"Fuck you, Rhodes," Kyle hissed, his eyes narrowing as he sized up the wiry little shithead before him. He certainly didn't look like the drugged-out prostitute he'd pretended to be on the street. He was now dressed in an expensive suit and tie, his bleached blond hair fashionably styled. "What the hell do you want from me?"

Rhodes clucked his tongue. "It's not what *I* want," he corrected. "It's what my boss wants. You're interfering with his business, Agent Dawson. And, well, we just can't have that. Now, if you would be so kind as to put your weapon on the ground and kick it away from you?"

Kyle did as he was told, then straightened, his hands held out a little from his sides. "Whose boy toy are you, Rhodes?" he asked, slowly turning as Rhodes circled him. "Obviously, you're not who you pretended to be.

Were you using prostitution as a way to recruit fresh meat for the market? Or did you just like being manhandled by drunks in alleyways?"

Rhodes gave Kyle a tolerant grin. "Who doesn't like to be manhandled now and then? But you're correct—I wasn't quite who I made myself out to be. And when this job is over, I can retire quite comfortably."

"Who's providing this golden parachute?" Kyle demanded. "Who's paying you to do his dirty work?"

Rhodes gave Kyle a pitying look. "Really, Agent Dawson, do you think I'm going to just stand here and confess all my dirty little secrets? You've seen far too many movies."

"Then why bring me out here?" Kyle asked. "If you're going to kill me, you might as well get on with it."

Rhodes heaved a dramatic sigh. "Unfortunately, that's not for me to do. I'm supposed to wait until closer to when the hired help is scheduled to arrive. Can't have anyone stumbling onto your body, now can we?"

Kyle swallowed hard, wondering just who the hell Rhodes was expecting to show up. "Fine. We'll wait here. But let Miranda go. You don't need her anymore."

Rhodes turned to look the girl over with a glance that made Kyle's skin crawl. "Oh, I don't know…" Rhodes mused. "I might have use for her yet."

The girl shrank away from Rhodes's lascivious gaze, her trembling increasing.

"Leave her alone," Kyle hissed, trying to draw Rhodes's attention away from the girl. If he lived through this, he'd tear the little fucker apart for putting the poor girl through hell. She sent a pleading look his way. He met her gaze briefly, then turned back to Rhodes.

Kyle licked his lips, trying to come up with a way to stall Rhodes until he could figure out how the hell to get Peterman's daughter out of there without getting both of them killed. "Were you the one who sent the picture of the dead man to Abby?"

Rhodes inclined his head. "It's amazing what an attorney can smuggle to his client these days…"

"Where's the body now?" Kyle demanded.

Rhodes shrugged. "Oh, others handle those nasty little details, Agent. But I imagine Whitmore's probably alligator food."

So it was *Whitmore in the photo… Okay, so where the hell is Maxwell?*

At that moment, a watch alarm started beeping. "Ah, there's my cue," Rhodes announced. "Good-bye, Agent Dawson."

Kyle started as two shots rang out in rapid succession. For a split second he wondered if his body had already gone into shock because he felt no pain at all. But then he saw the bloodstain spreading across Rhodes's suit jacket. Kyle's head snapped over to Miranda Peterman. Her eyes were wide, terrified. She started screaming, wiggling to break away from Rhodes. He clung to her as his knees gave out beneath him and he slipped to the floor.

As his synapses began to fire again, Kyle's instincts kicked in and he rushed toward Miranda, snatching up his weapon as he went and arriving just in time to grab her around the waist and keep her from falling to the ground with Rhodes.

Tucking the girl in close to his body to shield her as much as possible, he trained his gun on the darkness where the shots must've originated.

"Federal agent!" he barked out, half dragging the terrified Miranda behind some nearby shipping crates that he hoped might offer them a little cover from the gunman. "Drop your weapon and come out with your hands where I can see them!"

As the man came out from the shadows, his arms raised, Kyle straightened, completely dumbfounded. "Holy shit."

Fielding offered Kyle a friendly grin. "Well, hello again, Agent Dawson. Good to see you alive and well."

Kyle started to pull away from Miranda, but she clutched his arm with her bound hands, tears streaming down her face as she vehemently shook her head, her eyes pleading with him not to leave her.

"It's alright, sweetheart," he soothed. "I'm not going anywhere."

He gently pulled away from her to better train his gun on Fielding. "What the hell are you doing here, Fielding?" But as soon as the words left his lips, Kyle made the connection. He cursed under his breath as Fielding's grin widened, then ground out, "*Independent contractor.*"

"See, this is why I've decided to like you, Agent Dawson," Fielding said, his tone jovial. "You're sharp as a tack."

Kyle reached into his jacket pocket to pull out his phone. "I want you to lie down on your stomach, Fielding, and lace your fingers behind your head."

Fielding gave Kyle a disappointed look. "Now, is that any way to treat the man who saved your life? *Three times?*"

Kyle frowned, confused. "What the hell are you talking about?"

"Ask Abby about the picture I sent," he said. "It's of the man who'd been sent to kill you the night of the thunderstorm."

"What?" Kyle sputtered. "How the hell…?"

"The second time was when I accepted a very sizable sum to murder all of you involved. But I've decided to decline to provide said services as I find my employer's lack of manners…unfortunate."

Kyle could do little more than blink in dismay. The guy was a total whack job.

Fielding gestured toward where Rhodes lay. "The third… Well, I think you and your friend there were probably the bodies I was supposed to dispose of, but since you're alive, I guess that won't be necessary."

When Kyle's frown deepened, Fielding jerked his chin toward where Peterman lay. "No *blood*, Agent Dawson. Kevlar, I imagine."

Kyle came out from behind the crate and took a couple of quick sidesteps toward Peterman but halted when Fielding started to reach into his pocket. "Hands where I can see them!"

Fielding tilted his head slightly. "I'm just going to give you my phone and the flash drive that Deputy Morrow was kind enough to provide in exchange for her sister's return," he assured Kyle. At Kyle's startled expression, Fielding offered another comforting smile. "As my employer didn't require that it stay in his possession, I thought you might like to have it back. And you'll find some interesting photos on my phone that might assist you in your investigation."

Kyle nodded. "Okay. But slowly."

Fielding reached into his pocket again and withdrew

the items. Then he slowly crouched down and set them on the concrete at his feet. As soon as he was standing again, Fielding inclined his head a little, taking a bow. "Now, if you'll excuse me, Agent, I suppose I should probably leave before you call the police."

"You aren't going anywhere," Kyle informed him. "I'm taking you in for questioning, Fielding."

"Good luck to you, Agent Dawson," Fielding said, talking over Kyle's protestations. "It's been a fine game. I do hope we get the chance to play again."

"Game?" Kyle repeated. "What the—"

At that moment, Peterman moaned. Kyle glanced toward him, just briefly, but when he returned his attention to Fielding, the man was gone, having vanished back into the shadows.

Kyle dropped to Peterman's side and rolled the man over. As Fielding had predicted, there was a bullet hole in Peterman's shirt but no blood, the bullet having been stopped by Peterman's vest.

"Jesus, Peterman," Kyle muttered. "You lucky bastard."

"My daughter?" Peterman moaned as Kyle dialed 911. "Where's Miranda?"

At hearing her father speak, the girl rushed out from behind the crate, sobbing as she fell to the ground on her knees beside her father.

"Nine-one-one, what's your emergency?"

Kyle closed his eyes with relief when he heard the 911 dispatcher's voice. "This is Agent Kyle Dawson," he said. "There's been a shooting."

Chapter 25

Abby was just finishing her ice cream when she heard the sound of an approaching car. Frowning, she glanced over at her sister. "Are you expecting anyone?"

Emma's brows lifted and she shook her head. "No. You?"

Abby's frown deepened. The only person she expected to show up at the cabin was Kyle, and he was obviously still in New Orleans. She got to her feet and set down her bowl, motioning for her sister to stay where she was. Emma nodded and glanced toward the stairs that led up to the second floor where Tyler was sleeping.

Abby held a finger to her lips, then turned and crept toward the front door, pausing at the credenza in the hallway where she'd stashed her gun after returning home from the store. She'd felt silly putting it there when the cabin was so secluded and not known to anyone who might harm them, but the pictures and texts had spooked her. And now that the gun was in her grasp and held down by her thigh at the ready, she was grateful for a little healthy paranoia.

She'd just reached the door when a heavy knock sounded on it, making her start with a gasp. She cast a glance over her shoulder to where her sister still sat in the kitchen, then stood on her toes to peer through the peephole in the door.

When she saw who stood on the other side, she could've fainted with relief. She unlocked the door and swung it open. "You scared the shit out of me, Gabe," she said on a laugh. But when she saw the solemn look on his face, her knees went weak and she had to force herself to stay on her feet. She swallowed past her dread and managed to squeak out, "Kyle?"

Gabe grasped her upper arm, giving it a squeeze. "He's fine. But there was an incident down in New Orleans. He tried calling but couldn't reach you, so he asked if one of us could drive up here."

The relief Abby felt as her adrenaline abruptly crashed had even more of an effect on her knees, and she grasped the front of Gabe's shirt with her free hand to keep herself from dropping to the floor. In a daze, she handed over her gun to him and let him lead her toward the living room.

"What happened?" she asked, her voice shaking with emotion she was barely keeping in check. "Is he hurt?"

Gabe sat down on the couch next to her. "No, he's okay. His former partner, Dave Peterman, was shot, but luckily he was wearing a vest and should be fine. Another man, Harlan Rhodes, was shot and killed— apparently by the same man who abducted Emma."

"What? Why would he shoot him?" Abby asked, shaking her head in confusion.

"He saved Kyle's life," Gabe explained. "He also returned the data that you exchanged for Emma and offered up some other damning evidence against your brother-in-law."

"I don't get it," Abby said. "Why abduct Emma and then help us?"

Gabe shook his head. "Kyle said the guy talked like it was all a game. I don't know."

"Where's Kyle now?" Abby demanded. "I want to talk to him, see him. When will he be home?"

"Tomorrow morning," Gabe told her. "He's taking the red-eye out of New Orleans after he debriefs with his former boss."

She nodded and got to her feet. "Okay. Let's go."

Gabe launched to his feet and caught her arm before she could take more than a couple of steps. "There's no sense in leaving tonight, Abby. You might as well get some sleep, and we'll head out in the morning. Kyle wanted me to stay here with you and Emma, just to be on the safe side."

"Curtis is alive then."

Abby and Gabe started and turned to see Emma standing in the entrance to the living room, her arms wrapped around her torso.

Gabe nodded. "Yes, ma'am. We believe that he orchestrated your abduction. And we suspect that he had intended for one of his associates to murder my brother and another FBI agent in New Orleans."

Emma swallowed hard. "And you think he might still come after us."

"I'm afraid so, Mrs. Maxwell," Gabe told her gently but without sugarcoating the truth. "Is there somewhere else you can stay temporarily until we apprehend your husband?"

"What if we never catch my brother-in-law?" Abby demanded before her sister could respond. "There's nowhere Emma and Tyler can go that he wouldn't know about. And he has the resources to go off grid for quite a while. Theoretically, he could bide his time for weeks, months, *years* before finally resurfacing."

Gabe ran a hand over his high-and-tight and then along the back of his neck, clearly concerned. "She can file a restraining order—"

"Oh, come on!" Abby interrupted, throwing her arms out to the sides in frustration. "You know those are just a formality. We can't do a damned thing to enforce them until something happens, Gabe. And then it could be too late."

Gabe looked oddly tortured, the muscle in his jaw twitching when he practically growled, "I know."

Abby briefly wondered what was behind the fierceness of his response, but her thoughts quickly returned to her concern for her family's well-being. "There has to be something we can do. Could Bradford be assigned to them again for a while?"

Emma blushed at the mention of Adam Bradford's name. "As much as I enjoy the company of Deputy Bradford," she said softly, "we can't live in fear forever, Abby. At some point, we need to get back to normal. *Tyler* needs to get back to normal. He's going to have enough to deal with when he learns the truth about his father."

Abby took a deep breath and let it out on a sharp sigh, trying to be understanding and supportive of her sister's newfound independence and resolve, but afraid she didn't quite understand what her husband was capable of. But her sister was right. There was only so much Abby or anyone else could do. They couldn't all be looking over their shoulders for the rest of their lives. "Okay," she relented. "After we leave tomorrow—"

"I'm not going anywhere." Emma drew up to her full height and lifted her chin a notch. "I'd like to stay here another day or two, enjoy the time with my son. He and I have a lot to talk about."

Abby glanced at Gabe, torn between wanting to make sure her sister stayed safe and her need to be with Kyle and see for herself that *he* was safe as well.

"You must be tired, Deputy Dawson," Emma said with a smile that Abby recognized as forced but anyone else would've seen as that of a consummate hostess. "Could I offer you something? Coffee?" Her grin grew. "Mint chocolate-chip ice cream?"

Gabe returned her smile. "Well, you've twisted my arm, Mrs. Maxwell. I think I'll take you up on that coffee. And *maybe* the ice cream."

Abby stood in the living room alone for several moments, listening as Emma chatted with Gabe in the kitchen. Abby closed her eyes, wishing for a little normalcy of her own. And a certain pair of strong arms wrapped around her, holding her through the night.

She opened her eyes on a sigh and went to the door to secure the lock, then took a moment to pull back the curtains and peer into the darkness.

The morning couldn't come soon enough.

～◦～

Kyle thrummed his fingers on the table, his patience wearing thin. And that wasn't helped by the fact that Skinner seemed completely unaware of the death beams Kyle was glaring at him.

"Let me get this straight," Skinner drawled, leaning back in his chair, the springs squeaking and grating on Kyle's already frayed nerves, "you expect me to believe that the scrawny little bastard you roughed up a few weeks ago actually got the drop on you and Peterman? *You* I can believe. But Peterman?"

Kyle had to physically bite his tongue for a moment to keep from telling Skinner what a first-class dickhead he was. His tone was measured and carefully respectful when he answered, "Peterman never would've allowed either of us to end up in that situation if his daughter's life had not been in danger. He and I have had our differences, but he's…" Kyle coughed, choking a little on the words stuck in his throat. "He's a good agent. And a good man."

Skinner regarded Kyle for a long moment, a smug smile tugging at the corners of his mouth. "Yeah, he is. And so are you."

Kyle's thrumming abruptly stopped. "Sorry, what?"

Skinner heaved a resigned sigh. "As much as I hate to say it, Dawson, I might've misjudged you. Well, not the part about you being a prick, so don't think we're having a *moment* here."

"Wouldn't dream of it," Kyle said, still stunned by the unexpected praise—qualified as it was.

Skinner gave him a tight nod. "You did one helluva a job on this case."

At this, Kyle managed a slight smile. "Thanks. But I can't take credit for work that isn't mine. All I did was connect a few more dots. Abby—Deputy Morrow—was the one who gave us the connection to Maxwell and Whitmore."

"Well," Skinner said, pushing away from the table and getting to his feet at last, "if this Deputy Morrow of yours decides she'd like to come work for the Bureau, you let me know. I'd be happy to put in a good word for her."

Kyle stood and extended his hand. "Yes, sir. I will."

"Sir?" Skinner chuckled as he shook Kyle's hand in a firm grip. "You sure you didn't take a blow to the head?"

"Well, damn it." Kyle sighed, shaking his head. "Now we're *totally* having a moment." He spread his arms wide and gestured with his hands. "Go ahead. Bring it in for a hug, sir."

Skinner spat out a curse under his breath and side-stepped Kyle's open arms. "Piss off, Dawson."

"Oh, come on," Kyle taunted, following after Skinner. "You know you want to."

"Good-bye, Dawson," Skinner called over his shoulder as he strode quickly from the room. "Don't hurry back now. I mean it."

Kyle laughed softly to himself as he watched Skinner take off like his tail was on fire and his ass was catching.

"You two kiss and make up?"

Kyle turned to see Peterman walking toward him. The man carried himself like every step was agonizing, wincing as he extended his hand to Kyle.

"Hard to tell," Kyle mused, glancing over his shoulder in the direction of Skinner's departure. "You know, he's always so good about hiding how he really feels about me."

Peterman's laugh ended on a groan.

"What the hell are you doing here, anyway, Peterman?" Kyle asked. "Shouldn't you be at home with your daughter or, shit, in the *hospital*?"

Peterman placed a hand on his heart and gave Kyle a solemn look. "Why, Dawson, I'm touched by your concern."

Kyle grinned and jerked his chin at Peterman. "How's your daughter? Is she gonna be okay?"

Peterman nodded, his mood becoming solemn once more. "Yeah, I think so. Eventually."

"I'm sorry, Peterman," Kyle told him sincerely. "If I hadn't acted like such an ass, maybe we could've taken down these bastards before anything happened to her."

Peterman shook his head. "Don't."

Kyle's brows came together in a frown. "Sorry?"

"Don't do that," Peterman told him. "You start doing that shit, Dawson, you'll torture yourself with the 'if we'd only got 'em sooner' bullshit until you lose your fucking mind. Just focus on the wins. You saved my baby girl's life. That's a win in my book."

Kyle nodded. "Glad I could help. But Curtis Maxwell is still out there. How many other little girls are going to have to suffer because he's a greedy son of a bitch?"

Peterman gave Kyle a pointed look. "Well, we're not going to find him standing in the hallway jaw jacking, are we? I need to get back home to Miranda and make sure she's doing alright. And last time I checked, Dawson, you had a plane to catch."

Chapter 26

"You'll be here until I get back?" Abby asked, sliding behind the wheel of her sister's SUV the next morning.

Gabe closed the door and waited for her to roll down the window before he leaned in on his forearms. "I'm not going anywhere, Abby. Now get outta here and go call my brother before he starts leaving a shit-ton of voice-mail messages on *my* phone looking for you again. I'll keep an eye on everything here."

She chewed her lip and cast a glance back toward the cabin. "What if I can't reach him? I can't keep leaving the cabin in search of a cell signal."

"Don't worry," Gabe said. "His plane was supposed to land a couple of hours ago. I'm sure he's already on the way home to rest up for when he sees you again."

Abby felt her cheeks go warm at Gabe's knowing wink. "I'll try not to be gone too long," she promised, starting up the SUV.

He shook his index finger at her. "I'm gonna hold you to that. Don't let him talk you into phone sex or anything."

She gave him a wry look. "Can't make any promises."

He grimaced and shuddered. But he was grinning when he patted the roof of the SUV with the palm of his hand and took a step back to motion her on.

As soon as she hit the main road, Abby fished her

phone out of her bag, checking for a signal. Still nothing. It'd be a few more miles. But that didn't make the
wait any more bearable.

A few miles later, she hit an area with a decent cell
signal, and her phone began to ping with notifications.
She whipped the SUV over to the side of the road and
put it in park.

Her lips curved into a grin when she saw a text message from Kyle.

> Just landed. Coming to the cabin. Will see
> you soon.

She checked the time stamp on the text message. He
was probably already an hour into the trip. She immediately dialed his number, her heart hammering in anticipation of hearing his voice again.

"Hey, beautiful," he said in greeting. "Did you get
my text?"

"Yes, just now," she said in a rush. "How was the flight?
Are you doing okay? Are you sure you're okay to drive?"

"The next time I go to sleep, I want it to be with my
arms around you," Kyle replied, his voice low and heavy
with meaning.

"How close are you to the cabin?" she asked, her
stomach fluttering.

"Should be there in a couple of hours."

"Okay. I'll see you there," she said. "But promise me
you'll pull over for a few minutes if you get too tired."

"Cross my heart."

She pulled a U-turn and made it back to the cabin in
record time. She filled Gabe in on her conversation with

Kyle—well, the part about him being en route to the cabin anyway.

"Are you *sure* you'll be okay?" Gabe asked, hesitating at the front door, clearly reluctant to leave Abby and her family alone at the cabin.

"We'll be fine," Abby assured him. "I'm going to just stay around here with Emma and Tyler for a couple more days, then we'll all head home. And Kyle should be up here before we know it." She glanced up at the sky, which was growing ominous as storm clouds began to roll in. "Let's hope he doesn't drive into one hell of a storm. Speaking of which, if you don't get out of here, you're going to get stuck in this mess."

"I'm not worried about a little rain, Abby," Gabe said, giving her a pointed look.

She glanced over her shoulder at her sister and nephew, then turned her attention back to Gabe and forced a smile. "I'll walk you out."

Emma and Tyler followed them out onto the porch, waving good-bye as Abby walked with Gabe toward his beat-up old Chevy pickup truck. Abby wrinkled her nose. "You sure this will make it all the way back to Fairfield County?"

Gabe grinned, showing his dimples. No wonder he had the ladies eating out of the palm of his hand. "Don't worry. The Rust Bucket still has some life in her yet. Besides, the Old Man would've shit himself if I'd driven the department Tahoe up here when I have a perfectly good vehicle of my own."

Abby made a show of giving the truck the once-over, then turned a doubting look on Gabe. "I've seen less rust at a junkyard. This thing is a relic. It should be in a museum."

He shook his head, then slammed his truck door. "Don't listen to her, baby," he purred to the truck. "Haters gonna hate."

She winced when he started up the truck. It growled and sputtered but finally roared to life, backfiring like a gunshot.

"Shut up," he murmured before she could even say a word. But then he suddenly sobered and leaned an arm on his open window, studying her for a long moment. "You really love Kyle, don't you?"

Abby nodded. "Yes. Very much."

He blew out a sharp sigh. "So…then why'd you dump him that summer? He was a fucking mess, Abby."

"I know," she admitted, shoving her hands into the pockets of her jeans. "So was I. Believe me. If I could do things over, I would."

Gabe's jaw tightened as he considered what she said. "He and I… We don't always get along."

She laughed. "You don't say?"

He couldn't help grinning, but then his expression turned somber again. "But I love the guy. He's my baby brother. And I hate to see him hurting. Don't break his heart again, Abby."

She held his gaze. "I don't plan to."

———

Kyle blinked rapidly, clearing his vision. He should pull over as he'd promised Abby, take a quick break, get some more coffee, but shit—he was already jittery from the amount of caffeine he'd consumed since leaving the airport.

He knew it would've been smarter to just head home, but he didn't want to wait any longer to see Abby. He wanted to hold her in his arms, kiss her long and deep, promise he'd love her forever, and ask her if there was any way she'd consider marrying his sorry ass. Yeah, he'd apologized for storming out, and everything seemed fine between them, but he needed to see her again, see the look in her eyes, and *know* that everything would be fine before he could believe it.

He checked his watch. He was still about an hour and a half away.

Damn.

He blinked again, his eyes grainy and burning with the need for sleep.

He saw a sign indicating that a rest stop was just a few miles ahead and sighed. Maybe if he just took a few minutes' break, grabbed another shitty cup of coffee from the rest stop vending machine, and walked around for a few minutes… He took the exit and parked in the empty parking lot just as rain began to fall, the steady rhythm making his lids droop. Thunder rumbled. A storm was moving in.

He grinned, remembering what had happened during the previous storm. With a sigh, he leaned his head back for a moment and closed his eyes, letting the memories of that night replay in his mind. He'd just sit here for a sec and listen to the rain. Just until his eyes stopped burning…

Kyle awoke with a start and cursed a blue streak when he saw the time. He'd dozed off for nearly an hour. He grabbed his phone and called Abby to let her know he was running late but wasn't surprised when it went to voice mail. He cursed again and peeled out of the parking space, eager to get back on the road. The roads were still wet from the rain that had passed through, forcing him to keep the Mustang at a reasonable speed instead of flooring it to get to Abby.

He wouldn't get to her any faster if he put the car into a ditch, he reminded himself. It was just an hour. What was an hour when they had the rest of their lives to be together?

Abby peered out the window again, searching for Kyle's car. He should've been there an hour ago. Now the sky was getting darker as storm clouds continued to roll in, and somewhere in the distance she could hear the rumble of approaching thunder.

"I'm sure he's fine," Emma told her. "Didn't you say you told him to pull over and rest for a bit if he got too tired?"

Abby nodded. She could only hope he'd taken that advice and hadn't fallen asleep at the wheel. She shuddered, pushing away the images that intruded on her thoughts. She should've asked Gabe to stay at the cabin. Then she could've asked him to go out and look for his brother along the road.

Because that wouldn't have been paranoid at all...

She took a deep, steadying breath and let it out slowly. He was fine. She was sure of it. He had to be.

"A storm's coming," she muttered. "I'm going to go get Tyler."

Emma gave her a sympathetic smile. "He's out in the side yard playing."

Abby found her nephew brandishing a stick like a sword as he battled invisible foes. She watched him for a moment, glad that he seemed to be unfazed by his world being turned upside down. Of course, getting an extended stay at a secluded lakeside cabin when he was supposed to be in school wasn't exactly a hardship.

"Hey, Captain Jack, you need to come inside," Abby called. "It's getting ready to storm."

Tyler immediately halted and gave her a frustrated look. "I'm not Captain Jack. I'm not a pirate at all. I'm Aragorn—and I'm fighting Orcs."

Abby grinned. Aragorn was a much better pick. Couldn't argue there. "Well, you still have to come inside, Strider. The Orcs will be there later."

His face lit up when he realized Abby had used the hero's other name in *The Lord of the Rings*. "You've seen the movies?"

"Yes." She laughed as he jogged toward her. "I've even read the books."

"There are books?" he asked, his brows coming together in a frown.

She dropped her head in mock despair. "Oh, Tyler. You and I are going to the public library when we get back to town."

Just then the sound of tires on the gravel road brought their heads around toward the front of the house. "That must be Kyle," she said, relief washing over her.

Tyler took off toward the front of the house. Abby jogged after him but slid to a halt when she saw that the car pulling up the driveway didn't belong to Kyle. Her heart began to pound and her breath caught in her lungs.

Tyler's face lit up when he realized it wasn't Kyle who had arrived. "Dad!"

"No, Tyler!" Abby called out, fear for her nephew making her bolt forward to intercept the boy before he could get to his father.

"But that's my dad!" Tyler cried, struggling to break free from her grasp in an effort to get to his father.

"Get in the house!" Abby ordered, dragging Tyler toward the porch and up the steps, while glancing over her shoulder to check Curtis's progress. She managed to get Tyler inside just as Curtis threw open the car door and got out.

For a split second their gazes met. His was cold, calculating. Furious. Abby's blood turned to ice. He was there to kill them. Or at least her.

"What's going on?" Emma asked.

Abby slammed the door and bolted it with trembling fingers. "He's here."

Emma didn't ask who Abby was talking about. The way her blood instantly drained from her face, she knew exactly who Abby meant. "Oh God."

"Hide until I draw him inside," Abby whispered in a rush, digging through the overnight bag she'd left by the front door and pulling out her weapon. "Then sneak out and get to your car."

"We can't leave you," Emma argued.

"Yes, you can," Abby insisted. "It's better if we split up. Now, I want you to drive to town. Call the police as soon as you have a signal and go straight to the police station. It's right on Main Street—do you remember?"

Emma gave Abby a wary, worried look. "Yes, but—"

"Go, Em. Now!"

Emma darted forward and grabbed Tyler's hand. "Come on, baby. We have to go."

"But it's *Dad*," he said, his voice breaking. "Why do we have to hide? Mom?"

Thunder rumbled so close that the windows rattled,

startling them all. This time Tyler needed no urging when his mother pulled his hand. As they ran to find a hiding place, Abby took up position in the adjacent room, her back pressed to the wall as she waited. She closed her eyes, taking a few shaky breaths to try to bring her nerves to heel.

"Let me in, Abby!" Curtis shouted, trying the door-knob and finding it locked. "I don't want to hurt you!"

Like hell.

Another roll of thunder almost muffled the gunshots, but Abby recognized the distinctive sound. She flinched when the front door burst open with such force that it slammed into the other side of the wall that Abby was pressed against.

She took several slow, measured breaths, watching for Curtis to walk past the entrance into the room, wait-ing for him to come inside so she could either get the jump on him or draw him farther into the house and give her sister time to get away. But he didn't move. She could sense him on the other side of the wall, waiting just as she was, no doubt taking in every corner of the cabin that he could see from his vantage point before coming farther in.

"I know you're there, Abby," he called out. "Why don't you come on out so we can have a chat?"

The rain portended by the thunder now began to fall, obscuring the sound of his movements. Abby strained to hear. Sweat began to form at the roots of her hair and at the back of her neck as she waited.

The floorboards in the hallway creaked loudly as Curtis shifted his weight. The bead of sweat at the base of Abby's neck slowly slid down her spine. She

shuddered and adjusted her grip on her weapon, edging
toward the entrance to the room.

"I know what you've been up to, Abby," Curtis called
out, closer now. "My associates have been keeping me
informed. I won't let you turn my family against me."

Abby bit the inside of her cheek to keep from yelling
at the son of a bitch and assuring him he didn't need
her help in that regard. He'd done a stellar job all on
his own. She continued to wait and listen, praying that
Emma and Tyler would stay hidden until she could draw
him further in.

"Emma!" he called, his voice competing with the
driving rain that pounded the roof. "Baby, I'm home!
Tyler! Where are you, buddy?"

Abby wanted to hurl. The audacity of this asshole,
acting like his wife and son should be rushing to greet
him with open arms after all he'd done to them—after
all he'd done to countless other innocent victims.

Abby waited, listening intently, but the silence wore
on. She couldn't sense any movement, couldn't get a
bead on his position. Any sound she might've caught
was drowned out by the storm raging outside.

Unable to take the waiting any longer, Abby inched
forward again and was on the verge of peering around
the wall when she heard a quiet shuffle in the foyer.

He was growing impatient. She could almost feel
his irritation at being delayed, being *denied*. Then
she heard his slow steps as he made his way deeper
into the entryway, coming to a halt just outside the
living room.

Abby held her breath.

"You're a clever woman, Abby," he called out

casually. "I'm sure we can sit down and talk about this and clear up any *misunderstandings*."

He paused as if he truly expected her to reply, then moved farther into the house, going down the hallway toward the kitchen. Abby took a deep breath and stepped into the hallway behind him, her gun raised.

"Don't take another step, Curtis," she barked. He instantly halted and started to turn around. "Hands where I can see them!"

He obediently lifted his hands, but when he slowly turned to face her, a smug grin curved his lips.

"You're under arrest," she informed him. "Get down on your knees and put your hands behind your head."

He gave her a patronizing look. "Abby, Abby, Abby," he said, shaking his head with each utterance of her name, his golden-brown hair still perfectly styled in spite of the wind and rain. "C'mon…you've known me for years."

Her face twisted in revulsion. "Oh, I know you better than you think. You *disgust* me, you son of a bitch. Now get on the floor!"

"I'm afraid not."

Her brows came together in an angry scowl. "You might've missed the part where I have a gun. And at the moment, that gun is aimed at the center of your chest."

He took a step forward, his arms held out in a conciliatory gesture. "Abby—"

"That's close enough!" she shouted. "Stay back, Curtis. I'm warning you."

He came to a halt again, his grin growing. "I just want to talk, Abby. Clear up a few things."

"Go to hell, Curtis," she spat. "I know all I need to."

He quirked an eyebrow at her. "Do you?"

"The only thing I don't understand is why you offed Whitmore to fake your own death," she admitted.

He chuckled. "Ah, yes, Preston. An unfortunate business. He began to have second thoughts when his godfather became suspicious. Whitmore thought that if he recommended you to look into things, your family loyalty would prevent us from being outed if you found the truth. Little did he realize you're a traitorous bitch."

Abby ignored his barb. "So you killed him."

"Oh, *I* didn't," he said with a shrug. "I have people to handle that sort of thing for me. But it offered a rare opportunity for me to make everyone believe I was dead, take my money, and disappear for a while to start over. Who wouldn't do the same if he found himself in such a situation? I just need to tie up one particularly troublesome loose end."

"I won't let you hurt Emma and Tyler," Abby spat. She thought she heard the soft rumble of the garage door rising under the sound of the thunder, but she couldn't be sure. She prayed Emma and Tyler were making their escape as she'd instructed them.

Curtis hadn't seemed to notice, his eyes still trained on her, his demeanor unconcerned. "I would never *harm* my wife and son."

"You'd just fake your own death and abandon them to clean up your messes, is that it?" Abby said, her tone dripping with disdain. "Don't you give a shit what this will do to your wife? Your *son*?"

He tilted his head to the side, regarding her with that patronizing look of his that made her want to nut punch him. "Don't *you*?"

Abby took a menacing step forward, her grip on the gun tightening. "That's *all* that matters to me, asshole."

"And yet if you go forward with all of this nonsense, my assets will be frozen, my properties confiscated," he pointed out. "Your sister and nephew will be completely destitute. They will have nothing."

"You're wrong," she argued. "They'll have *me*."

He chuckled, shaking his head pityingly. "Oh, Abby. No, they won't."

Abby heard the floor creak and spun around. The shot ripped through the flesh of her left arm. She reflexively fired the gun, putting two rounds in the center of Curtis's bodyguard's chest. Arlo stumbled back a couple of steps, his eyes wide with surprise, but in his shock he managed to fire two more wild rounds before his gun slipped from his fingers and hit the hardwood floor.

Abby heard Curtis grunt as one of the rounds struck him. But glancing behind her to assess the situation cost her. In spite of being severely—perhaps mortally—wounded, Arlo lunged forward, wrapping his powerful arms around her and throwing her to the side, back toward the living room. But the momentum carried him with her. Abby's gun was jarred from her grasp as she and Arlo tumbled to the ground.

She struggled to wiggle out from under the unconscious bodyguard, Arlo's weight on her chest making it difficult to breathe. She shoved at him with her wounded arm and stretched out her free hand, her fingers straining to reach her gun just a few inches away.

Movement out of the corner of her eye caught her attention. Curtis came limping toward her, snatching up Arlo's gun from the floor. His face was twisted with fury, blood stained his thigh where Arlo's shot had caught him, and his hand shook as he raised the gun.

Abby frantically tried to pull herself toward her own weapon, panic giving her an extra surge of adrenaline as her heart beat furiously, pounding in her ears. Her fingers had just reached the butt of her gun when she heard a male voice shout, "Maxwell!"

Her hand closed around her weapon, and she brought it up just as Curtis whirled around, gun aimed at the person who'd called his name. Abby fired a split second after another shot rang out. Curtis's body jerked with the impact. For a moment he stood there, his eyes wide, his face slack. Then his knees buckled and he fell to the floor.

Abby's entire body began to tremble as relief washed over her, but she kept her weapon trained on the entrance to the living room, poised to protect herself again if necessary.

"Abby? It's me! I'm coming in, sweetheart."

Kyle.

She lay back on the floor with a little sob of relief. A moment later, his beloved face was peering down at her, his expression taut with concern.

"Curtis?" she managed to croak out, her throat dry.

Kyle gently took her weapon and set it aside. "Dead."

She closed her eyes and nodded. In the next second, Arlo's deadweight was rolled off her and Kyle was dragging her into his arms, covering her face with kisses and capturing her lips in a brief, hard kiss that stole her breath.

When it ended, he scooped her into his arms and rose to his feet, cradling her against his chest. "It's alright, sweetheart," he murmured against her hair. "I've got you. And I'll never let you go."

Chapter 27

KYLE HAD JUST FINISHED WRAPPING ABBY'S ARM when the first of the local police arrived. He kissed Abby on the forehead. "Stay here," he murmured against her skin. "I'll handle this."

He turned to go but Abby grasped his hand and twined her fingers with his. "I'll come with you."

Her hand was cold in his. Her body still trembled, but her gaze was steady, determined, as she pushed back from the kitchen table and got to her feet. *God, he loved her.* He had to work to suppress a proud grin as he said, "Okay. But you let me know if it's too much."

She pressed her lips together and nodded.

"*Police!*" came a voice from the front porch.

Kyle grabbed his badge from his pocket and crept slowly forward, keeping Abby slightly behind him, just in case these local boys got a little too eager for action. "We're Agent Kyle Dawson with the FBI and Deputy Abby Morrow with the Fairfield County Sheriff's Department. We're coming out."

Kyle blinked against the sunlight that was breaking through the few remaining rain clouds as they made their way out to the porch.

"We got a call about a domestic," one of the officers—a kid who looked like he was fresh out of the academy—informed him. "What the hell is the FBI doing here?"

Kyle shared a glance with Abby. "It's a little complicated. Two assailants have been shot and killed inside." When the rookie stared at Kyle like he might vomit on his shoes, Kyle bent forward a little and said quietly, "You'll want to call it in and get a team out here."

The kid gave him a terse nod and walked a few steps away to call in to dispatch.

"My sister," Abby said in a rush, clutching at the arm of the other officer. "Emma Maxwell. Where is she? Is she okay? Where's my nephew?"

He gave her a sympathetic look. "She's fine, Deputy. Mrs. Maxwell and her son are at the station. They're pretty shaken up but they're unharmed."

Abby released the officer and Kyle led her over to the porch swing where he pulled her down onto the seat beside him. He put his arm around her and drew her in tight against him, careful of her wounded arm.

"Are *you* okay?" he whispered.

He felt her shudder against him, but she nodded.

"How's your arm?" he asked as more sirens approached.

"Just a scratch," she murmured. "I think it's probably already stopped bleeding."

"We'll have the paramedics take a look when they get here, just in case." Kyle jerked his chin as the rookie came up the steps and sent Kyle a grateful look. As soon as the kid was inside, Kyle chuckled. "God, it doesn't seem like that long ago that we were that guy, fresh-faced and eager to make the world a better place. Didn't take long to figure out it was even worse than we'd thought."

Abby pulled back so that she could peg him with a stern gaze. "There are always going to be more assholes like Curtis and Preston Whitmore out there," she said.

"But we're making a difference, Kyle. What happened today—what we put *an end to* today—it means Rosalie Sparks didn't die in vain. You kept your promise to bring her killer to justice."

He studied her face for a moment, letting his gaze travel over every beloved inch, then reached up and caressed her cheek with the backs of his fingers. "When I saw Maxwell standing there with that gun on you... it scared the shit out of me, Abby. Jesus. If I ever lost you..."

Kyle looked away and cleared his throat. But she put her fingers under his chin and turned his face back to hers before leaning in and pressing a long, lingering kiss to his lips.

"It's over," she assured him, nestling close. He wasn't sure if her words were meant more for him or for her. But he'd take them anyway.

———

Three days later...

Abby brushed her hands on her jeans, having loaded the last of Curtis's things into the moving truck that was going to put them in storage until his affairs could be put in order. The house staff had been dismissed with letters of glowing recommendation. Since Curtis's will would be in probate until the legal system could determine how to dispose of the assets acquired as the result of his criminal activity, there were no funds to support Emma and Tyler. And only the items from the house that had belonged to the Morrow family prior to Emma's marriage or that Emma could prove she'd purchased were allowed to stay with her. The rest was forfeit until further notice.

"I'm so sorry about all of this, Emma," Elle McCoy was saying for the hundredth time that afternoon, feeling guilty because of her role in the legal process. She'd come over to help load the truck and to help Emma move to a house owned by Mac Dawson until she could come up with a more permanent solution.

"Don't worry about it, Elle," Emma said. "You can take everything for all I care. I don't want anything that I shared with that man." She cast a look over at Tyler where he was sitting on the front steps, his shoulders slumped, the truth of what his father had done barely even making sense to his young mind. "I have the only thing he gave me that is of any value."

Elle briefly squeezed Emma's arm. "If there's anything I can do—"

"You can grab one of these boxes and make yourself useful, sweet cheeks," Gabe interrupted, straining to carry a heavy box of books to the moving van containing Emma and Tyler's things.

"Bite me, Dawson," Elle shot back, but she moved to go grab a box anyway.

Gabe chuckled and offered Abby a conspiratorial wink. "She wants me."

Kyle was shaking his head as he sidled up to her. "I think that's about everything. I just have—"

Abby turned to see what had caused his words to die abruptly on his tongue and could feel the charge in the air around Kyle even before she recognized the approaching car as belonging to Mac Dawson.

"Shit," Kyle huffed.

"You're going to have to talk to him some time," Abby reminded him quietly. "You can't keep dancing around the tension between you."

Since everything that had happened at the cabin, Abby had devoted nearly every moment to helping her sister and nephew cope with their loss and assisting them in making plans for their future. That meant she and Kyle *still* hadn't had a chance to talk about where things were between them, and she felt a twinge of guilt at her own hypocrisy. But when she slipped her hand into Kyle's, silently offering him support as they walked out to meet Mac's car, she could feel something shift within him.

Mac's face was stoic as usual, revealing nothing as he got out of his department Tahoe and came toward them. "Just wanted to stop by and make sure Emma has the key to the house."

"She does," Abby assured him. "Thanks so much for doing this, Mac. It means a lot to Emma and to me."

He gave a terse nod, acknowledging Abby's gratitude, but it clearly made him uncomfortable. "Just helping out is all. It's not Emma's fault what happened."

Abby gave Kyle a subtle prodding in the ribs, then widened her eyes at him and sent a glance Mac's way.

Kyle took the hint and cleared his throat. "Sadie and Joe are having a cookout next weekend since the last one they tried got derailed on account of everything that's happened. You coming?"

Mac turned his gaze back to Kyle and stared at him for a moment before giving him a terse nod. "Guess I might stop in."

The three of them stood in awkward silence until a

honking horn brought their attention back around to the moving vans. "Get your asses in gear!" Gabe shouted. "Daylight's wastin', and there's no way I'm letting Tom drive one of these vans. He'd have it in a ditch in no time."

"Piss off, Gabe!" came Tom's muffled response from inside the van's cab.

"Need I remind you of a certain joyride in a VW bus when we were teenagers?" Gabe asked.

"Excuse me, sir," Kyle muttered to his father, turning to go break up the argument that was brewing between his big brothers. "Duty calls."

"Kyle."

Abby stiffened, her gaze darting back and forth between the two men. She wasn't sure what she expected, but in all the years she'd known the Dawsons, Mac had never once referred to Kyle by his first name.

"Yes, sir?"

Mac put his hands on his hips and suddenly took a great deal of interest in a clump of dirt at his feet. "I, uh, gave a friend of mine at the Bureau a call. Seems you'll be reporting to him in your new assignment."

Abby felt Kyle tense and squeezed his hand tighter.

"And?"

Mac cleared his throat a couple of times, kicking at the clump of dirt with his toe. "Told him he's getting one hell of an agent and that he'd better treat you well or he'd have *me* to answer to."

Abby's gaze snapped to Kyle's face to gauge his reaction. For a long moment, he stared at his father in stunned silence. Then he extended his hand. Mac hesitated for a moment but then clasped his son's hand in a firm handshake.

Abby could hear the emotion in Kyle's voice as he said, "Thanks, Dad."

Mac gave Kyle a nod and turned back to his car, but there was no way Abby was going to let him get away that easily. "Mac!" she called, jogging the couple of steps to him. When he turned around, she threw her arms around his neck and hugged him tightly.

"Oh, well now," he muttered, giving her an awkward hug. "What's this all about?"

She pulled back and pressed a kiss to his cheek. "Thank you," she whispered. "For raising such an amazing son."

With that, she turned on her heel and jogged back to Kyle, lacing her fingers with his once more as they headed toward Emma's moving van.

"What was that all about?" he asked.

She shrugged. "Just saying thank you. That's all."

That night, Abby lay in Kyle's arms, her head resting on his chest. Every muscle in his body ached after moving several vanloads of Emma and Tyler's belongings out of her house and then getting her settled. But it was all worth it. He would've done it for anyone who needed his help, but today's work had the added benefit of allowing him to shoulder some of the burden that Abby had taken on in her determination to look after her family. Besides, if all went as he hoped, Emma and Tyler would be *his* family too soon enough.

He trailed his finger lightly over Abby's arm, avoiding her still-healing wound from a few days before. "You awake, sweetheart?"

She stretched, moaning a little with pleasure. "Barely. I thought you'd be too tired after everything today to be so…*energetic* tonight."

He grinned. "What can I say? The thought of getting you naked later was all that kept me going today."

She chuckled, low and sexy, nuzzling closer and melding the soft curves of her body into his. Instantly, he felt desire stirring deep in his belly. Good God, the things this woman did to him. He couldn't get enough of her.

So when she lifted her face to his, seeking his kiss, it was impossible for him to resist—not that he'd wanted to. He grasped the back of her neck, deepening the kiss, drawing her closer until she was stretched out on top of him. Her soft moan of pleasure as she slowly sheathed his throbbing cock nearly undid him.

He sat up, wrapping her legs around his waist and grinding his teeth together to keep from giving in to the release building at the base of his spine. "Jesus, Abby," he ground out. "I love being inside you."

She let her head fall forward so that her mouth was near his ear, her breath hot against his skin. Another little moan escaped her as her muscles began to tense, and then she cried out as her release shook her, drawing Kyle along with her.

For several moments, they clung to each other, panting, hands gently sliding over sweat-slicked skin. When their heartbeats finally began to slow, Kyle pressed a kiss to Abby's shoulder.

Then he pulled away just enough to run his fingers through the length of her silky hair, assuring himself that the beautiful woman in his arms was real and not an illusion. "I love you," he told her. "I want to spend every day of the rest of my life loving you."

"I love you, Kyle," she breathed, her fingers trailing along the curve of his jaw, her eyes filled with the truth of her words. "I want that too. I want to start over. I want to see if we can have a life together. But I know that you wanted to be somewhere more exciting and make a name for yourself away from your father's shadow. Please just promise me that you won't let me get in the way of your dreams. I don't want to be what keeps you here when you want to be somewhere else."

Kyle took Abby's face in his hands. "There's nowhere else I'd rather be than right here. With *you*." He captured her lips in a heated kiss, making sure she had no lingering doubts. When he finally ended the kiss, he pressed his forehead to hers, not sure if he deserved this much happiness but determined to hang on to it for dear life anyway. "And as for my dreams…the most important dream I ever had was *you*."

Acknowledgments

It is with great respect and gratitude for those in law enforcement that I write the Protect and Serve series. As such, I have done my best to present the information in the story accurately and realistically. However, there may be times when I had to bend the rules of police procedure just a bit for dramatic effect or when said procedures varied or sources conflicted.

I owe a special debt of gratitude to my technical advisers: Deputy S., Detective L., and Sheriff B. Thank you for answering my questions and for giving me a small glimpse into your world. Any errors in the story are my own.

I also need to give a shout-out to my dear friend and tireless agent, Nicole Resciniti, whose faith in me never wavers. This series never would have come to be without her. Love you, Nic! In addition, I would be remiss if I didn't thank my incredible team at Sourcebooks, especially my amazing editor, Cat Clyne, who isn't afraid to push me out of my comfort zone.

And, as always, thank you to my husband and our darling boys. There's no way I could do this without your love and support. You are my sun, moon, stars.

Author's Note

For the purposes of this series, I have created fictional Fairfield County, Indiana. All of the places, events, and people therein are products of my imagination.

Kate SeRine's pulse-pounding
Protect & Serve series continues with

Safe from Harm

Coming Spring 2016

"Heart-pounding action and steamy sexual tension.
This series is a must-read!"

—Julie Ann Walker, *New York Times* bestselling
author of the Black Knights Inc. series

～～～

There's something about prosecuting attorney Elle McCoy
that Deputy Gabe Dawson just can't get enough of. Even
with Gabe's family legacy in law enforcement and a promising
career, Elle's smart, sassy rejection of all his charm makes Gabe
want her even more.

But Gabe's confidence is shaken when he's shot on the steps
of the courthouse, protecting Elle from a terrorist intent on
revenge. Worse, Elle isn't out of danger yet. But as they race
to counter the terrorist's next move, Gabe determines to prove
to Elle—and himself—that he's a man worthy of her.

For more Kate SeRine, visit:

www.sourcebooks.com

About the Author

Kate SeRine (pronounced "serene") has been telling stories since before she could hold a pen. When she's not writing, you'll find Kate reading every book she can get her hands on, watching low-budget horror movies, or geeking out over pretty much any movie adaptation of a comic book. As long as action and suspense are involved, she's in!

Kate lives in a smallish, quintessentially Midwestern town with her husband and two sons, who share her love of storytelling. She never tires of creating new worlds to share and is even now working on her next project—probably while consuming way too much coffee. Kate is also the author of the award-winning paranormal romance series, Transplanted Tales.

Connect with Kate at www.kateserine.com, Facebook.com/kateserine, or on Twitter @KateSeRine.